I0823713

THE BARK BEFORE THE DAWN

Also by Sarah Fox

The Magical Menagerie Mysteries

MURDER MOST OWL *
DEAD MEN WAG NO TAILS *
TAILS FROM THE CRYPT *

The Wyatt Investigations Mysteries

DEFINITELY MAYBE NOT A DETECTIVE

The True Confections Mysteries

SIX SWEETS UNDER
BAKING SPIRITS BRIGHT
BOULEVARD OF BROKEN CREAMS

The Literary Pub Mysteries

WINE AND PUNISHMENT
AN ALE OF TWO CITIES
THE MALT IN OUR STARS
CLARET AND PRESENT DANGER
THROUGH THE LIQUOR GLASS

The Pancake House Mysteries

CREPES OF WRATH
FOR WHOM THE BREAD ROLLS
OF SPICE AND MEN
YEAST OF EDEN
CREPE EXPECTATIONS
MUCH ADO ABOUT NUTMEG
A ROOM WITH A ROUX
A WRINKLE IN THYME

The Music Lover's Mysteries

DEAD RINGER
DEATH IN A MAJOR
DEADLY OVERTURES

* *available from Severn House*

THE BARK BEFORE THE DAWN

Sarah Fox

First world edition published in Great Britain and the USA in 2026
by Severn House, an imprint of Canongate Books Ltd,
14 High Street, Edinburgh EH1 1TE.

severnhouse.com

Copyright © Sarah Fox, 2026

Cover and jacket design by Piers Tilbury

All rights reserved including the right of reproduction in whole or in part in any form. The right of Sarah Fox to be identified as the author of this work has been asserted in accordance with the Copyright, Designs & Patents Act 1988.

British Library Cataloguing-in-Publication Data
A CIP catalogue record for this title is available from the British Library.

ISBN-13: 978-1-4483-1546-8 (cased)
ISBN-13: 978-1-4483-1901-5 (paper)
ISBN-13: 978-1-4483-1547-5 (e-book)

This is a work of fiction. Names, characters, places and incidents are either the product of the author's imagination or are used fictitiously. Except where actual historical events and characters are being described for the storyline of this novel, all situations in this publication are fictitious and any resemblance to actual persons, living or dead, business establishments, events or locales is purely coincidental.

No part of this book may be used or reproduced in any manner for the purpose of training artificial intelligence technologies or systems. This work is reserved from text and data mining (Article 4(3) Directive (EU) 2019/790).

All Severn House titles are printed on acid-free paper.

Typeset by Palimpsest Book Production Ltd., Falkirk, Stirlingshire, Scotland.
Printed and bound in Great Britain by TJ Books, Padstow, Cornwall.

The manufacturer's authorised representative in the EU for product safety is Authorised Rep Compliance Ltd, 71 Lower Baggot Street, Dublin D02 P593 Ireland (arccompliance.com)

Praise for Sarah Fox

"Feels more like a warm dose of sunshine . . . A quirky, breezy, feel-good read"
Booklist on *Tails from the Crypt*

"A well-balanced small-town cozy offering a hint of romance and a whiff of local color . . . For cozy fans who like their mystification with a little magic"
Kirkus Reviews on *Tails from the Crypt*

"A charming cozy full of unexpected surprises, romance, magic—and murder"
Booklist on *Dead Men Wag No Tails*

"This delightfully warm and charming series starter is filled with romance, murder, and magic"
Booklist on *Murder Most Owl*

"Cozy fans will find plenty to like"
Publishers Weekly on *Claret and Present Danger*

"[The] charming atmosphere, solid plotting, and several enticing recipes are sure to please cozy fans"
Publishers Weekly on *The Malt in Our Stars*

About the author

Sarah Fox was born and raised in Vancouver, British Columbia, where she developed a love for mysteries at a young age. When not writing novels, she is often reading her way through a stack of books or spending time outdoors with her English springer spaniel.

www.authorsarahfox.com

For Trixie and Orion

ONE

A resounding crack cut through the warm Florida air.

"Best sound in the world," my boyfriend, Callum McQuade, said as we watched a baseball sail over the field before it hit the grass. "Come on, Javi," he called out to the young man who'd hit the ball. "You can do better than that. Georgie wants to see you hit a homer."

Javi Fuentes, member of the Major League Baseball team the Toronto Blue Jays, gave no indication that he'd heard Callum. But when one of his teammates threw him an easy pitch a second later, the crack of ball against bat was even more impressive, like a rich thunderclap. I held my breath as I watched the ball arc up into the air and soar clear out of the park. Maybe that wasn't so difficult for a professional player, considering that this was a small ballpark with hardly any seating beyond the outfield, but even in a large stadium, it would have been a home run by a long shot.

I jumped to my feet and clapped with genuine delight as Callum and the other guys present cheered and whistled.

"That's more like it," Callum said as he sat down on the bench in the dugout.

Javi walked over our way. "You think you're gonna just sit there and watch?" He held out his baseball bat, his dark brown eyes twinkling with good humor. "Nah. Get out here and show us what you've got, McQuade."

I smiled when Callum's eyes lit up.

"Do you mind?" he asked me.

"Of course not," I replied.

I already knew that watching Callum swing a baseball bat was like watching poetry in motion. He'd retired from his professional baseball career nearly two years earlier, but he still had his own batting practice sessions and he played the game for fun whenever he had the opportunity. I couldn't get enough of seeing him in his element, and watching him here, in an honest-to-goodness ballpark with a handful of his former teammates around him, sent a happy thrill through me.

"Come on, Georgie," Javi invited. "You need an on-field view for this."

My smile brightened and I followed Callum as he jogged up the steps from the dugout and onto the field.

A few days ago, when Callum and I first arrived in Dunedin, Florida, shyness had made me reserved around the professional ball players I'd only ever before seen on television. Although I was still my usual introverted self, hours spent with Javi and some of Callum's other former teammates now had me feeling far more at ease with the group.

Callum and I would be leaving that afternoon, flying back to our home on the Oregon coast, but I'd eagerly agreed to spend more time at the ballpark when Javi extended the invitation to us the night before. We'd already watched a team practice and a couple of spring training games. We'd also spent time with the guys away from the ballpark. This, however, was the first time I'd had a chance to set foot on the actual field.

I gazed around in wonder as I emerged from the home team dugout. The view was certainly different from down here than it was in the stands.

"Don't hurt yourself, old man," Javi teased as he handed the bat over to Callum.

"Hey, watch your mouth," Ozzie O'Malley, one of the team's veteran members, cautioned. "I'm a year older than him."

"That's why you're ancient and McQuade's just old."

"Settle down, boys." Callum gave the bat a practice swing, a grin on his face. "Let's see who can make it three out of three."

"You're on." Javi crossed his arms, ready to watch Callum's attempt.

Maybe it was silly, but a sudden case of nervous jitters upped my heartrate. Although the friendly competition had no stakes other than boasting rights, I still wanted Callum to win.

Just one of many signs that I was crazy in love with him.

Callum set up at home plate and took a couple more practice swings before nodding to Paco Arenas, another former teammate who stood on the pitching mound. Paco threw the first pitch and I watched with rapt attention as Callum swung the bat and made contact. The ball flew out of the park over left field.

I cheered, unable to contain myself.

The next impact of bat against ball didn't have quite the same rich sound, but the ball still had enough oomph to get over the back wall. Just barely, but it got there. Callum's third hit sounded more like the first, and the ball arced easily out of the park.

I ran over to hug him as he left home plate. He laughed and lifted me off my feet, holding me with one arm.

"Still got it," he said as he handed the bat over to Ozzie.

"Or maybe your girl's just good luck," Ozzie said as he approached home plate.

"She is," Callum said, looking me in the eyes as he addressed his friend. "But that doesn't mean I needed any luck."

I gave him a quick kiss and held his hand as we watched the rest of the informal competition unfold. Ozzie's first and third hits flew over the back wall, but the second one fell just short. He endured a lot of ribbing for that from his teammates, but he still had a smile on his face.

Javi took his turn last. I don't think anyone was surprised when he hit three easy home runs in a row.

"A tie," Callum said to Javi, offering him his hand.

Javi reached out as if to shake it, but snatched his own hand back at the last second. He laughed at Callum, then pulled him into a hug.

"Don't be a stranger, man," Javi said before releasing him.

Callum spent several more minutes saying goodbye to his friends.

"Is it hard to leave?" I asked as we walked out of the ballpark a little later, my hand in his.

"Sure," he replied. "I love those guys, and the game. But I'm also glad to be heading home."

I smiled at that. "Same. We'll be met by some very excited animals."

He mirrored my smile. "Can't wait."

Neither could I.

By the time we reached the airport in the early afternoon, bubbles of excitement fizzed and frothed inside of me. I'd enjoyed every minute of our vacation, but I missed all the animals that lived on the farm with us, especially my dogs, Flossie and Fancy, and my kitten, Stardust. My aunt Olivia, who owned the farm, had texted me daily updates to keep my worries at bay, but nothing could beat in-person snuggle time with my fur babies.

I knew Callum missed the animals too. He loved my dogs and cat—the feeling was mutual—and he had a strong connection with all of the residents of my aunt's animal sanctuary. Auntie O had hired him a year ago to manage the farm, shortly after he retired from his professional baseball career. He'd grown up on a ranch in Colorado and loved working with animals of all kinds.

As we stood in line to check our baggage at the airport, I texted my aunt to let her know that our flight was currently listed as on time. Even so, we wouldn't arrive back in Twilight Cove until late at night. But if nothing delayed our planned arrival time, Auntie O would leave Flossie, Fancy, and Stardust in the farmhouse before she went to bed in the carriage house. That way, my animals would be there when we got home.

After sending the text message, I tucked my phone away and inched forward as the line moved along. I caught sight of something in Callum's wavy blond hair and brushed it away.

"Sunflower seed?" he asked.

"A typical hazard of hanging out with Javi, I'm guessing." I ran my fingers through his hair, checking for other stowaway seeds, but found nothing more.

"I'm just lucky it wasn't Gatorade."

Javi had upended a package of sunflower seeds on Callum's head when we'd first arrived at the ballpark that morning. Totally on brand for Javi, according to Callum.

"I really like him," I said, as I leaned into his side.

"I'm glad." Callum slipped an arm around me. "He's practically your kid brother now."

I smiled. "I'm good with that."

"Just wait until he starts dumping sunflower seeds in *your* hair."

I laughed.

The line moved again and soon we had our turn at the counter. We checked our suitcases and then wandered through the terminal, Callum now free of luggage and me with just a tote bag. I stopped to check out some new fiction releases in one of the shops while

Callum bought a package of gum for the flight. As I moved out of the little store, a woman with long, curly red hair bumped into me, nearly knocking my bag to the ground.

"I'm so sorry!" she apologized, her blue eyes wide.

"No worries," I assured her as I adjusted the strap of my tote.

She flashed me a grateful smile and then hurried off.

I stared after her, an unsettled feeling niggling at me. I could have sworn that I'd seen fear in the woman's eyes. Knowing there wasn't anything I could do about it even if I were right, I tried to shake off my concern.

"Everything OK?" Callum asked, joining me outside the shop.

"All good," I replied as he took my hand.

More than an hour later, as we stood in line to board the airplane, a flash of red hair caught my eye. The same woman who'd bumped into me earlier was waiting in another line to board a flight to Charlotte, North Carolina. She glanced around and kept playing with the strap of her purse. She definitely struck me as nervous. Maybe she just didn't like flying?

As she drew closer to the boarding gate, she seemed to settle, no longer fidgeting or looking this way and that. The line for our flight to Portland moved forward and I handed the airline employee my phone so she could scan my boarding pass. In the last second before I stepped out onto the jet bridge, I looked for the redheaded woman again, but she'd already disappeared, no doubt boarding her own flight.

The woman drifted out of my thoughts as Callum joined me on the jetway and took my hand again.

Together, we boarded the plane, both of us eager to get home.

TWO

By the time we arrived in Twilight Cove, midnight had come and gone. That didn't bother Stardust or the dogs. They heard us coming and burst out the back door of the farmhouse as soon as I opened it.

"Whoa, there." Callum scooped Stardust up off the porch before she could get trampled by the excited springer spaniels.

"A-woo!" Fancy, my brown-and-white spaniel, cried out in greeting.

Flossie, her black-and-white sister, danced around and barked, excited energy radiating off of both dogs.

We spent a good ten minutes hugging, petting, and snuggling the three animals. They eventually calmed down, but Flossie's and Fancy's tails continued to wag. My heart felt warm and full. If I'd had any doubts about whether this was where I truly belonged, this homecoming would have cured me of that.

After we got our suitcases into the farmhouse, Callum took the dogs out in the yard for a few minutes and then we all headed upstairs to bed. Callum and I crashed immediately, with both dogs and Stardust snuggled up on the bed with us, instead of on the dog bed they usually shared in the corner of the room.

Waking up to dog kisses and a kitten pouncing on my blanket-covered legs brought a sleepy smile to my face the next morning. Callum and I weren't exactly bright-eyed and bushy-tailed, having managed only a few hours of sleep after our trip home, but we both greeted the day happily. We spent extra time on our morning farm chores, visiting each animal and letting them know how much we'd missed them. We tended to the donkeys, goats, chickens, alpacas, and horses. Flossie, Fancy, and Stardust hung out with us the entire time, sometimes snoozing and sometimes sniffing at interesting scents. Or, in Stardust's case, chasing and pouncing on bugs.

After I'd finished my usual chores, Callum struck out into the fields to check all the fences while I dropped in at the carriage house to see Auntie O.

I greeted her with a hug when she opened the door. Her blue eyes were bright with happiness and she returned my hug with vigor.

The spaniels, Stardust, and I joined my aunt in the carriage house for a cold drink while I told her about my time in Florida with Callum. I also got her to update me on all the farm animals and everything else I'd missed while away.

"Tessa dropped these off for you the other day," Auntie O said, getting up to fetch something from across the room.

"Our tickets to the museum's fundraiser?" I guessed when I saw her pick up two small rectangles of sturdy paper.

"It's a good thing you ordered them before you went away." My aunt handed me the tickets. "Apparently, they sold out a few days ago."

Twilight Cove's museum had decided to hold a 1920s-themed fundraising party. Tessa, my best friend, had been looking forward to the event for months. She loved vintage fashion and already had a flapper dress that she planned to wear to the party. I still needed to find an appropriate outfit, but I hoped I could track one down either at the local vintage clothing shop or online. I needed to get on with my search, though, since the date of the event was fast approaching.

Auntie O and I chatted for a while longer before I returned to the farmhouse, where I attempted to get settled back into my writing routine. I loved my career as a screenwriter, focusing mostly on thrillers and the occasional romance movie for television, but I struggled to get anything done that day. I answered a few work-related emails and read over the half-finished script that I'd worked on before leaving for Florida, but that was pretty much the extent of my productivity for the day. My brain was still stuck in vacation mode. Hopefully, over the next day or two, I'd get it switched firmly back into writing mode.

Putting aside my work, I instead focused on unpacking and doing laundry. Callum and I had arrived home so late that we'd simply left our bags by the door and changed into sleepwear before falling into bed. Once I had a load of clothes in the washer and had returned my emptied suitcase to the attic, I decided to drive into town for some groceries.

"Want to come with me?" I asked Flossie and Fancy after telling them my plans.

Flossie barked and Fancy let out a long, "A-woo!"

The next instant, they stood at the back door, tails wagging.

I smiled and grabbed their leashes. "Silly question, right?"

Stardust gave a tiny meow and rubbed up against my ankles.

"I'm sorry you can't come," I said, my heart melting as I picked her up and gave her a cuddle. "But maybe you can keep Auntie O company."

My aunt was happy to have the kitten stay with her while she baked and worked on financial matters for the animal sanctuary. When I left the carriage house, Auntie O was sitting at the kitchen table, her laptop in front of her and her reading glasses on, with Stardust curled up on her lap.

After the short drive into town, I parked on Main Street and the dogs and I walked first to the bakery and then to the grocery store. The dogs waited outside—in the company of a store employee who was enjoying some fresh air on her coffee break—while I grabbed a few items to restock my refrigerator. Then the three of us ambled down the road toward Déjà Brew, the local coffee shop, all the while enjoying the fresh ocean air and the view of the water.

As soon as Genesis—the new owner of Déjà Brew—saw me outside the coffee shop with the dogs, she hurried out with a bowl of fresh water for Flossie and Fancy. They greeted her with wagging tails before taking a drink and flopping down on the sidewalk. Genesis had bought Déjà Brew from its former owners at the beginning of the year, but I'd known her since the previous summer. She was dating my friend Cindy Yoon, and both Genesis and Cindy had come out to play baseball with Callum and me and some of our other friends during the summer and fall months. Now that we were back from our vacation, Callum hoped to start up the practices again.

I tied the spaniels' leashes to a metal loop that Genesis had recently installed by the door and followed her inside.

"How was Florida?" Genesis asked as she prepared my London fog latte. She wore her many braids twisted up into a large bun on the top of her head, and had multiple, colorful bangles on her wrists.

Although customers occupied several tables, I was the only person at the counter, giving us a chance to chat.

"Great," I replied. "The weather was amazing and we had a fun time. Callum got to see a lot of his friends and former teammates."

And I hadn't once worried that he'd decide he wanted to stay in Florida—and the professional baseball world—instead of returning to Twilight Cove with me. I'd entertained worries of that variety several months ago, but I was glad that my confidence in our relationship and in his expressed happiness with his new life had grown enough to silence those anxious thoughts.

Genesis snapped a lid onto the take-out cup that held my freshly made latte. "There was a woman in here asking about Callum first thing this morning."

"Someone local?" I asked.

Genesis shook her head as she slipped a cardboard sleeve onto the cup. "I've never seen her before. She said she'd heard he lived in Twilight Cove and asked if he ever hung out here at the coffee shop. I got the feeling she was trying to get me to tell her how to find him. Other than saying that he comes in here now and then, I didn't tell her anything."

"Thanks for that," I said with appreciation as she handed over my drink. "She's probably a fan. All the ones I've met have been nice, but you never know when someone might get a little too obsessive."

"That's what I was thinking. You don't need any crazies showing up at the farm looking for him."

The mere thought of that happening ignited a flicker of alarm inside of me. I quickly snuffed it out.

"Anyway," Genesis continued, "I probably won't see her again, but if I find out she's been asking more questions, I'll let you or Callum know."

I thanked her again and said goodbye before returning to my waiting dogs.

I considered taking the spaniels down to the beach for a walk before heading home, but then I remembered the groceries sitting in the trunk of my car.

"Home first, then a walk," I decided.

"A-woo!" Fancy said with a wag of her tail, no doubt in response to the "W" word.

We stopped off at the farmhouse long enough for me to put

away the groceries, move my clothes from the washing machine to the dryer, and to finish off my drink. Then we set off through the woods, heading for the ocean. I wore a sweater and a jacket, finding the Oregon spring weather distinctly chilly after the warm Florida sun. Twilight Cove's weather forecast consisted mostly of rain for the next week or two, so I wanted to make the most of the current day, with its overcast sky but no precipitation.

Flossie and Fancy didn't seem to mind the spring temperatures. As soon as we reached the beach, they ran straight for the ocean and splashed around while I walked along the wet sand. When we got back to the farm, I had to hose off and towel dry the dogs before letting them in the house, but they didn't mind.

Once inside, I noticed that Callum had retrieved his suitcase in my absence. He lived in the small cabin located beyond the barn, although he'd spent most nights at the farmhouse with me over the past few months. Now that we'd gone on a trip together and had spent almost every minute of the past week in each other's company, I had a restlessness growing inside me. I didn't want us living in two different places, even if they were on the same property. I loved falling asleep in his arms each night and waking up next to him every morning. I loved *him*.

Maybe it was time for me to take the lead and let him know how I was feeling. A sudden case of nerves skittered through me, but I calmed myself down without too much difficulty. I truly believed that the two of us were on the same page with our relationship. My brain loved to fret, but in this case, I felt certain that any worries would be for nothing.

After fetching Stardust from the carriage house, I jogged upstairs to find my carry-on bag, which I'd left on a chair in my bedroom. I fished out the mystery novel I'd started reading on the plane, and also removed my sunglasses and the snacks and bottle of juice—nearly empty now—that I'd bought in the departure lounge at the Tampa airport. Then I stashed the bag in my closet and got settled on the couch in the living room as the first drops of rain pattered against the roof.

I'd made it through half a chapter of the mystery novel when Flossie and Fancy raised their heads from where they lay on the rug near the unlit fireplace. I didn't pay much attention until Flossie let out a low growl. Then Fancy did the same.

"What's wrong, girls?" I asked with surprise.

They rarely ever growled, and I wondered if they'd heard some distant thunder that my own ears couldn't detect.

They both jumped up and hopped onto the loveseat by the front window, their noses pressed to the glass. I set my book aside and joined them there. The rain had started out as a gentle shower, but now it poured down in sheets. I peered through the gray gloom toward the road. All seemed quiet and still out there, aside from the rain.

Flossie let out another low growl.

I spotted a flicker of movement by one of the lilac bushes at the western edge of the property.

"Is that someone in our yard?"

As if in response to my question, Flossie and Fancy ran to the front door. Flossie let out a volley of barks while Fancy threw back her head and howled. Stardust, startled by all the noise, jumped off the couch and shot up the stairs to the second floor.

Another flicker of movement drew my attention back to the window.

I saw a flash of a cobalt blue rain coat.

This time I had no doubt.

Someone was lurking behind the lilac bush, watching the farmhouse.

THREE

I considered opening the front door to let the dogs loose, but I quickly scratched that plan. I didn't know who was out there and what their intentions might be. The last thing I wanted was for the dogs to come to any harm. Still, I didn't like the thought of somebody skulking around the farm, so I darted into the kitchen and grabbed the dogs' leashes before returning to the living room. I clipped the leads onto the spaniels' collars and opened the front door.

Flossie and Fancy nearly pulled me right off my feet. I scrambled to keep up as they flew off the front porch and across the wet lawn. A car engine roared to life nearby. We rounded the lilac bush in time to see a dark blue sedan peeling off along the road, too fast for me to get a look at the license plate.

The spaniels put their noses to the ground and sniffed around the shrubs, but no one remained in our front yard. I let Flossie and Fancy sniff for another couple of minutes, and they followed the scent trail to the edge of the road, no doubt where the car had been parked.

The rain poured down harder, so I persuaded the dogs to accompany me back to the house, where I had to towel them off once again. Even after I switched out my rain-soaked clothes for a dry outfit and added a cozy hoodie on top, I couldn't shake off a chill of unease. Maybe the prowler had an entirely innocent reason for standing out in the front yard, but I couldn't think what that might be, especially since they'd taken off so quickly once I'd opened the door.

I told Callum about the incident when he joined me at the farmhouse for dinner that evening. He seemed puzzled, and a little worried, but not alarmed.

"I'll keep an eye out for prowlers," he said, "but hopefully whoever it was won't be back."

"Genesis mentioned that a woman at the coffee shop was asking about you. Maybe it was the same person. A fan hoping to catch a closer look."

A crease appeared between Callum's eyebrows. "Maybe. If you see someone hanging around again, it might be best to call the police. If nothing else, that might discourage the person from coming back."

I agreed with that plan, but I hoped it wouldn't be necessary.

Once I'd shared the incident with Callum, my burden of worry eased and I didn't spend much time thinking about it further. The next day, I had far better luck with getting back into my writing routine and I spent a solid few hours pounding out pages to add to my latest screenplay.

In the afternoon, I shut down my screenwriting software, gave Stardust a cuddle, and made sandwiches for Callum and me to eat for lunch. After our quick meal, we spent a few minutes chatting with Conrad Rigsby, our neighbor from across the street, who'd stopped by to borrow a post pounder so he could repair one of his fences.

Once Conrad left, Callum took Flossie and Fancy with him to the barn, where he planned to clean out the stalls. He would meet me in town later with the dogs, so I could bring them home and he could coach the girls' softball team at the local high school, a new endeavor of his. In the meantime, I would pay a visit to the local vintage clothing store, Vintage Vibes, to start my search for an outfit for the museum's fundraising party.

Vintage Vibes sat between an outdoor sporting goods store and a dentistry office, half a block away from Main Street. I'd visited the store a couple of times previously, but only ever to accompany Tessa on her mission to find clothes, never to buy for myself. Shopping wasn't my favorite pastime, and I would have preferred to have my best friend's company, but she was still at work, teaching English and drama at the high school.

While it turned out that Emily—the owner of the shop—didn't often have 1920s clothing items in stock, she'd recently acquired several outfits either from or inspired by that era, hoping to cater to the many locals who planned to attend the museum's upcoming party. Although Emily had only two flapper dresses in my size, the small selection didn't bother me in the least, because I fell in love with one on first sight.

The dress had a stretchy teal lining that hugged what few curves I had and reached down to just above my knees. Attached to the lining was a black tulle overlay adorned with black and gold sequins arranged into Art Deco-inspired patterns. The black fringe at the bottom added several inches of length, and the sequins shimmered and sparkled in the light whenever I moved.

"Georgie, it's like the dress was made for you," Emily gushed when I stepped out of the changing cubicle at the back of the store. "You look amazing!"

Of course she wanted to make a sale, but her compliment struck me as genuine. Even if she hadn't said anything, my own opinion would have been enough to sway me. I loved the look and feel of the dress. Although it was a Great Gatsby-inspired costume rather than a true vintage garment, that didn't bother me in the least. Most likely, it kept the price down. For a dress I'd likely wear only once, that added to the appeal.

"I've got some elbow-length black gloves that will elevate the outfit." Emily disappeared around a corner and out of sight.

While she was gone, I turned in a slow circle in front of the full-length mirror, assessing how I looked from various angles. I still loved the dress after that extra scrutiny.

I used my phone to snap a photo and sent it to Tessa. I knew she'd want to see what I'd chosen as soon as possible.

Emily reappeared as I sent the text, carrying two pairs of black gloves. One pair encased my hands like regular gloves and stretched up past my elbows. The other set also reached up over my elbows, but had only a section of black lace to cover the back of each hand, with a small loop to hook over my middle finger to hold it in place. Those gloves left my palms and fingers bare, which I preferred, so I ended up purchasing that pair with the dress.

I took a look at the men's outfits Emily had in stock, including a pinstriped suit with matching waistcoat. Unfortunately, she didn't have anything that would fit Callum, who stood over six feet tall. Hopefully we could find him something online.

I left Vintage Vibes with my costume stashed safely in a reusable shopping bag. Instead of climbing back into my car when I left the shop, I walked over to Main Street and Déjà Brew. Luck was with me, and I found Genesis behind the counter rather than one of her employees. I ordered a steamed milk for myself and a coffee for Callum.

"You know that lady who was in here asking about Callum yesterday?" I asked Genesis as she prepared the drinks.

Her brown eyes filled with concern. "Has she caused any trouble?"

"I'm not sure," I replied. "Someone was lurking around the farmhouse yesterday, but I didn't get a good look at them. Was the woman wearing a blue raincoat when you saw her?"

Genesis set the two drinks on the counter. "She was. I remember thinking how the beautiful color matched her eyes."

"It could have been the same person, then."

Genesis snapped lids on the drinks. "That's creepy. Did you tell the police?"

"All I saw was a flash of a blue coat, and she wasn't far onto our property, so I didn't see any point. But now that I know that it was probably the same woman . . ."

"Maybe you should tell Brody."

Brody was a local police officer and a friend.

"I can provide him with a description," Genesis offered. "Actually, I've still got the security footage from that day."

"I'll talk to Brody and let him know that you have the footage. I don't know if he'll want to do anything unless her behavior escalates." Which I hoped it wouldn't.

"In the meantime," Genesis said, "how about I send you a couple of stills from the video? That way you'll know who to watch out for if she's still hanging around town."

"That would be great. Thanks, Genesis."

She promised to text me the photos later in the day.

With the two drinks in hand, I walked back to my car and drove straight over to the high school to meet Callum and the dogs. I didn't tell him about my conversation with Genesis. I didn't want to distract him from his coaching and I figured the information could wait a couple of hours.

Flossie, Fancy, and I hung around for a while and the dogs lapped up the attention the teenage girls from the softball team showered upon them. Then, with a wave, we set off along the street, heading in the direction of my car, which I'd parked two blocks away from the school. Apparently, parking spots were hard to come by around the time school let out for the day.

We'd almost reached my red Honda Civic when Flossie and Fancy lurched off to the left, tugging me around a corner.

"Hey, where are you going?" I asked, surprised.

The spaniels pulled so hard that I had to break into a jog to keep myself from falling flat on my face.

"Fancy! Flossie! No pulling!" I chastised.

In response, they slowed their pace, the leashes slackening in my hand. They kept going forward, however, and they glanced back at me as if trying to urge me to move faster.

A hint of worry crept into my chest, but I didn't try to make the spaniels stop or turn back. They were smart dogs, and I'd learned to pay attention when it seemed like they were trying to tell me something.

They led me farther along the sidewalk and then across the street. After a few more paces, Flossie and Fancy stopped and sat down. They glanced up at me and then focused their brown eyes straight ahead. We'd arrived at a cute motel painted turquoise with white trim. Emergency vehicles sat in the middle of the parking lot, some with their lights flashing. A door to one of the ground floor rooms stood open, and two police officers were outside, talking.

"I wonder what happened," I said to the dogs. "I hope nothing too terrible."

Despite that hope, the fact that multiple police cruisers had arrived on the scene made me worry that something serious had occurred. I couldn't tell what was going on from our vantage point, and I wasn't about to move closer and get in the way, so I didn't see any point in hanging around. Besides, knowing the way the local grapevine worked, I'd probably hear all about the incident by the next morning.

"Ready to go home?" I asked the spaniels.

I worried that they might not want to leave, but they jumped to their feet and turned back the way we'd come. With one last glance at the emergency vehicles, I walked with them to my car.

Once I'd shut Flossie and Fancy in the back and I'd settled in the driver's seat, I checked my phone. Genesis had texted me the pictures she'd promised.

I tapped on one of the two photos, enlarging it on the screen.

Startled, I stared closer at the picture.

The woman wore a blue coat that matched the color I'd seen near the lilac bushes outside the farmhouse. She was white, maybe about forty years old, and she had gorgeous, curly red hair.

But what really caught my attention was the fact that I recognized her.

She was the same woman who'd bumped into me at the airport in Tampa.

FOUR

"I don't understand."

I studied both photos again before staring out the windshield.

"Woo," Fancy said softly from the back seat as Flossie nudged my cheek with her nose.

I gave Flossie a pat on the head and set my phone in one of the cup holders.

I wanted to talk to Callum, but that would have to wait. I didn't want to interrupt the softball team's practice, which would run for another hour. My mind whirring, I drove back to the farm and took the dogs for a long walk through the woods before tackling the evening farm chores. By then, I'd started to doubt myself.

After feeding the donkeys, I took out my phone and stared at the photos again.

Maybe I was mistaken. Perhaps the curly red hair had caused me to erroneously believe that the two women were the same person.

As I stood there in the middle of the barn, studying the photos, Callum walked in. Instead of the hoodie he'd worn at the baseball field, he now had a flannel shirt buttoned up over his gray T-shirt. He also wore his cowboy hat. The sight of him never failed to set off butterflies and a warm glow in my chest, although this time I could still feel an undercurrent of worry beneath the pleasant sensations.

Flossie and Fancy intercepted Callum, their tails wagging. He stopped to greet them, but then he came straight over to me.

"How was practice?" I asked as I stepped into his arms, longing to be close to him.

"Great," he said as I rested my cheek on his shoulder. "It's a good group of girls and they're having a lot of fun so far. Best of all, Roxy's taken on a leadership role, helping out the girls who've never played softball before."

I raised my head so I could see his face. "That's good to hear."

Roxy Russo had started volunteering at the animal sanctuary back in the summer. She didn't have the easiest home life and had spent most of her time alone when I'd first met her. She'd been doing better at school lately and had gained a lot of confidence. I'd grown fond of her, so I was happy to hear that she was continuing along a positive trajectory.

"She really seems to be making friends," Callum added.

I smiled and wrapped my arms around him. "That's very good news."

My smile faded and I let out a sigh as I leaned into him.

He ran a hand down my back. "Something wrong, Georgie?"

It didn't surprise me that he'd caught on to my worries so quickly. He'd become adept at reading me.

"Mmm." I didn't feel like letting go of him, but I forced myself to step back out of his arms and answer him properly. "Something's strange, at the very least. Remember yesterday's prowler?"

Concern showed in Callum's green eyes. "Did they come back?"

"No. Not that I know of, anyway. But I asked Genesis if the woman who was asking about you wore a blue raincoat, like the prowler."

"I'm guessing she did."

I pulled my phone from my pocket and showed him the clearest of the two photos Genesis had sent me. "This is a still from the coffee shop's surveillance footage."

He studied the photo for a second before raising his eyes to meet mine. "And she's the prowler?"

"The coat's a match, but otherwise I can't be sure. The thing is, I saw this woman at the airport."

"In Portland?" he asked, surprised.

"Tampa. She bumped into me while you were buying gum."

A line appeared between Callum's eyebrows. "And now she's here in Twilight Cove? You think that's too much of a coincidence?"

"I'm worried that it is," I admitted. "What if she's obsessed with you?"

"Was she on the same flight as us?"

"That's what makes it even creepier. I saw her boarding a flight for Charlotte. So she couldn't have simply followed you from the airport in Portland. She would have had to fly from Charlotte over to this side of the country and then drive to Twilight Cove. It's not impossible for someone to find out that you live in this town."

"Definitely not."

Doubts assailed me again. "But maybe I'm wrong. Maybe it's not the same person."

Callum searched my eyes. "Did you feel certain when you first saw the photo?"

"Very certain. It wasn't until I got home that doubt started creeping in."

"If your gut feeling told you that it's the same woman you saw in Florida, we shouldn't dismiss it."

"If I'm right, that means she tracked you all the way from Florida, asked about you at the local coffee shop, and then showed up here in our yard." A chill ran down my spine. "That's seriously creepy."

"We should let Olivia know," Callum said. "Send her the picture so she knows who to watch out for. I'll tell her to call the police if she sees the woman near the farm."

"Should we tell Brody too?"

"Definitely."

Anxiety set my stomach churning.

"Hey." Callum pulled me close again. "She's probably harmless. We're just being cautious."

"Have you ever had serious problems with fans before?" I asked, drawing comfort from his embrace.

I knew he still got asked for autographs and photos, but whenever fans had stopped him in my presence the interactions had been positive.

"Not to the point of criminality or making me seriously fear for my safety." He stepped back and took hold of my hands. "And this is probably nothing too serious either. But for your sake, and Olivia's, I want to make sure the police know what's happened so far."

"I'll text Brody and send him the pictures as soon as I'm back at the house," I assured him. "Then I'll start making dinner. Soup or spaghetti?"

"Whichever is easiest."

"Spaghetti it is." I had homemade sauce in the freezer, whereas I would have had to make the soup from scratch.

Callum kissed me before releasing my hands. "I'll get on with my work here so I'm not late joining you."

"Come on, girls," I called to Flossie and Fancy.

The spaniels trotted along with me as I headed for the barn door.

"Hey, Georgie?" Callum called.

I paused and looked back.

"Everything will be fine," he said.

I sure hoped he was right.

Despite Callum's assurances that everything would be OK, I couldn't stop thinking about the red-haired woman, even after I'd texted Brody and set about preparing dinner. I hoped I'd made a mistake and the lady from the airport wasn't the same woman as the one from Déjà Brew. Yet, even if they were two different women, that didn't change the fact that the redhead who'd asked Genesis about Callum had shown up at the farmhouse. That in itself creeped me out.

As I defrosted the homemade spaghetti sauce and heated a pot of water, questions circled in my mind. Had the redhead at the airport bumped into me on purpose? If so, why would she do that? Perhaps she'd been watching Callum and me and surmised that I was his girlfriend, and that had stoked fires of jealousy in her.

Except, I hadn't seen any hostility or animosity on her face when she'd bumped into me, or when she was waiting to board her plane. Instead, I'd seen fear in her eyes.

Could she have feared that Callum and I might catch on to her plan to follow him home?

Maybe, but somehow that explanation didn't sit right with me.

Of course, I couldn't expect to make sense of the actions of someone unstable enough to follow a former MLB player all the way across the country to show up on his front lawn.

When Callum came into the farmhouse kitchen a while later, I smiled, my anxiety immediately dropping a notch or two. Just having him close by made me feel calmer, even though my worries still lingered. Unfortunately, while we cleaned up after our meal, my anxiety ratcheted up again. Not so much because of the red-haired woman, but because of my relationship with Callum.

I wanted him to move into the farmhouse full-time, but inviting him to do so would be offering a new level of commitment to our relationship. I was already plenty committed and knew he was too, but how could I take that next step when I still had secrets that I was keeping from him? I didn't want to hold anything back from Callum, but I also didn't want him thinking I was losing my mind.

I glanced over at Flossie and Fancy as I loaded our plates into the dishwasher. They were snoozing away peacefully with Stardust curled up between them. They didn't seem to have a care in the world. I wished I could say the same about myself.

I shut the dishwasher and dried my hands, trying to rein in my worries. I didn't want Callum catching on to the fact that I had something weighing on my mind.

It was too late for that, as it turned out.

"You've got worry written all over your face," Callum said, taking my hand and tugging me closer so he could wrap his arms around me.

"Clearly, I should never play poker, because I was trying to hide it."

Although I spoke the words in jest, Callum's green eyes held no humor.

"I don't want you trying to hide your feelings from me, Georgie," he said.

My stomach flipped at his sincerity, and at the way his eyes burned softly into mine.

I put a hand to his face and stroked my thumb over the blond stubble on his jaw. "I love you, Callum McQuade."

"Likewise, Georgie Johansen."

He kissed me in a way that eclipsed all my worries and troubles, at least for the moment.

"What can I do to help calm your anxiety?" he asked, still holding me close.

I relaxed into his embrace and nestled my head against his shoulder. "You're already doing it."

Flossie and Fancy raised their heads and jumped to their feet. They ran to the door as the sound of an approaching vehicle reached my ears.

"Who is it, girls?" I asked the spaniels as I released my hold on Callum.

Their tails wagged and Fancy threw back her head and let out a long, “A-woo!”

“Somebody we know, then,” Callum surmised.

We took a quick look out the window. A police cruiser drew to a stop in the driveway.

“Brody?” I guessed, based on the dogs’ excitement.

“Yep,” Callum said a second later as we watched our friend climb out of the vehicle.

I scooped up Stardust, who’d woken up during the dogs’ excitement, and Callum opened the back door. The dogs shot outside to meet Brody.

A few drops of rain pattered down from the dark sky, so we invited him inside as soon as he’d finished greeting the dogs. Flossie and Fancy clattered into the house ahead of him and danced around our feet.

“Sorry to interrupt your evening,” Brody said as he shut the back door behind him.

“You’re always welcome here,” I assured him. “Is this about the texts I sent you earlier?”

Brody nodded and ran a hand over his short, dark hair. “Can you tell me more about what’s been going on?”

We invited him to sit at the kitchen table and offered to make him some coffee. He declined the drink, but took a seat. Callum and I joined him, and the dogs settled down beneath the table. As soon as I set Stardust on the floor, she hopped up onto Brody’s lap with a purr, bringing a smile to his face.

While he stroked Stardust’s gray fur, I relayed the story, starting with the red-haired woman bumping into me at the airport in Tampa, and including every detail I could think of, though there weren’t many.

“Do you think she could be stalking Callum?” I asked.

“It’s possible that she was,” Brody said, his expression serious, “but we can’t be certain.”

“Was?” I echoed. “Has she left Twilight Cove?”

Evidence of her departure would definitely help me to feel more at ease.

“No,” Brody replied, “but she won’t be bothering you again.”

Something in his voice sent a zip of unease through me.

"Why's that?" Callum asked. I could tell from the glance he sent my way that he shared my sudden apprehension.

Brody held up his phone. Displayed on the screen was a grainy photograph, one of the two I'd sent him earlier.

His next words sent a cold quiver down my back.

"This woman was found dead at the Sea Breeze Motel."

FIVE

"Dead of natural causes?" I asked, once I'd recovered from the initial shock of Brody's announcement.

"Early indications point to foul play," he replied.

"Do you know who she is?" I realized that I'd used the present tense and corrected myself. "Who she was?"

Callum took my hand in his, and it was only then that I realized I'd curled my fingers into a tight fist. I relaxed my hand, letting my fingers entwine with his.

"We don't yet have a formal identification," Brody said, "but we do have a preliminary one, thanks to her motel registration and her driver's license and credit cards. I can't share her name with you at this point, but I can tell you that she was a resident of Tampa and just checked into the Sea Breeze Motel yesterday."

"But you don't know why she was in Twilight Cove?" Callum asked.

"We're still looking into that. We're hoping her next of kin might know why she was in town and what connections she might have to people here."

"Please tell me that Callum isn't a suspect," I said, my voice strained.

"Why would I be?" Callum asked, taken aback. "Because she might have been stalking me? I never even set eyes on her."

"At this stage, we don't have any suspects," Brody replied. "But since the two of you did have a link to her, as tenuous as it might be, you'll likely need to provide your whereabouts at the time of death."

My stomach churned, making me wish I hadn't just eaten. "When did she die?"

Brody scratched Stardust between her ears, getting a blissful purr out of her. "Early this afternoon. We don't have a more specific time of death yet. The post-mortem will take place tomorrow."

I sent an uneasy glance at my boyfriend. "Callum was coaching softball at the high school this afternoon, and I was shopping at Vintage Vibes for a while. When I left the shop, I saw the emergency vehicles at the motel."

"Before coaching, I was here at the farm," Callum said. "First, with Georgie, and later Olivia helped me out in the barn. I was only alone long enough to drive over to the school."

"And I was alone to drive to Vintage Vibes, but that's it," I added. "If it's just the afternoon that we need to account for."

"Once we have a time of death, you'll need to provide formal statements. At this point, I just wanted to make sure I had all the information you could give me." Brody pushed back his chair and got to his feet. "I'm sorry I cast a pall over your evening."

"No need to apologize," Callum said as we stood up too.

Brody set Stardust gently on the floor. "I'll be in touch."

Callum walked him out, but the weight of the news lingered well after his departure. Hearing about the woman's death had fed my anxiety, giving it a burst of unfortunate energy. I tossed and turned after going to bed, unable to stop worrisome thoughts and questions from circling around and around in my mind.

Who was the dead woman? Why was she in Twilight Cove? Who had killed her and why? Would Callum and I end up as official murder suspects?

I had no answers to those questions, but that did nothing to stop them from keeping me awake, and eventually my restlessness woke Callum.

"Hey," he said sleepily, shifting closer to me. "Can't sleep?"

"I'm sorry for waking you."

"Don't be." He opened his arms. "Come here."

I snuggled up to him. In the warmth and safety of his embrace, I finally drifted off to sleep.

We didn't hear from Brody again until the following afternoon. I took a break from writing—losing myself in my latest thriller helped me forget about my worries—and checked my phone to find a text message that he'd sent twenty minutes earlier, asking if I could attend the police station sometime in the next few hours. Before responding, I walked out to the barn to find Callum. He checked his phone and found he'd received the same message.

"Want to go now?" Callum asked.

"The sooner the better."

I hoped that the police now had a time of death for the mystery woman, because I wanted to know if Callum and I had alibis that would keep us free of suspicion.

Callum took a few minutes to change his clothes and then we headed into town together, leaving the dogs and Stardust at the farmhouse. I'd talked to Auntie O about the death first thing in the morning, but all she'd heard from other sources was that there'd been an incident of some sort at the motel. If there were any other details traveling through Twilight Cove's grapevine, they'd yet to reach our farm on Larkspur Lane.

At the police station, Brody led me to one interview room while another officer took Callum elsewhere in the building. Once again, I told Brody everything I could about the red-haired woman. This time, he made an audio recording and took notes.

"Can you please tell me your whereabouts between the hours of one thirty and two thirty yesterday afternoon?"

I almost sighed with relief. "Callum and I were eating lunch together until quarter to two. Then Conrad Rigsby—from across the road—stopped by for about ten minutes. After that, I was alone for five to seven minutes while I drove into town. The rest of the time, I was shopping for a dress at Vintage Vibes."

And Callum, I knew, had worked in the barn with Auntie O after Conrad's brief visit. Neither of us had had an opportunity to harm the dead woman.

"Does the name Nina Hartmann mean anything to you?" Brody asked next.

"No," I replied. "Was that the victim's name?"

Without answering my question, Brody produced a photograph from a manila folder and slid it across the table toward me. It was a picture of the redheaded woman, but a selfie this time, and far clearer than the stills Genesis had acquired from Déjà Brew's security footage.

"This is a better picture of her," Brody said. "Looking at the photo, do you remember seeing this woman before she bumped into you at the airport in Tampa?"

I scrutinized the photo, but I had no other memories of her.

"No," I replied. "But seeing this photo makes me more certain than ever that she's the same woman that I saw in Tampa. I'm not sure if this is important, but I could have sworn she was scared of something—or someone—at the airport."

"Any idea why?"

"None." I looked down at the photo again, a wave of sadness for the woman rushing over me. "Do you know yet if she had some reason to be in Twilight Cove other than looking for Callum?"

"We're still looking into what brought her here," Brody said. Then he wrapped up the interview.

"Are Callum and I off the suspect list?" I asked once he'd stopped recording our conversation.

"As soon as we can confirm your alibis, you will be."

I was glad that Brody clearly had no doubt that he'd be able to confirm our alibis, but his colleagues would need proof before eliminating us as suspects. Particularly the state police, who had arrived in town to run the investigation.

"Can you tell me anything about Nina Hartmann, other than her name?" I asked, even though I doubted he'd be willing to share any further details.

"Not much. We've contacted her family in Tampa, and they expressed surprise that she was in Twilight Cove. They don't know of any reason why she would have traveled here."

I thought for a moment. "She must have left North Carolina for Oregon right after arriving in Charlotte."

"She booked her flight to Portland shortly after landing in North Carolina."

"So her trip out this way probably wasn't planned in advance," I said. "But if she had no connection to Twilight Cove and came here only because she was stalking Callum, why did she end up dead?"

"That's exactly the question that my colleagues and I are working to answer. Meaning," Brody added with a pointed stare, "you don't need to."

I'd earned that admonition by getting involved with previous murder investigations, but I didn't think he had anything to worry about this time.

"I know," I assured him. "And as long as Callum and I get struck from the suspect list, I'll have no reason to get involved. I'll still be curious about what happened and what Nina's intentions were, but I'm more than happy to let the police find those answers."

"Glad to hear it."

When Callum and I left the police station a few minutes later, sadness and relief took turns as my dominant feeling. My sadness was for the dead woman, who'd clearly met a horrible end, as well as for her family and friends, who now had a terrible loss to deal with. My relief, on the other hand, was for Callum and me. I had no doubt that Brody and his colleagues would soon confirm our alibis, so I no longer had to worry about suspicion hanging over us.

Of course, that didn't mean my incessant curiosity had taken a vacation, but I was quite content to let the local and state police solve the mystery of Nina Hartmann's death.

SIX

Before heading back to the farm, Callum and I stopped at the Pet Palace to buy some kibble for Flossie and Fancy.

"You didn't bring my favorite spaniels?" Cindy Yoon, the store's owner and my friend, asked with disappointment when we walked into the shop.

"They'll be upset too, once they find out we were here without them," Callum said.

Flossie and Fancy loved visiting the Pet Palace, partly because they enjoyed the attention they received from Cindy and partly because they usually ended up getting a treat.

"And they'll definitely know," I added.

A few quick sniffs of our shoes and the dogs would realize we'd visited their favorite store without them.

Callum settled an arm around my waist as we journeyed farther into the shop. "We'd better go home armed with apology gifts."

We took care of that first, choosing a couple of paw-shaped cookies with dog-friendly icing on them. I added a package of dried sardines for Stardust. The dogs liked those too and would no doubt help the kitten eat them.

"Did you hear there was a murder at the Sea Breeze Motel yesterday?" Cindy asked when Callum set a large bag of kibble on the sales counter, next to the treats. "It's so scary."

"There's a bit of a story to that," I said as I pulled out my credit card.

"Really?" Cindy asked with interest. "I haven't even heard who died."

"A woman from out of town," Callum said.

"Was it the same woman who might have been stalking you?" Cindy asked Callum with surprise. "Genesis told me about her."

The bell above the door jingled as two customers entered the shop.

"We'll tell you the rest another time," I promised in a whisper.

Cindy nodded with understanding and called out a greeting to the new customers.

After I paid for my purchases, Callum hoisted the bag of kibble up onto his shoulder like it hardly weighed anything and we said our goodbyes to Cindy.

A fizzy sort of happiness bubbled up inside of me as we reached Callum's vehicle.

"What's that smile for?" Callum asked, loading the bag of kibble into the back of the truck.

I shook my head, though I couldn't suppress my smile. "You'll think I'm silly."

"Impossible." He wrapped his arms around my waist and kissed me below my left ear.

"OK, then." I summoned up my courage. "I like doing ordinary things with you. I like doing everything with you, of course, but even doing mundane things with you is nice."

"Because they're ordinary couple things?" he guessed.

I nodded.

Ordinary *family* things, I almost said, before holding the words back.

I couldn't do that. I couldn't think of Callum as my family until I was completely honest with him. Secrets had no place in a fully committed relationship.

Instead of meeting his gaze, I toyed with the buttons on his flannel shirt and moved to safer conversational ground. "There's something else we should do today, once we get home."

"Does it involve you taking off my shirt?" he asked with a grin. "And maybe the rest of my clothes?"

I swatted his arm as my cheeks heated. "No! We need to buy you a costume for the museum's party."

"Hm. That doesn't sound nearly as fun." He leaned in close and whispered in my ear. "But maybe there'll be time for both."

"Callum!" I stepped back from him, fighting another smile. "We should go. The thoughts you're thinking aren't suitable for downtown Twilight Cove."

He opened the driver's door and grinned at me over the roof of the truck. "I'll try not to break the speed limit."

Still smiling, I shook my head and climbed in the passenger side.

The smile slipped off my face when I shut the door and glanced out the window. A young man—maybe about twenty years old—in torn jeans and a gray bomber jacket was standing on the street corner, watching us. Even when I caught him staring, his gaze didn't waver. He had a slender build and pale skin, and his dark brown hair flopped down over his forehead. I'd never seen him before. There was something unsettling and calculating about the way he watched us so overtly.

"Do you know that guy?" I asked, giving a discreet nod in the young man's direction.

Callum took a second to study him, a frown appearing on his face. "Never seen him before."

The guy finally turned away, disappearing around the corner.

I nearly shivered. "Creepy."

"Maybe he wasn't looking at us," Callum said, starting the truck's engine.

I didn't say so, but I didn't buy that.

I just hoped Callum didn't have another baseball-crazy stalker.

Callum and I spent the evening snuggled up on the couch. A crackling fire added to the coziness of the living room while warding off the damp chill of the rainy evening. Flossie and Fancy lay on the rug, snoozing away, while Stardust purred on my boyfriend's lap. Callum had his arm around me as I used my laptop to search the internet for men's 1920s costumes.

"That one," Callum said, pointing to an outfit after we'd scrolled through dozens of options.

I pictured him in the costume and smiled. "Good choice."

The ensemble he'd pointed to consisted of cuffed, pinstriped trousers and a matching waistcoat. The available accessories included a fedora and white spats that he could wear over any black dress shoes. I added all of the items to the shopping cart and checked out.

As an introvert, I typically didn't gravitate toward parties, but I was looking forward to this one. I loved the 1920s theme and couldn't wait to see everyone's outfits.

Once we'd purchased the costume, I shut down my laptop and set it on the coffee table. I leaned against Callum's chest and ran a hand over Stardust's fur. She purred louder, closing her hazel eyes in bliss.

"I approached Olivia again about my proposal to fund the sanctuary," Callum said as I watched the flames dancing and popping in the fireplace.

"And?" I asked.

"She's agreed to hear me out. I'll give her the full proposal sometime this week."

Auntie O had turned down his offer to fund the sanctuary in the past. Callum already lived rent-free in the cabin beyond the barn in exchange for managing the farm. He wouldn't accept a salary for his work, so my aunt didn't feel right taking more money from him. Callum, however, loved the sanctuary and didn't want us to have to rely on fundraising to keep it going.

I didn't know exactly how much money Callum had—I'd never asked—but I knew he was a multimillionaire, thanks to his lucrative career playing major league baseball. He'd set up his parents and sister financially, and I knew he supported several charities.

I didn't mind that he wanted to finance the sanctuary because that meant my aunt wouldn't have to worry about that side of the operation. After the death of her husband, she'd received a large life insurance payout, which had allowed her to retire early from her teaching job and set up the sanctuary. Even so, caring for all the animals was a costly endeavor. We'd already held one recent fundraising event to help cover the cost of upkeep and veterinary care.

I could, however, also understand my aunt's hesitation to accept Callum's offer. She didn't want to take advantage of his generosity, especially when he already gave so much to the sanctuary, and I suspected that she also worried about potential relationship complications. After all, Callum was already the farm's manager and now he was my boyfriend. If he also became the sanctuary's benefactor, that added another layer of complexity.

Although it was uncharacteristic for me—a practiced worrier—I'd decided not to trouble myself about the subject. If Auntie O wanted to talk things over with me, I'd be happy to act as a sounding board, but I wanted her to come to a decision that she would feel fully comfortable with going forward.

"Do you think there's any chance that she'll agree?" Callum asked, stroking a wavy lock of hair away from my face.

"There's a chance," I said. "She just needs to figure out if she can feel comfortable with every angle of it."

"She's doing good work here, and I've got more money than I need. It just feels right to me."

I turned my head so I could smile up at him. "You're a good man, Callum McQuade."

He was about to say something in response when his phone vibrated on the coffee table. Then my phone chimed.

We both reached for our devices at the same time.

"I'm also an unsuspicious man, apparently," Callum said as he read his new message.

I knew then that he'd received the same text as Brody had sent me.

The police had confirmed our alibis.

We were officially off the suspect list.

SEVEN

After spending several hours writing the next day, I took the dogs out for a walk, desperate for some fresh air and a chance to stretch my legs. It had rained all night, leaving the path through the woods muddy, but the clouds had parted to reveal the sun, and I wanted to take advantage of the break in the wet weather.

Flossie and Fancy didn't mind the mud and, with my sturdy boots on, I didn't either. Birds sang in the trees around us and sunlight filtered through the dripping canopy as we followed a familiar trail to our favorite secluded beach. As we made our way out of the forest and onto the sand, the dogs charged off ahead of me, chasing away a seagull that was bobbing in the water near the shore. Then they raced up and down the beach before running back my way and sitting at my feet.

"Are you having fun?" I asked as they looked up at me expectantly.

Flossie shifted her gaze to my jacket pocket.

Plastic rustled and the bag of dog treats I had tucked in the pocket inched its way out into the open.

I clapped a hand over the bag before it could tip out onto the ground.

"Flossie!" I admonished. "That's very cheeky!"

"A-woo," Fancy said, likely in support of her sister.

A spike of fear shot through me and I glanced around. Thankfully, we were alone. Cliffs bookended this section of beach, limiting its accessibility. I was extra grateful for the seclusion now.

Flossie had first demonstrated her ability to move objects without touching them several months ago. I didn't know if it was a new power of hers, or one she simply hadn't used in front of me before. Soon after meeting the spaniels, I'd learned that they could do more than the average dog. Fancy, for instance, could camouflage herself and emit a blue glow. Flossie could undo any lock with the touch of her paw, but I wondered now if her telekinesis was evidence of an escalation of the power that allowed her to manipulate locks.

"I can't condone such behavior," I scolded, though not too harshly. "So you'll have to do something for me before you get a treat."

After all, I didn't want them developing a habit of helping themselves to snacks whenever they wanted.

Still seated, Fancy scooted closer to me with undisguised eagerness.

"That goes for you too," I told her.

She grumbled in complaint.

I picked up two pieces of driftwood and gave each one a good toss. "Go fetch!"

The dogs bounded off.

Moments later, they galloped back along the wet sand, each carrying a piece of driftwood. They dropped them at my feet and then sat and looked up at me, their tongues lolling out as they waited.

"Good girls," I praised. "Now you can have a treat."

I doled out the small dog cookies and returned the bag of treats to my pocket, zipping it shut to make it more secure.

"There's something I need to talk to you about," I said as I struck off along the shoreline, the dogs trotting along beside me. "I need to tell Callum about your special abilities. I'm scared to do it, because he might not believe me. He might think I'm losing my mind. I don't want to change our relationship in any sort of negative way, but I also can't keep the secret from him any longer."

"Woo," Fancy said.

Maybe it was going too far to think she was agreeing with me, but I thought so anyway.

"It would be a lot easier to get him to see that I'm not completely nuts if you two were willing to demonstrate your powers for him," I continued. "And I know I'm always cautioning you to be careful in public, but this is for Callum's eyes only. Maybe for Auntie O one day too, but let's start with Callum for now."

I glanced down at the dogs. They trotted along happily, seemingly unburdened by any worries.

"Any chance you'd be willing to help me out?" I asked.

They glanced up at me with their soulful brown eyes, but in

no way indicated if they were agreeing, disagreeing, or if they even understood anything I'd said.

I sighed and drew to a stop, the toes of my boots barely out of reach of the gentle, lapping waves.

Flossie and Fancy trotted into the shallows and splashed about.

There could be no guarantee that the spaniels would show Callum what they could do. I'd just have to take the leap on my own and hope that our relationship survived.

The risk terrified me, but I knew there was no real alternative.

As I stood on the sand, gazing out at the Pacific Ocean and breathing in the wonderfully fresh—and slightly chilly—air, a great horned owl soared overhead. The dogs stopped their splashing and looked up to track the owl's flight path.

Shading my eyes from the sun, I smiled and called out, "Hello, Euclid!"

Still in the water, Fancy threw back her head and bayed.

The owl circled above us once more before disappearing over the trees.

Euclid wasn't just any great horned owl; I considered him a friend, and I knew the spaniels did too. Dorothy—the woman Flossie and Fancy had lived with before I adopted them—had enjoyed a close relationship with the owl, who would perch on her windowsill, and even on her shoulder. After Dorothy's death, Euclid had helped me survive an almost deadly encounter with a killer, solidifying my bond with the bird.

Sometimes I didn't see him for days on end, but he always stopped or swooped by for a visit before too much time passed. He'd led me to helpful clues more than once while I was looking into local murder cases, and I wondered if his appearance now was his way of telling me that I was making the right decision by opening up to Callum.

There was no way for me to know that for sure, but there was one way to find out if telling Callum the truth was the best move: share the dogs' secrets and see what happened.

As Flossie, Fancy, and I turned for home, I resolved to raise the subject with him that very night.

"Brody texted me earlier," Callum announced that evening when he arrived at the farmhouse for dinner.

"Have the police solved the murder?" I asked, hopeful.

"He didn't mention the murder." Callum washed his hands at the kitchen sink. "He invited me to go play pool with him and Nicholas tonight. Do you mind if I go?"

"Of course not." I glanced at the dogs as I set a casserole dish full of mac and cheese on the table.

So much for my plan to tell Callum about the spaniels' special abilities. I didn't want to drop that surprise on him right before he was going out with his friends. The news would throw him for a loop, no matter how well he took it.

"You sure?" Callum asked as he took cutlery out of a drawer. "You could come with me, if you'd like."

"And intrude on your guys' night out?" I said with a smile. "No, thanks. I'll be fine here with the dogs, Stardust, and a good book."

Flossie barked, sounding like she concurred.

On his way to the table with the knives and forks, Callum stopped to give me a lingering kiss. "I don't know how late I'll be, so I'll sleep at the cabin tonight so I don't disturb you or the animals."

I acknowledged that with a kiss of my own, careful to hide my disappointment.

If I wanted him to stay at the farmhouse every night, I needed to extend an invitation for him to move in, and I couldn't do that until we talked about Flossie and Fancy. Something which, now, would have to wait.

Nevertheless, I vowed not to delay the task for long.

If Callum was here with me the following evening, we would have that conversation.

After dinner, Callum took the dogs out for a couple of minutes and then came back in the house to kiss me goodbye. I spent a quiet and cozy evening with the dogs and Stardust, finishing up a good mystery novel while the animals snoozed.

Then Stardust insisted on a wild round of playtime, zooming around the house with the dogs in pursuit. Finally, they all settled down, and we headed upstairs to bed.

It took a while for me to drift off to sleep. My thoughts kept churning about the news I was going to share with Callum. Finally, after tossing and turning, my mind quieted and sleep overtook me.

Later, my eyes flew open in the darkness and I lay still, my heart thudding. Something had woken me, but I didn't know what.

I heard nothing, so I checked the digital clock on the bedside table.

Eleven twenty-one. I'd slept for less than an hour.

I glanced around the room, lit only by the glowing numbers on the clock. All appeared to be well. The dogs and Stardust had forgone their shared bed in the corner of the room to snuggle up with me. The spaniels lay sprawled out on their sides, taking up a good two thirds of the bed, while Stardust lay curled up on Callum's pillow.

I was about to turn over and go back to sleep when Flossie raised her head and let out a low growl.

A chill ran through my bloodstream.

"What is it, Flossie?" I asked.

She held still. I hoped she'd put her head down and go back to sleep, but instead she growled again.

Fancy raised her head and growled too.

Fear slithered through my stomach.

Both dogs jumped up, leapt off the bed, and ran out of the room.

My chest tightened.

I threw back the covers and grabbed my phone from the bedside table before hurrying out into the hallway, making as little noise as possible.

I followed the dogs' low growls into one of the spare bedrooms at the front of the house. Flossie and Fancy had their front paws up on the windowsill and their noses pressed to the glass. I crept over their way, staying off to the side of the window as I peered out into the night. Aside from the outlines of trees, I couldn't see anything in the darkness.

Flossie let out a sharp bark. She and her sister pushed off from the windowsill and ran for the door. They clattered down the stairs to the main floor, with me scurrying after them.

The spaniels tore across the kitchen to the back door, where they barked furiously. They weren't the happy or excited barks that heralded the arrival of someone they knew. These were guard dog barks, and the sound sent tremors of dread through me.

Still clutching my phone, I tiptoed over to one of the kitchen windows. As soon as I glanced through the glass, I pulled back sharply.

A dark figure stood on the back porch.

EIGHT

I hesitated, not wanting to call 911 only to find that it was Callum on the porch.

Then the logical part of my brain kicked in.

Of course it wasn't Callum. The dogs wouldn't be so agitated if they knew who it was. They definitely believed the person didn't belong here.

I retreated to the staircase, tucking myself out of sight of anyone who might peek in through the windows, and tapped my phone's emergency call button with a trembling finger. Although whispering felt appropriate in the circumstances, I had to speak loudly to be heard over the volley of frantic barking.

I reported the prowler to the emergency operator and provided the farm's address.

A brief pause in the dogs' barking had me hoping the prowler had left.

Then the back door rattled in its frame.

Flossie and Fancy resumed barking, even more ferociously this time.

A shadow slipped past one of the windows.

I dashed across the room and peeked outside in time to see someone vault over the porch railing. The prowler hit the ground and took off at a run.

I darted into the dining room, heading straight for the front window. Flossie and Fancy scrambled along with me, nearly tripping me in their haste. When I looked out into the darkness, I spotted the figure sprinting toward the road. They disappeared from sight a moment later.

After I'd relayed the prowler's direction of flight to the emergency dispatcher, I sank down to sit on the dining room floor, my back leaning against the wall. My heart pounded so fiercely that I feared it might give out.

Flossie and Fancy gave up on looking out the window and descended on me, covering my face with kisses.

"It's OK. It's OK," I said, stroking their fur. "Good girls."

The emergency operator stayed on the line with me until a police cruiser pulled into the driveway. Only then did I find the strength to climb to my feet. I told the dogs to wait indoors while I went out to greet the officers. Flossie and Fancy barely managed to sit and stay when I gave them those commands. They clearly wanted to burst out of the house and chase down the prowler, but I didn't want them disappearing into the darkness or getting hurt if they managed to catch up to the trespasser.

I spoke briefly with Officers Perlman and Escobar before they asked me to wait inside while they had a look around. The dogs and I watched from the window as the beams of their powerful flashlights swept around the property. The officers checked as far off as the barn, which I appreciated.

I phoned Aunt Olivia to make sure she was OK. My call woke her up, but once she heard why I was checking on her, she wanted to jump out of bed and come over to the house. I managed to convince her to stay put, though that was likely only because the officers came back to the kitchen door and reported that the prowler seemed to be well and truly gone. They promised to patrol the area and swing by the house several more times through the night, and then they left.

After locking the door behind them and checking all the other doors and windows on the main floor of the house, I sent a quick text message to Callum.

Are you back?

His reply came a few minutes later, after I'd returned to bed.

Not yet. Can't sleep? Want me to come home?

I desperately wanted him to come home, but I also didn't want to spoil his rare night out with his friends, and I didn't want to be needy.

No worries. Have fun, I wrote before setting my phone aside.

When morning arrived, I greeted it reluctantly and with bleary eyes. The dogs and Stardust, however, seemed to be no worse for wear after the excitement in the middle of the night. They made sure I didn't laze about in bed, no matter how much I was tempted to do exactly that.

As soon as I opened the back door, the dogs shot outside.

Leaving Stardust in the house, I followed them. They sniffed around the porch and then scurried down onto the lawn, their noses to the ground the entire time.

I trailed after them as they stayed on the scent, rounding the corner to the front of the house. When the spaniels got close to the road, I called out to them, making them wait until I'd checked for traffic. I didn't see or hear any vehicles, so we crossed Larkspur Lane together. The dogs led me to a maple tree that stood directly across the road from the farmhouse. They sniffed at the base of the trunk, then sat down.

"Woo-woo," Fancy said.

Flossie barked and stood up, pawing at the ground before looking at me.

"What is it?" I asked as I approached.

When I reached the spot beneath the tree, I crouched down and something caught my eye. I pushed aside a few blades of grass to reveal what looked like a shard of purple plastic.

"Is this important?" I asked the dogs.

Flossie barked and wagged her tail. I used my phone to take a picture of the plastic shard. There was a fancy "F" written in black on the fragment, but if it was the start of a word or name, I couldn't tell, because the rest was missing.

I left the piece of plastic in place—in case it turned out to be evidence—and called the non-emergency number for the police and reported what the dogs had found when following the prowler's scent. I didn't know how long it would take for an officer to stop by, so I decided to get on with my day. I yawned my way through a quick breakfast of toast and jam and then pulled on my boots and coat before making the short trek out to the barn.

Flossie and Fancy ran off ahead of me, still showing no signs of suffering from lack of sleep. Although I trudged across the yard, I smiled as soon as I stepped into the barn. Callum was already at work, fixing one of the stall doors. He put aside his drill and a new set of hinges, giving the dogs a good pat before greeting me with a kiss.

"Did you have fun last night?" I asked as I leaned against him.

"We had a good time." He wrapped an arm around me. "Did you manage to get some sleep after you texted me?"

"About that . . ."

The sound of tires crunching over the gravel driveway caught my attention. The dogs charged out of the barn and Callum and I followed at a walk.

"The police?" Callum said with confusion when he saw the cruiser pulling to a stop by the farmhouse.

As we walked over to greet the officer, I gave Callum a quick rundown of what had transpired the night before.

"Georgie." Callum took my hand and tugged me to a stop so he could look me in the eye. "I'm so sorry I wasn't here."

I squeezed his hand. "It's OK. We're all fine."

I could tell he wanted to say more, but Brody climbed out of the police cruiser, so I slipped my hand out of Callum's and led the way over to the vehicle.

Brody had heard about the prowler, so I took him across the road and showed him the piece of purple plastic.

"Of course, I can't say for sure that the prowler dropped this," I said, "but Flossie and Fancy followed the person's scent right to this spot."

"Clever dogs," Brody praised the spaniels, much to their delight.

He snapped some photos and then bagged the tiny piece of evidence. I appreciated that he'd taken those steps, even though I knew that there probably wasn't much chance of identifying the prowler, especially since the case wouldn't be a priority for the police when they had a murder to solve.

"If not for the fact that she's dead, I would have thought the prowler was the redheaded woman," Callum said as we all crossed Larkspur Lane to return to the farm.

"I sure hope you don't have two stalkers." I remembered the creepy guy I'd seen in town. "But maybe there is another one."

I told Brody about the guy dressed in the bomber jacket and the way he'd watched Callum and me, or just Callum. I described him as best I could and added that I'd never seen him before that sighting two days ago.

"Do you have any leads on who might have killed Nina Hartmann?" Callum asked.

"The investigation is still in its very early stages," Brody replied in his typical uninformative way.

I tried a question of my own. "Did she have children?"

"No children, no spouse," Brody said as we reached the police cruiser. "She's got an elderly father and a sister in Tampa. The sister is scheduled to arrive in Twilight Cove this afternoon."

My heart ached for the woman who'd lost her sister. Even if the murder victim had been stalking Callum, her death was still a terrible tragedy.

Brody took his leave, and Callum and I walked back toward the barn together while the dogs bounded off in the direction of the carriage house, no doubt looking for Auntie O.

"Are you sure you're OK?" Callum asked, taking my hand. "You must have been terrified last night."

"It was definitely scary," I admitted, "but Flossie and Fancy are great guard dogs when they need to be. The way they were barking, they sounded much bigger and meaner than they actually are."

"Then they deserve extra treats today."

"I'm sure they won't argue with you," I said with a smile.

"Is it OK if I stay over tonight?" Callum asked. "The prowler's not likely to come back, but I'd feel better if I were with you at the house. Plus, I don't like spending nights away from you."

"The feeling's mutual. I'm meeting Tessa for dinner, but I won't be out late."

"Have a good time. For now, I'd better get back to that stall door."

As he disappeared into the barn, I turned and took in the sight of the yellow-and-white Victorian farmhouse. I hoped Callum was right and the prowler wouldn't return, but for some reason, an ominous weight sat heavily in my stomach.

NINE

I met my best friend, Tessa Ortiz, on Main Street shortly after she finished work for the day. Most of the shops would close within the next hour or two, but that still gave us time to take care of an important task before we had dinner at the Moonstruck Diner.

Auntie O's birthday was coming up in a few weeks and I didn't want to leave shopping for her gift until the last minute. The last time I'd seen Tessa, she'd suggested getting my aunt a set of earrings, and she'd offered to go to the local jewelry store with me. We both found parking spots close by and walked together to the small shop.

An electronic bell sounded when we opened the door and classical music played quietly in the background. The only person in the store was a man in his fifties, wearing a suit and standing behind the sales counter. He introduced himself as Anton, the proprietor, and offered us assistance, but we were happy to simply browse for the time being.

Although I'd already decided to choose earrings for Auntie O, we ended up looking at necklaces and bracelets as well. The display cases were full of gorgeous pieces, but when we came upon a counter-top turnstile showcasing different animal earrings, I knew for certain that I'd come to the right place.

"Check these out," I said, moving closer to the display.

"Classy yet whimsical, and so very Olivia," Tessa said with approval.

The selection of earrings included silver koala bears, white gold honeybees, and sapphire-and-silver jellyfish. I looked through all of the options twice before deciding on a set of delicate hummingbirds made from sterling silver, topaz, and opal. Olivia loved hummingbirds and put out a feeder for them every spring and summer.

"She'll love them," Tessa said when I made my choice.

She wandered off to look at a display case full of bracelets while I approached the sales counter.

"Did you find something, Georgie?" Anton asked.

"You know my name?" I said with surprise.

"Oh . . ." He faltered before saying, "I'm acquainted with your aunt."

That didn't surprise me. Auntie O had lived in Twilight Cove for decades and seemed to know just about everyone.

"These are for her birthday." I set the earrings on the counter.

"A wonderful choice," Anton said with a smile. "And made by a local artist."

"Even better."

As I paid for the earrings, someone entered the shop. Anton called out a greeting, but I didn't glance at the other customer until Tessa and I left the store. I caught a glimpse of a woman with black hair, wearing a dark blue leather jacket and carrying a takeout coffee cup. Just before the door drifted shut behind us, I heard the woman say to Anton, "Do you ever purchase jewelry from individuals?"

Tessa and I crossed Main Street and walked down the hill to the Moonstruck Diner, our favorite place to meet up for a meal. I loved the retro style of the diner with its black-and-white checkered floor and its turquoise-and-white booths. Customers could also sit at the turquoise-and-chrome counter, and the jukebox by the door still worked.

As usual, Tessa and I chose to sit in a booth, where we'd have more privacy. The owner, Jackie, came by to take our orders and to chat for a minute.

"Did you ladies hear about the murder at the Sea Breeze Motel?" she asked in a hushed voice once we'd given her our orders.

"It's so scary and sad," Tessa said.

I hadn't yet had a chance to tell Tessa about the tenuous connection that Callum and I had to the dead woman.

"Definitely scary," Jackie agreed, "though it sounds like it was probably a targeted murder. I hope that means no one else is at risk."

Her statement awakened my curiosity. "Why do you think it was a targeted killing?"

"I'm friends with Kevin and DeeDee, the owners of the motel. Dee told me that the dead woman was staying there, and her room was ransacked the day before the murder. The victim complained to her about it. Dee called the police, but the woman said she didn't think anything was missing."

"That's strange," I mused. "Why break in and not take anything?"

"I don't know, but if trouble followed her to Twilight Cove, then hopefully the killer has already left town." Jackie considered what she'd said. "At the same time, I want the police to catch the culprit. I hope they can still do that if the killer's no longer here." She barely paused for a breath before adding, "I'll have your drinks for you in a moment, ladies."

She swept off to greet a group of four customers who'd just arrived at the diner. After that, she brought the two glasses of cherry lemonade that we'd requested.

While we waited for our food orders to arrive, I filled Tessa in on my experiences with the dead woman, Nina Hartmann.

"Creepy," she said, after I told her about the fact that Nina had likely lurked near the farmhouse before her death. "She followed you and Callum all the way across the country and spied on you? That's extreme."

"There was a prowler at the farmhouse last night too."

"What?" Tessa exclaimed. "Georgie, that's terrifying."

"Thank goodness for Flossie and Fancy," I said. "They barked up a storm."

A troubled frown appeared on Tessa's face as she thought things over. "But it couldn't have been Nina last night."

"No." Unease hummed through me, not for the first time that day.

"Do you think both prowler incidents could be somehow related?" Tessa asked.

"I don't see how." Yet, I'd wondered about it myself.

Thinking about the murder and the previous night's prowler wreaked havoc on my stomach and threatened to destroy my appetite, so I asked if we could change the subject.

"Of course," Tessa said, her serious expression transforming into a smile. "I want to hear all about your trip to Florida."

Jackie delivered our food and, while we ate, I shared stories from my vacation. By the time we left the diner, the sun had set and the sky had turned a deep shade of blue. I said goodbye to Tessa and drove home, looking forward to spending the rest of the evening with Callum, the dogs, and my sweet kitten.

I'd almost reached the farm when a large bird swooped down in front of my car, not so close as to risk getting hit, but near enough to catch my attention. My car was the only one on the road, so I slowed to a crawl and soon found that my initial impression was correct—it was Euclid who'd flown by. Now he sat on a fence post at the side of the road, looking right at me. Or, right at my car, at least.

I pulled over and climbed out of the vehicle.

"Hey, Euclid. What's up?" I spoke quietly, even though there were no people around to hear me. Great horned owls, I knew, had incredibly acute hearing.

His head swiveled and dipped down so he was looking at the ground. He returned his intelligent gaze to me, and I felt like he could see right into my soul. A second ticked by, then another, before he spread his wings and took off, climbing up into the air before soaring over the nearby woods.

Larkspur Lane had no streetlamps, and my car's headlights were of limited help, so I switched on my phone's flashlight app and aimed the beam at the ground below the fence post where Euclid had perched. At first, I saw nothing. Scraggly bushes had grown along the fence, almost swallowing it up in places. I pushed aside some damp branches and aimed the light into the brush.

It didn't surprise me when I found something. Euclid always had a reason for leading me somewhere. Even so, my stomach gave a little flip when I spotted a smartphone in a blue case with the brand's logo in one corner. Euclid wouldn't have cared about me finding the phone if it had simply been lost by a random person.

I reached for the device, but then stopped myself, not wanting to touch it if it was evidence in a police investigation. Letting the branches fall back into place, I took stock of my exact location. I was standing across the road and one property down from Auntie O's farm, a short walk away from where the spaniels had found the fragment of purple plastic.

Could last night's prowler have dropped the phone?

I called the police station's non-emergency number and asked to speak to Brody. When he came on the line, I told him what I'd found and where.

"Best not to touch it," Brody advised. "I'll be there in a few minutes."

After ending the call, I realized I had no way to explain to the police why I'd stopped on the side of the road. If I told them that Euclid had signaled for me to stop and look around, they'd think I'd lost my mind. Even Brody would think so. I couldn't help but wonder—yet again—if Callum would have the same reaction.

I made a quick decision and drove my car to the farm. I fetched Flossie and Fancy, as well as the reflective vest and headlamp that I kept in the trunk of my car. Callum wasn't at the house, so I didn't have to explain why I was suddenly rushing to walk the dogs down the road in the dark. We'd just reached the fence post where Euclid had perched—marked by a purple glove I'd grabbed from my car—when Brody's police cruiser drove into view.

After I'd greeted him, I gave him the very brief story I'd prepared, saying that the dogs had shown a keen interest in the bush by the fence while we were out walking. It wasn't a total lie, since Flossie and Fancy had sniffed at the area as soon as I brought them over that way, but I made it sound like that was when I'd discovered the phone. As much as I didn't like having to fib to a friend, I didn't know what else to do.

"I'm sorry if I'm being paranoid," I said as Brody pushed aside the scraggly branches. "It's just that, after everything that's happened recently, I worried it might be related to the prowler incident. I probably should have just picked it up and brought it to the station."

Brody shone his powerful flashlight at the phone when I pointed it out. "No, you did the right thing, Georgie."

"You think it might be the prowler's phone?" If it was, that would certainly help the police identify the person.

"Actually," Brody said as he pulled on a pair of gloves. "I think you might have found the murder victim's phone."

TEN

On the weekend, Auntie O and I drove to Twilight Cove's museum so we could help out with the preparations for the fundraising party. Tessa had also signed up to volunteer, and met us there. A converted barn housed the museum's exhibits and archives, but an old Victorian house on the property also belonged to the museum.

The house had been owned originally by Franklin Joseph Elmore, a wealthy businessman involved in the timber and rail industries. The Elmore family had donated the property to the town many decades earlier, and now the main floor of the house was occasionally used for special events, such as the upcoming 1920s-themed party.

I'd never before set foot inside the Elmore house, so when I arrived there with Auntie O, I took a moment to drink in the sight of the gorgeous hardwood floors, crown molding, tiled fireplaces, and plaster ornamentation on the ceiling. The antiques in the rooms off the foyer were also a sight to behold. I'd already heard from Auntie O—who knew the organizer of the event—that much of the furniture was original to the house and would be stored elsewhere on the premises during the party so as to avoid any potential damage. Less valuable pieces would be moved in for the purpose of the event as needed.

"I have some great news," Gillian Fisher, who was spearheading the event, said once Auntie O, Tessa, and I had arrived. "A collector of antiques with a particular interest in the Art Deco era has agreed to lend us some reproduction furniture for the party."

"She's a collector of reproductions?" Tessa asked with surprise.

"She has plenty of antiques that are the real deal, so I'm told," Gillian explained as she led us to her office, tucked in a back corner of the Victorian, "but she used to rent reproductions out for theater and film projects. That was before she became incredibly wealthy and was able to collect real antiques."

"Do you think she'd be willing to share some pointers on how to become incredibly wealthy?" Tessa asked in jest.

Gillian smiled and unlocked the door to her office. "The story goes that she was an aspiring actress and singer. She met with moderate success back in the 70s, but she got rich by marrying a wealthy and successful film director. He was twenty years her senior and, when he passed away, Angelica inherited everything."

Tessa sighed. "Somehow I doubt there's a rich film director waiting to sweep me off my feet."

"You never know," Gillian said with a wink.

"But how about a handsome police officer?" I whispered as Gillian and Auntie O preceded us into the office.

"If only," Tessa whispered back.

Tessa and Brody had been friends for a long time, but over the past year or so, Tessa's feelings for him had developed beyond friendship. She'd shared that secret with me and only me, because she firmly believed that Brody didn't feel the same way. I had my suspicions that she wasn't altogether right about that—not anymore, at least—but time would tell if their relationship would evolve in a romantic direction.

Gillian invited us to take seats and checked her phone as she scooted around behind her desk. "Oh, shoot," she said as she looked at the screen.

"What's wrong?" Auntie O asked.

"It's Angelica Bergstrom, the woman I was just telling you about. We made arrangements for her to come and have a tour of the Elmore house today, but she just texted to say that she's having car troubles. She's requested that someone pick her up from the Gilmore Hotel, but I've got the volunteer meeting."

"Could one of us pick her up instead?" Tessa asked.

Gillian smiled with relief. "That would be such a great help."

"I can go," Tessa offered. "Although, the upholstery on the passenger seat of my car is held together by duct tape. That might be a little too rustic for a wealthy woman."

"Oh . . ." From the way Gillian's face fell, it was clear that she feared the same.

"I can go," I said. "My car isn't fancy, but it's in good shape."

"Much better than my old clunker," my friend agreed.

Gillian's relief made a comeback. "Oh, thank you, Georgie."

She looked to Tessa. "Actually, perhaps both of you should go in Georgie's car. Would you mind stopping on the way to the hotel to pick up dishes and cutlery from a local donor? We'll use it for the fundraising party and future events as well. I'm afraid there are several boxes, though."

"The two of us should be able to handle that," Tessa said, looking to me for confirmation.

I agreed, so Gillian texted both Angelica and the donor of the dishes to let them know that we would be stopping by soon.

Several other volunteers arrived then, so Tessa and I quickly took our leave so Gillian could get the meeting started. Auntie O stayed behind to take part in the meeting and promised to share any important information we might miss.

It took only three minutes for Tessa and me to reach our first stop, where we transported several heavy boxes from a stately, two-story home to the trunk of my car. Thankfully, the elderly donor of the dinnerware had a dolly for us to borrow, otherwise Tessa and I would have struggled to move the boxes.

Once we had everything loaded into my car, we thanked the woman and carried on toward the Gilmore Hotel, perched on a hill overlooking the ocean. On the way to the hotel, I told Tessa about the phone I'd found and what Brody had said about it.

"If it is the murder victim's phone, that's super creepy," Tessa said. "Do you think she dropped it there when she was watching the farmhouse?"

I slowed the car before making a left turn. "I don't know how else it would have ended up there. It might not help the police with their investigation, but at least they won't be wasting time looking for the phone anymore."

After bagging the device at the side of the road, Brody had told me that the police had been on the lookout for Nina Hartmann's phone, since one hadn't been found among her belongings at the murder scene. Nina's sister had told the cops that the phone had a bright blue case with the same brand name as the one at the side of the road.

"Maybe it'll contain information that will lead the police to a suspect," Tessa said. "Or to someone who knows something helpful, at least."

"Let's hope so."

The sooner Nina's killer was caught, the sooner everyone in town could relax.

"Have you ever been inside?" Tessa asked as we pulled into the Gilmore Hotel's semicircular driveway.

"I've only ever driven by," I replied, craning my neck to get a good look at the building through the windshield. "Looks swanky, though."

"The swankiest place to stay in Twilight Cove."

I pulled to a stop near the front doors. We climbed out of the car, and I handed my keys over to the valet. When we entered the lobby, a sparkling fountain caught my attention first. Then I took in the sight of the white marble floors with black accents, and the lush green potted plants. I didn't know the cost of a night's stay at the Gilmore, but I suspected it was far more than I'd be willing to fork out.

Gillian had provided us with Angelica Bergstrom's room number, so Tessa and I took the elevator up to the fourth floor and knocked on the door to her suite. It swung open and the scent of flowery perfume wafted out into the corridor. The woman before us had short, honey blonde hair styled into large curls, and wore a long-sleeved, dove-gray dress. She had pearls at her throat and a white Pomeranian tucked under one arm.

She stroked the fur on the tiny dog's head. "The ladies from the museum, I presume?"

"We're volunteers, yes," Tessa said. "I'm Tessa Ortiz and this is my friend Georgie Johansen."

"Angelica Bergstrom," the woman said, before opening the door wider and setting her dog on the floor. "Please, come in. I just need a moment to finish getting ready."

We entered the suite to find ourselves in a tastefully furnished sitting area. Sunlight broke through the clouds and streamed in through the French doors that led out to a generous balcony with a stunning ocean view. Whitecaps dotted the waves and a seagull wheeled through the air.

The Pomeranian let out a series of yapping barks, aimed at Tessa and me, nearly bouncing off the floor with each one.

"That's enough, Birdie," Angelica admonished. "These are nice people."

Birdie let out another few yaps, until I crouched down and held my hand out, talking softly to her.

She inched closer and finally allowed me to stroke the silky fur on her head.

"What a cutie," Tessa said, crouching down beside me.

As Angelica packed a phone and a few other items into her handbag, Birdie approached Tessa and gave her hand a cautious sniff.

"See, Birdie. New friends." Angelica pulled on a wool coat and scooped her dog up into her arms.

"How long are you in town for?" Tessa asked as we walked to the elevator with the wealthy collector and her Pom.

"Just until tomorrow morning," Angelica replied. "I meant to stay another day, but my plans changed. It's a lovely town."

"Do you live in Oregon?" I asked as we boarded the elevator, realizing that Gillian hadn't told us much about the woman at all.

"I split my time between Gold Beach and New York City."

By car, Gold Beach was about two and a half hours down the coast from Twilight Cove.

"I love to be near the ocean," she continued, "and there's just something about the Oregon coast that resonates with my soul."

"I know what you mean," Tessa said with a smile. "I've lived here all my life and wouldn't want to be anywhere else."

The elevator doors opened and Angelica stepped out first. As I followed, my shoelace slapped against the marble floor, alerting me to the fact that it had come undone.

"I'll just be a second, Tessa," I said, moving off to the side so I wouldn't block the way to the elevators.

She nodded and hurried after Angelica, who'd nearly reached the hotel's front doors.

I stopped next to a potted palm tree and crouched down to tie my shoe. A woman wearing a red dress and matching stilettos stood on the other side of the plant, speaking into her cell phone. I hardly noticed her until she said, "The murder of my sister has been such a shock, Detective. I'm sure you can understand that having her personal effects turned over to me would be a comfort in this challenging time."

I slowed my lace-tying, my interest piqued. The woman had her back to me but, through the palm fronds, I could see that she had dark hair worn in a sleek, chin-length bob.

"Of course," she said after a pause, crying quietly now. "I know you're working hard to find her killer and I appreciate that."

During another pause, I switched feet and retied the lace on my other shoe to buy me some time. Tessa and Angelica had already disappeared outside.

"All right," the woman said as she gave a delicate sniff. After another short pause she said a tearful thank you and ended the call.

I stood up as she turned around and strode toward the elevator.

She didn't so much as glance my way, but I didn't fail to notice that she was completely dry-eyed.

ELEVEN

"You think she was fake-crying?" Tessa asked after we'd returned to the Elmore house, where Gillian was now taking Angelica—and Birdie—on a tour of the Victorian while they chatted about the fundraising party.

"It sure seemed like it," I replied.

The volunteer meeting had wrapped up in our absence, and Tessa, Auntie O, and I were unloading the last of the donated dinnerware from the trunk of my car and moving it inside with the help of three dollies belonging to the museum.

Auntie O had disappeared into the Elmore house with her latest load while Tessa and I shifted the final boxes from the trunk to the waiting dollies.

We transported the boxes to Gillian's office and stashed the dollies in the basement. Auntie O had stopped to chat with Gillian and Angelica, so Tessa and I hung out on the front porch as we waited for her.

"Maybe we can find out the name of Nina Hartmann's sister from social media," Tessa suggested as we sat on the porch swing.

"Good idea."

I pulled out my phone and searched for social media accounts under Nina Hartmann's name. I found several for people with the same name that weren't the right Nina. Then I finally landed on an account with a profile picture featuring the red-haired woman.

"This is her."

Tessa scooted closer so she could see the screen of my phone. "At least she doesn't have thousands of friends and followers."

"True, but all these profile pictures are tiny."

I scrolled slowly through all of Nina's connections. Just as an ache began behind my eyes, I found a promising profile. I clicked on it so I could see a larger version of the photo.

"I just caught a glimpse of the woman's face, and she's wearing sunglasses in this picture, but it could definitely be the same woman," I said. "She's got the same hairstyle."

"Scarlett Nicholson," Tessa read off the screen. "Not the same last name, but one or both of them could have married and taken their spouse's name."

"Scarlett says right here in her bio that she's married and has a son, so you could be right about that."

I exited the web browser and shut off the screen. My eyes immediately felt better.

"Not that it matters," I said. "I don't need to be looking into this murder. I can leave it to the police this time."

"Are you sure?" Tessa asked, skeptical. "Mysteries are like magnets for you."

I tucked my phone in my jacket pocket. "I can't deny that I'm drawn to the puzzle of it, but I'm not a fan of the dangers involved in investigating murders. I've had enough excitement in my life lately with that prowler who came by a few nights ago."

Tessa buttoned up her coat against the damp breeze. "That was definitely creepy. I hope the police catch whoever it was."

I had the same hope, but it was a slim one. Unless the prowler came back—which I definitely didn't want to happen—or got caught snooping around someone else's house, the culprit would likely never be identified.

Auntie O exited the Elmore house then, and she and I chatted about more pleasant topics as I drove the two of us to Déjà Brew on Main Street. It seemed like half the town had the same idea. The coffee shop was packed, with every table occupied and a line at the counter. Genesis worked briskly to fill drink orders, along with two of her part-time employees.

While Auntie O and I waited for our turn to order, I texted Callum to ask if he wanted me to bring him back a coffee. He replied moments before I put my order in.

After paying, I moved down the counter to wait for the drinks. I had a good view of the front door from there. Two customers left the coffee shop and, as the door drifted shut, a young white man with sandy hair elbowed it open. I'd never seen him before, yet when his gaze slid my way, he came to an abrupt halt. He whipped around and darted out the door before hurrying up the street.

I barely had a chance to register his odd behavior before a barista set the drinks we'd ordered on the counter before us. Auntie O picked up her pistachio latte and I grabbed my matcha latte and Callum's coffee. Then we made our way around the growing line near the cash register and pushed open the door. Once outside, I glanced up the road, but the sandy-haired man had disappeared from sight.

When we got back to the farm, Auntie O headed for the carriage house and I climbed the steps to the back porch of the farmhouse. As soon as I opened the door, Flossie and Fancy burst out and danced around me with excitement. After I'd given them enough attention to satisfy them, they bounded down the steps to explore all the smells in the yard. I carried on into the house and found Stardust batting a toy around the kitchen and Callum drinking down a glass of water by the sink.

"How was volunteering?" he asked as he placed his empty glass in the dishwasher.

"Not bad. The Elmore house is really beautiful. It's going to be a great venue for the party."

I handed him his coffee and he thanked me.

My stomach flipped as I played with the lid on my own cup. I couldn't put off our chat any longer. "There's something I need to talk to you about."

Callum leaned against the kitchen counter and took a sip of coffee. "OK. Is everything all right?"

I didn't know how to answer that question. Everything was OK at the moment, but would that still be true in a few minutes? That would depend entirely on how he reacted to what I had to share with him.

My stomach churned and I set my latte on the kitchen table. No way could I handle any sort of food or drink at the moment.

"Georgie?" Callum set aside his own drink and crossed the room to put his hands on my shoulders. "You look worried."

I tried to smile, but failed. "I have something important to tell you, but I'm nervous about how you'll react."

His forehead creased with concern before he enveloped me in a hug. "I don't want you to ever be scared of telling me what's on your mind."

I couldn't draw the usual comfort from his embrace. I was a jittery bundle of nerves, unable to stay still, so I stepped back and tried to take a deep breath. That proved difficult, with my chest growing tighter with every passing second.

"Let's sit outside." Maybe I could breathe more easily out there.

That didn't turn out to be the case. I sat down on the porch steps and Flossie and Fancy cantered over my way. Callum sank down next to me as I stroked the spaniels' fur and tried to calm my nerves.

He rested a hand on my knee. "Georgie?"

Even though I couldn't meet his eyes right then, I could hear the concern in his voice and I knew it wasn't fair to keep him in suspense. I met Flossie's gaze, then Fancy's, silently begging them to help me out.

"You know how smart Flossie and Fancy are, right?" I began.

The spaniels wagged their tails at the sound of their names.

"The smartest dogs I've ever met," Callum replied, giving them each a pat on the head.

"Well," I hedged before continuing, "there's more to it than that."

"A-woo!" Fancy interjected.

I rested a hand on her head. "I can't explain how it's possible, but they've both got unusual abilities. Maybe even magical abilities." Now that I'd started sharing the secret, words tumbled out of me. "Flossie can unlock doors and move things with her mind. Fancy can camouflage herself and glow with a blue light.

"I know it sounds crazy," I continued. "But I swear it's for real. I think their abilities have something to do with Witch's Peak, the place where Dorothy found them when they were puppies. Near where I found Stardust back in the summer. I've been watching Stardust to see if she has any special abilities, but so far, I haven't noticed any." I paused to take a breath.

"Georgie . . ."

"Maybe they'll show you what they can do." My words came out with an undercurrent of desperate hope. I couldn't look at Callum yet, so I kept my eyes fixed on the dogs. "Flossie? Fancy? Will you show Callum what you can do?"

They gazed up at me, but didn't move.

I bounced to my feet. "Maybe if I lock the door, Flossie will open it."

"Georgie . . ." Callum said again.

I'd almost worked up the courage to turn and meet his gaze when Flossie gave a bark and Fancy let out an excited howl. They took off, racing over to the driveway. Gravel crunched and Roxy appeared on her bicycle, riding onto the farm. Another girl on a bike followed. She had a blonde braid trailing down her back. As she got closer, I recognized her as one of Roxy's softball teammates.

Flossie and Fancy ran to meet the girls and raced alongside them as they pedaled over toward the house. I'd been so wrapped up in my worries that I'd forgotten Roxy was coming to volunteer at the sanctuary that afternoon.

She hopped off her bike while it was still moving and dropped it on the lawn. The other girl disembarked more carefully and propped up her bike with the kickstand. While she and Roxy crouched down to greet the dogs, I tapped my fingers against my leg, needing an outlet for the nervous energy that threatened to short-circuit my body.

I sensed Callum get up from the steps and move to stand next to me. He rested a hand on my lower back as the girls finished fussing over the spaniels and straightened up.

"Hey," Roxy greeted, as the other girl gave us a shy wave. "Izzy's interested in volunteering here too. Is it OK if she kind of shadows us today?"

"Hi, Izzy," I said, surprised that my voice didn't sound strange. "Of course it's OK, as long as that works for Callum."

"It's great," he said. "We'd love to have you as a volunteer, Izz."

That brought a smile to the blonde girl's face.

"Are we fixing that fence today?" Roxy asked.

"After we take care of the goats' hooves," Callum replied.

"You'll love the goats," Roxy said to Izzy.

"Do you want me to give you a hand?" I asked Callum, without meeting his gaze.

My phone buzzed on the porch railing where I'd left it.

"Sorry. Just a second." I darted up the steps, missing the comforting touch of Callum's hand on my back as soon as it was gone.

I read the text message I'd received from Genesis.

"Everything OK?" Callum asked.

I realized I had a frown on my face and smoothed out my expression. "I need to run into town to see Genesis. Unless you need me here?"

"The girls and I can manage," Callum assured me.

"But I can't stay too late," Roxy said. "My dad's in town and he's taking me out for dinner."

Which meant I had no time to steal Callum away to continue our conversation right then.

"All right," I said, trying to sound normal. I gave the dogs each a kiss on the snout. "I'll see you later."

I reached for the door, intending to dash inside to grab my coat and car keys.

"Georgie, wait," Callum requested.

I paused, apprehensive.

He jogged up the steps while Roxy and Izzy played with the dogs on the grass.

With Callum face-to-face with me, I finally looked into his green eyes. They held no judgment, but they were definitely troubled.

My stomach clenched.

He took my hand. "We'll talk more later, OK?"

I nodded as I swallowed a lump in my throat.

"I love you, Georgie," he said, before giving me a kiss on the cheek.

"I love you too," I whispered.

He squeezed my hand and set off for the barn with Roxy, Izzy, and the dogs.

I watched him go, wondering if our love for each other would be enough to get us through this.

TWELVE

It took a concerted effort to focus on the road as I drove into the heart of Twilight Cove. My thoughts wanted to spin like a fierce whirlwind and I fought off wave after wave of near panic. I tried to convince myself that it was for the best that Callum and I hadn't finished our talk. He probably needed time to process everything I'd told him.

After some time to reflect, would he be more or less likely to think I'd lost my mind?

I really had no idea, and the text message I'd received from Genesis only added fuel to my spinning thoughts. She'd said that something strange was going on and asked if I could meet her at Déjà Brew. She hadn't provided any other details.

Fortunately, the drive took only a few minutes, although that was plenty of time to work myself into worried knots. At least talking to Genesis would help to distract me from obsessing over how I might have messed up my relationship with my boyfriend.

I parked down the street from the coffee shop and walked quickly up the hill. When I entered Déjà Brew, I found that the crowd had thinned out in my short absence. Patrons occupied about half of the tables and only one person stood at the counter. One of the part-time employees was looking after that customer, so as soon as Genesis saw me, she waved me over.

"Carly," she said to the young barista, "I'll be in the office for a bit. Just holler if you need me."

She opened the bar flap so I could join her behind the counter, and then she led the way into the back corridor.

"Can I get you something to eat, Georgie?" she offered over her shoulder.

"No, thanks," I replied. "I'm good."

The mere thought of trying to eat anything set my stomach churning.

"You've got me a little worried," I confessed as I followed her into a small office. "Are you all right?"

"I'm fine," she assured me. "And I'm sorry for worrying you. It's probably nothing serious. It's just . . . something happened that struck me as a little odd and I thought you should know about it."

She grabbed her laptop off the desk and gestured for me to join her on the loveseat pushed up against one wall.

"You know how the murder victim was here asking questions about Callum before she died?" When I nodded, she continued, "Another woman came in and asked about him a little while ago."

"Do you have any idea who she was? What kind of questions did she ask?"

Genesis opened her laptop. "I tried to get information out of her after she brought up Callum's name. She asked if it was true that he worked at an animal sanctuary and if the farm was open to tourists. When I asked what name to write on her cup, she hesitated for a second and then told me her name was Jane. It felt like a lie, and I got a weird vibe from her. She claims she's here on vacation, but I'm not so sure. I asked her where she was visiting from and she got all tight-lipped, took her drink, and left."

"I probably would have assumed that she was simply a fan hoping to catch a glimpse of Callum while in Twilight Cove," I said, "but with the red-haired woman asking questions and then getting killed, and having another prowler at the farmhouse . . ."

"There was another prowler?" Genesis asked with surprise. "Not the redhead a second time?"

"The other prowler came at night, after Nina Hartmann was killed."

"Nina . . . that's the dead woman?"

I nodded. "This is all starting to feel pretty creepy."

"Even for me, and I'm not the subject of the questions or the target of any prowlers." Genesis tapped a few keys on her laptop and moved her finger along the trackpad. "I haven't had a chance to check the security footage yet, but she must have been caught on camera."

"I appreciate you sharing this with me," I said.

Genesis pulled up the security footage and zoomed through it to find the right spot.

"Here we go," she said as she stopped the video, before letting it play at normal speed. She pointed at the screen as a woman entered the coffee shop and approached the line at the counter. "That's her."

The current angle didn't provide a good view of the woman's face, but something else certainly caught my eye.

"I think I've seen her before," I said. "Or at least, a woman with the same jacket and similar hair."

The individual on the surveillance footage had straight black hair and wore a dark blue leather jacket, just like the one I'd caught a glimpse of at the jewelry store.

"Any idea who she is?" Genesis asked.

"Unfortunately, no. And it's hard to see her face."

"Let's move it ahead a bit." Genesis fast-forwarded the footage.

After paying for her order, the woman moved down the counter to wait for her drink. Genesis stopped the footage at that point and then rewound it by a few frames.

"There. That's a pretty good look at her face." She zoomed in. "Even better now."

"That's great." I studied the woman's features. She was Asian and possibly in her late thirties, but her jacket remained the only thing familiar to me. "I don't recognize her, though. You've never seen her in here before?"

"Not here at the coffee shop and not anywhere else, but I guess that isn't surprising since she said she's from out of town. Do you want me to email you a copy of this frame?"

"Please. It'll be good to have on hand just in case she pops up again."

Genesis tapped keys on her laptop. "Maybe there was a post online about the fact that Callum's living in Twilight Cove and that's why visitors are suddenly coming here and asking about him."

"Could be," I said, though she didn't have me convinced.

"Of course, that would be easier to believe if Nina Hartmann hadn't ended up dead."

"Exactly." I sighed. "Maybe the murder is completely unrelated to the fact that she asked questions about Callum, but not knowing if that's the case is what's so unsettling."

"I can only imagine. Do you want me to tell Brody about this woman?"

"I'll fill him in," I said. "Could you save this footage, just in case we need it later?"

"You bet. And if I learn anything more about the woman, I'll let you know."

"Thanks, Genesis."

She emailed me the photo and I left the shop while she got back to work. Once seated in my car, I brought up the picture on my phone to study it once again. Although a bit on the grainy side, it was still a decent photo. I opened my internet browser and uploaded the file for an image search. The results consisted of pictures of dozens of women who clearly weren't the one in the original photo.

Giving up on figuring out the woman's identity—at least for the time being—I texted Auntie O to let her know I was in town and to ask if she needed anything. She replied right away, requesting a slice of pizza from the local pizza parlor so she wouldn't have to cook dinner that evening.

For the first time since leaving the coffee shop, I took in my surroundings. The sun was sinking low over the ocean and shadows were lengthening all around. I hadn't realized how late it was getting.

I stopped by the pizza parlor and bought an entire pizza, since I didn't feel like cooking either. I hoped to share the food with Callum as well as Auntie O, but I didn't know if he'd want to spend time with me that evening. The only way to find out was to get home and talk to him.

Once I had the pizza in hand, I drove home and parked next to the farmhouse. I glanced over at the carriage house, but decided to let the dogs out before taking dinner to my aunt. Callum had clearly returned to the house at some point, because the kitchen lights were on and the dogs' dishes sat on the floor, licked clean. He'd left Stardust's dish on top of her cat tree—to prevent Flossie and Fancy from gobbling the kitten's food—and it was also empty, save for a few crumbs.

"Where is Stardust?" I asked the dogs after hugging and petting them, and receiving sloppy kisses in return.

Their unconditional love and enthusiastic affection eased the worry in my heart, just a little.

The spaniels didn't give any indication of their feline sister's location, but I noticed light spilling out of the living room. I wandered in there and stopped a few paces over the threshold.

Callum lay on his back on the couch, sound asleep, with Stardust curled up on his chest. Normally, such a sight would have brought a smile to my face. In my current state of emotional turmoil, it brought tears to my eyes.

I blinked them away and switched on a lamp before turning off the overhead light. Then I tiptoed back to the kitchen. I left one light on in that room and turned off the others before grabbing the pizza box and herding Flossie and Fancy out the back door.

"Everything OK?" my aunt asked a while later as we ate pizza at her kitchen table.

I glanced down at my plate. I'd managed only two bites of pizza in the time it had taken her to eat an entire slice.

"I guess I've got a lot on my mind," I said, not wanting to lie but also not wanting to talk about the root of my main worries.

I took out my phone and showed her the picture that Genesis had sent me, telling her how the mystery woman had asked about Callum at the coffee shop, just like the dead woman had.

"Let's hope it's just a coincidence that two people have shown such interest in Callum in recent days," Olivia said. "But maybe you should tell Brody, just in case."

"I've been meaning to text him. I'll do that as soon as I get back to the farmhouse."

I closed the pizza box, intending to take the leftovers back to the house for Callum to reheat. My stomach flipped at the thought of continuing our earlier conversation. I dreaded what he might say, but at the same time, I desperately wanted to know what was going on in his head.

After saying good night to my aunt, I left the carriage house with the dogs and walked across the yard. Flossie and Fancy brushed past me and nearly tripped me when they stopped abruptly, right in the middle of the driveway.

They tensed, and Flossie let out a low growl that sent a chill slithering down my spine.

I grabbed their collars, not caring that the pizza box tumbled to the ground.

"What's wrong?" I whispered.

The spaniels tried to lunge ahead, but I held them back, not wanting them to run headlong into danger.

The back door to the farmhouse slammed open and a shadowy figure shot out, leaping over the porch steps to the ground.

Flossie and Fancy strained against my hold and barked frantically.

The figure looked back in our direction, but never slowed down, running for the road.

"Oh no." Fear threatened to steal all the oxygen from my lungs. "Callum and Stardust."

Still holding onto the dogs' collars, I ran awkwardly, bent over at the waist.

When we reached the porch, the dogs stopped pulling and aimed their noses at the back door. Fancy let out a worried whine that made my insides quiver.

"Stay," I instructed the dogs.

I carefully let go of their collars, relieved that they didn't try to run after the fleeing intruder.

Quietly, I opened the back door and stepped into the house.

My heart lurched, and nearly stopped.

Callum lay on the kitchen floor, blood glistening on his forehead.

THIRTEEN

"Callum!" Shattered glass crunched beneath my feet as I stepped into the farmhouse. I put out a hand and spoke to the dogs over my shoulder. "Stay."

Flossie and Fancy whined, but sat on the porch and stayed put.

I crossed the kitchen in three quick strides, my heart squeezing with fear. I nearly cried with relief when Callum sat up on his own, just as I reached him.

"Cal?"

"I'm OK," he assured me. He touched his forehead and winced. His fingers came away smeared with blood.

I grabbed his other hand as he started climbing to his feet.

"Maybe you should stay sitting," I said, worried by his injury.

"I'm all right, and I'd rather sit on a chair."

I gave him a hand up and pulled a chair out from the kitchen table. He eased down onto it and I gently ran my hands through his hair, checking for other cuts on his head.

He captured one of my hands in his, stopping my inspection. "Hey. Georgie." He put a hand to my cheek. "I promise I'm all right."

I realized then that I hadn't managed to keep my tears at bay. A fat one rolled down my face. I wiped it away.

"You got hit on the head," I said, stating the obvious.

"They didn't knock me out. Just took me by surprise."

I pulled out my phone and reluctantly slid my hand out of his. "I'm calling the police."

The dogs whined out on the porch, but I told them once again to stay put. I didn't want them hurting their paws on the smashed glass. I flicked on the overhead light and saw that the broken glass had come from the window nearest the back door. The intruder must have climbed in that way.

"What happened?" I asked as I woke up my phone.

"I was asleep on the couch," Callum replied. "I woke up to the sound of breaking glass. I jumped up and came in here to see what happened, and somebody dressed in black lunged at me. They hit me before I even got a good look at them. Then they took off out the door."

"Stardust?" I asked, worried.

"She ran the opposite way when we got startled awake."

I gave Callum's shoulder a squeeze on my way to the living room. Two eyes glowed from beneath a chair on the far side of the room. I breathed a sigh of relief, glad that the kitten had gone into hiding at the first sign of trouble.

I placed my call to 911 on my way back to the kitchen.

"Are you sure there are no other intruders in the house?" the operator asked after I'd explained the situation.

"I'm pretty sure there was just the one person," I said, looking to Callum for confirmation.

He nodded his agreement.

Nevertheless, the operator asked us to wait outside.

Before leaving the house, I returned to the living room and nudged the chair aside. I scooped Stardust into my arms and gave her a kiss on the head before setting her in the downstairs bathroom and shutting the door. I didn't want her venturing into the kitchen and hurting her paws on the broken glass. I also didn't want her getting scared and running off when the emergency vehicles arrived.

When I returned to the kitchen, Callum was on his feet. He appeared steady and unshaken, but I put an arm around him anyway and walked with him out onto the porch. As soon as Callum was seated out there, the dogs fussed over him, whining and licking his hands.

About five minutes later, sirens wailed on Larkspur Lane. A police cruiser pulled into the driveway, followed by an ambulance.

Lights switched on in the carriage house and Aunt Olivia emerged, puzzled and concerned. I jogged across the yard to fill her in on what had happened and assured her that nobody was badly hurt. By the time I'd brought her up to speed, another police cruiser had arrived on the farm, this one driven by Brody. While the police searched the house and yard, the paramedics checked over Callum.

"It's not a deep cut," one of the paramedics declared, after cleaning the injury on Callum's forehead. "It doesn't need stitches."

"You should still go to the hospital," I said, holding Callum's hand while the paramedic bandaged his cut.

Callum gave my fingers a squeeze. "I don't need to. It was just a glancing blow and I'm sure I don't have a concussion."

The paramedics left the decision up to Callum.

He stood at the base of the porch steps with me, his arms around my waist. "If you really want me to go, Georgie, I will."

I tried my best to corral my worries and not let them run wild. I managed to calm myself enough to offer a compromise. "How about if you feel dizzy or sick or get a headache, you let me know and I'll drive you to the hospital?"

He gave me a quick kiss. "I promise I'll tell you if I feel any of those things."

Somewhat reassured, I stepped out of his loose embrace and provided a statement to one of the officers.

Later, when Brody emerged from the house, I approached him with my phone out.

"I'm guessing you didn't find anything inside," I said.

"We'll dust the windowsill and inner door knob for prints, but Callum thinks the intruder was wearing gloves. And whoever it was had their face covered. There's not much to go on, but I'm glad things didn't turn out any worse."

"Me too." I wrapped my arms around myself, shivering in my jeans and hoodie, only partly from the damp chill in the air.

"Maybe you should wait in the carriage house," Brody suggested. "It's not very warm out here."

"There's something I need to tell you first." I filled him in on the latest woman to ask questions about Callum at the coffee shop. Waking up my phone, I pulled up the photo of the woman in the leather jacket and showed it to him. "Don't you think something strange is going on? Two different people have been asking about Callum and now we've had three incidents of prowlers at the farm."

"It's extremely concerning," Brody said. "Can you email me this photo? I'll also get the original footage from Genesis tomorrow, but it'll be good to have the picture now."

I emailed it to him right then and there.

The ambulance and one of the police cruisers left the farm and I managed to convince Auntie O to go back to bed. Brody and Callum boarded up the broken window with a piece of plywood while I swept up the glass. After Brody left, I ran the vacuum through the kitchen to make sure I didn't miss any shards.

Once I felt confident that I had the house free of broken glass, we let Flossie and Fancy inside and I released Stardust from the bathroom. She crept cautiously into the kitchen with her tail down and her ears flattened. Flossie and Fancy trotted over to her and nuzzled their noses into her fur. She immediately relaxed and purred.

I'd retrieved the pizza from the lawn earlier and had stowed it in the carriage house's refrigerator until Auntie O went back to bed. Fortunately, the box had stayed closed when it tumbled out of my hands, so we slid the pizza into the oven to reheat it. After all the excitement, I was hungry enough to eat another slice, and Callum had missed dinner altogether.

The animals told me that they hadn't eaten either, a claim that Callum refuted, but I gave them each a treat. We all deserved something after the evening we'd had.

With the dogs and Stardust satisfied and dozing in the corner, I paced the kitchen while we waited for the pizza to heat up.

"Hey." Callum caught my arm as I passed by him. "You'll wear a hole in the floor."

"Sorry." Exhaustion would probably overtake me soon, but for the moment nervous energy bounced around inside of me, making it difficult to stay still.

Callum wrapped his arms around me and I leaned gratefully against his chest.

"I'm so glad you're OK," I whispered.

"And I'm so glad that you and the dogs weren't in the house."

"The prowler might have been watching the place. If they saw me go over to the carriage house with the dogs, they probably thought the house was empty." I shook my head, even as I kept it resting against his chest. "I don't understand what's going on."

Callum rubbed comforting circles on my back. "Neither do I." He stepped back and looked me in the eye. "I know it's been a crazy evening, but we need to talk about the stuff you told me earlier."

I tensed, not sure that I was feeling up to hearing what he had to say. But I also wasn't feeling up to waiting and worrying.

"Don't look so scared," he said gently. "We're good, Georgie."

"I haven't ruined everything?" I asked, still worried. "You don't think I'm completely crazy?"

"No and no." He kissed my forehead. "The dogs having magical abilities . . . that's not exactly easy to wrap my head around."

"I swear I'm not making it up."

He rested his hands on my upper arms. "I know you're not."

I stared into his eyes, trying to read what was coming. "You're not going to break up with me?"

He gathered me into another hug. "Georgie, you're the love of my life. I'd have to be a complete fool to walk away from you."

I relaxed against him, a little at least. "But do you believe me? About Flossie and Fancy?"

"I believe you. Does my brain feel like it's being twisted in new directions? Yes. But I know you wouldn't lie to me and it's not the first time in my life that I haven't been able to explain something. Besides, there are certain things that make a lot of sense now."

"Like what?" I asked, curious.

"One day I was fixing the lawn tractor. I tried to grab a wrench while still holding parts in place with my other hand, but I couldn't reach the tool. I set down the tractor parts and looked for the wrench, only to find that it was now within easy reach."

"Was Flossie nearby, by any chance?"

"Sitting and watching my every move."

We both looked at the black-and-white spaniel. She wagged her tail.

"And then there was the time I was carrying groceries from my truck to my cabin and dropped my keys in the grass," Callum continued. "Flossie and Fancy were there. I couldn't see my keys right away, so I set the groceries on the porch while I had a look around. Next thing I knew, the cabin door drifted open. At first, I wondered if someone had broken in, but the place seemed untouched. I figured I must have forgotten to latch and lock the door—even though I remembered doing both—and a gust of wind had blown it open. Except, it wasn't windy."

"You never mentioned that at the time."

"I convinced myself that I'd had a moment of forgetfulness, because that was the only explanation that made sense. Until today."

"You know the great horned owl that hangs around the farm sometimes?" I asked, deciding to get everything out in the open all at once.

"He's got magical abilities too?"

"I'm not sure," I said. "But he's definitely unusual, and crazy smart. He led me to the murder victim's phone the other day, and he's led me to other clues in the past."

"But why that owl and our dogs?" Callum asked.

"I don't know for sure. Euclid—that's the owl—was friends with Dorothy. She found Flossie and Fancy up in the hills where, apparently, ley lines converge. Does that mean anything to you?"

"Lines of magical energy?"

"That sounds about right. Maybe Euclid and the dogs were all at Witch's Peak when something magical happened. It's the only explanation I can think of."

"It's far better than any I can come up with."

I closed my eyes as I held onto him. "Thank you for believing me."

"Thank you for sharing this with me. You don't ever have to keep anything from me, Georgie."

I smiled against his chest, a heavy weight gone from my shoulders.

I'd taken a leap of faith and I'd landed safely.

FOURTEEN

The rest of the weekend passed without incident, though I often found myself on edge, especially when alone in the farmhouse. Callum installed security cameras at the front and back of the house, and that nudged my fear down a notch, but I couldn't be sure that the sight of the cameras would be enough to scare off the prowler if he or she returned.

I texted Brody the day after the break-in to ask if there had been other similar incidents in the neighborhood or if Auntie O's farm seemed to be the sole target. He replied that the latter was the case. That ratcheted my sense of unease back up again. I feared that Callum was the target of everything that had happened so far, and I didn't like to let him out of my sight.

On Monday afternoon, the high school softball team was scheduled to play its first real game of the season. I probably would have tagged along even if I weren't worried about Callum's safety, but I hoped that I would provide an extra set of eyes and ears to make sure nothing bad happened while he was focused on coaching the team.

Flossie and Fancy came to the ballpark too and I sat at the bottom of the bleachers so they could lie on the grass by my feet. A few students and a handful of parents showed up to watch the game along with us. I clapped and cheered for all the girls on Twilight Cove's team, but I cheered especially hard when Roxy hit the ball far out into left field and made it safely to third base, batting in two runners. Flossie and Fancy joined in the cheering, Flossie with a series of excited barks and Fancy with a long, happy howl that made everyone around us laugh.

By the fifth inning, the dogs had grown restless and I needed to stretch my legs, so we took a short walk before returning to the bleachers. I wasn't quite ready to sit down again, so we stood off to the side of the seats, watching the action on the field.

Flossie and Fancy flopped out on their sides for a snooze, but they bounced to their feet when someone strolled up to stand next to me.

"It's always fun to watch kids play, isn't it?" the woman said.

I glanced her way, about to respond, and did a double take.

It was the woman I'd seen at the jewelry store. The one who'd asked questions about Callum at Déjà Brew. She wore the same dark blue leather jacket as before and she had her black hair tied up in a ponytail.

"Um . . . yes, it's great," I said as my brain whirled. "Do you have a kid out there?"

"No. I was just passing and thought I'd watch for a bit. It brings back good memories from my childhood." She kept her eyes fixed on the game as she spoke, but I had my doubts about the veracity of what she'd told me.

"I'm Georgie," I said, hoping she'd provide me with her name.

It took a second, but she looked my way with a smile and offered, "Hailey."

Not Jane then. But was Hailey just another false name?

As she turned her attention back to the game, I glanced at the dogs. They sat in front of me, watching Hailey. They didn't appear upset or on edge, but they were definitely alert.

"That's Callum McQuade, isn't it?" Hailey asked after a few beats of silence, her gaze fixed on my boyfriend where he stood in the home team's dugout.

Alarm bells clanged in my head. "Are you an MLB fan?" I asked, rather than answering her question.

She shrugged. "I watch games now and then. What brought him to Twilight Cove?"

The dogs shifted at my feet. They could probably sense my increasing tension.

"You'd have to ask him that," I said, regarding her with ever-increasing suspicion.

Hailey just smiled. "I won't bother him. I thought he was in Florida, possibly working for the Blue Jays during spring training? But maybe he was just there for a visit."

I didn't respond. She was fishing for information, but why? And the fact that she knew Callum was in Florida recently made the alarm bells in my head ring even louder.

I tried to refocus on the softball game. The teenage girl at home plate hit the pitch thrown her way. The ball sailed toward second base. I watched Roxy jump to catch the ball, clapping when she closed her glove around it. When I glanced to the side again, I realized Hailey had left.

I spun around and spotted her striding toward the parking lot.

I glanced back at the game, then at Hailey again. She climbed into a black car.

"What do you think?" I asked the dogs.

They wagged their tails and Flossie gave a woof.

That made up my mind.

I jogged over to the parking lot, with the spaniels bounding along at my side. Callum and I had driven to the ballpark in separate vehicles, in case the dogs and I didn't want to stay for the entire game. Although I would have liked to watch more innings, I knew I'd struggle to concentrate after the conversation with Hailey.

If none of the previous incidents had occurred, her questions about Callum still would have put me on edge, but in the context of everything that had happened lately, her behavior had me on high alert.

With the dogs in the back seat, I started up my car and drove out of the parking lot, relieved to find Hailey's black car still in sight when I turned onto the road. I kept a bit of distance between us as I followed her toward the outskirts of town.

As I drove, I pondered whether Hailey could have been the intruder who broke into the farmhouse and attacked Callum on the weekend. She certainly appeared athletic enough to run as fast as the intruder had when he or she fled the farm. I tried to picture the black-clad figure clearly in my head, but no matter how hard I tried, I couldn't be sure if the person had been a man or a woman.

Hailey had a similar build to the burglar, but was she tall enough to be a match?

She'd stood right next to me at the ballpark, so I knew she was shorter than me. Maybe around five foot six in contrast to my five foot nine. My impression was that Saturday night's intruder was taller than Hailey, but I couldn't be sure. Everything had happened so fast. I really hadn't seen much more than a dark blur.

My unease intensified as I followed Hailey's car north, in the general direction of Auntie O's farm. Had she decided to break into the farmhouse while Callum and I were at the baseball game?

I realized that I'd drawn closer to Hailey's car than I'd intended. She'd paused at a stop sign and I'd almost caught up to her. As I slowed down, she suddenly flicked on her signal and turned left. When I reached the stop sign, I had to wait for another car to pass through the intersection. By the time I made a left turn, Hailey had zoomed off into the distance. She made another quick left, heading back toward the center of town. When I reached that corner, the black car had disappeared from sight.

Had she realized that I was tailing her and ditched her plan to head for the farm?

Maybe, but I couldn't be sure.

That seemed to be the story of my life lately.

I couldn't be certain of who was involved in all the strange happenings or why.

Those loose threads and unanswered questions chafed at me. Unsolved mysteries of any kind drove me nuts. When mysterious events put people I cared about in danger, the unanswered questions plagued me with even greater intensity.

Giving up on trying to find Hailey's car again, I swung by the farm to make sure she hadn't taken a circuitous route there. All seemed quiet. The doors and undamaged windows remained locked and the board over the broken window appeared undisturbed.

Auntie O wasn't home, which was probably for the best. I didn't much like the idea of her being there by herself when someone with nefarious intentions had an unusual interest in the place.

I considered returning to the ballpark, but I felt torn between doing that and staying home to keep an eye on the farm. Fortunately, Tessa texted me to ask if I was watching the game, because she was about to leave the school building and head over to the ballpark. In my reply, I told her I'd just arrived home. I sent her the photo of Hailey from the coffee shop's security footage and asked her to watch out for the woman because of her unsettling interest in Callum.

Tessa agreed, and that allowed me to feel better about staying at the farm. I sent Callum a quick text message to let him know where I'd gone, and reminding him to stay vigilant, but I didn't mention why I'd returned home. I'd tell him about Hailey and her questions when I saw him in person.

Stardust was glad to have me home and I spent nearly half an hour tossing her toys across the living room floor so she could scamper around and pounce on them. Flossie and Fancy joined in the fun now and then, bringing a smile to my face.

I had a fright when I heard footsteps on the front porch and the dogs barked up a storm, but when I peeked out the window, I saw a parcel delivery van driving away. Sure enough, someone had dropped a package by the front door. It was addressed to Callum, from the online store where we'd purchased his costume. Nothing nefarious there.

Still, it came as a relief when Callum finally arrived home. I told him about Hailey and he encouraged me to text Brody with the information. As I did so, I received an incoming text message from Callum's mother.

I smiled as I read it. "Your mom just messaged me to say thank you for the postcard we sent from Florida."

Callum checked his phone. "She did the same to me."

"Speaking of postcards . . ." I looked at the French memory board hanging on the kitchen wall. I'd purchased a postcard that I'd intended to add to the board, which already displayed cards from a few trips I'd taken in years past. "What did I do with the one I bought in Tampa?"

"Woo," Fancy said.

"Does that mean you can lead me to it?" I asked. Then I smacked a hand to my head. "Never mind. I remember now. I put it in the outer pocket of my carry-on bag."

I jogged upstairs, with Flossie and Fancy clattering along behind me. I dug the bag out of the closet and slid a hand into the unzipped outer pocket. My fingertips touched the postcard, but also something else. Puzzled, I closed my hand around the mystery item and pulled it out of the pocket.

I sank down to sit on the floor as I stared at the object resting on my palm.

Suddenly, some of the recent incidents made far more sense.

FIFTEEN

"Have you ever seen this before?" I asked Callum when I returned downstairs, holding out the object I'd found in my bag.

It was a fancy brooch, glittering with diamonds and a dazzling emerald. I didn't know if the gemstones were real, but they sure looked pretty enough to be genuine.

"No," Callum replied. "Is it yours?"

"Definitely not. I found it in the bag I used for my carry-on."

Callum's forehead furrowed with confusion. "How did it end up there?"

"I think Nina Hartmann put it in my bag."

A hint of alarm flashed in his green eyes. "The dead woman?"

"At the Tampa airport, when she was very much alive."

I reminded him about Nina bumping into me. It had seemed like an innocent accident at the time, but I no longer believed that.

"Is this why Nina came to Twilight Cove?" Callum asked as he peered at the brooch. "And why this house has been a magnet for prowlers and burglars?"

"It must be." I paced the kitchen as I tried to piece everything together in my head. "I think Nina must have recognized you at the airport. It would have been easy for her to figure out that you and I were together."

Although we'd separated briefly while Callum bought a pack of gum at one of the shops, we'd spent most of our time in the airport side by side, and often holding hands.

"And since she recognized me, she figured there was a good chance she could track me down to get this brooch back," Callum surmised.

"Exactly." I stopped pacing. "She got on her flight to Charlotte as planned, possibly already knowing that we were heading for Twilight Cove. With a little searching online, she probably could have figured out that you live in this town now."

Callum continued outlining the theory. "So when she got to Charlotte, she booked a flight to Oregon. Then she just had to figure out where, exactly, we live in Twilight Cove."

"Which is why she asked about you at the coffee shop. Maybe at other places around town too."

"And somehow she found out that we live here on the farm," Callum said.

"She came to watch the house, waiting for an opportunity to get the brooch back. But Flossie and Fancy knew she was lurking out in the yard."

Fancy gave a quiet "A-woo" from the dog bed in the corner.

I smiled at her and her sister. "You're such clever girls."

She and Flossie wagged their tails before settling back in for a snooze.

My smile faded as I realized something. "This could be why Nina was killed." The brooch sat heavily in my hand.

"Somebody else wanted it," Callum guessed. "And still wants it."

"If that's true, then these jewels must be the real deal. What do you think the brooch is worth?"

We both stared at the piece of jewelry. The jewels glittered and gleamed in the rays of golden light cast through the window by the setting sun.

"That's a lot of diamonds," Callum said, "and the emerald is impressive. I'm no jeweler, but if the gems are real, it could easily be worth tens of thousands of dollars. Maybe even more."

Threads of unease snaked through my stomach. "I guess I shouldn't have touched it, but I didn't even know what it was until I pulled it out of my luggage."

I set it on the kitchen table and grabbed a Ziploc bag from a nearby drawer. Before sliding the brooch into the bag, I snapped a couple of photos of it with my phone.

"We'd better call Brody," Callum said. "Or the detective in charge of the murder investigation."

I tried Brody's personal number first. When I got no answer, I tried the police station's non-emergency number and found out that Brody was on duty, but out on a call. I left a message, asking him to phone me back when he had a chance.

"We could always take it right to the police station," Callum suggested.

Doubt crept in at the edges of my mind. "What if it's a fake and we're wrong about all of this?"

He put an arm around me. "I have a feeling we're right. Everything that's been happening lately makes a lot more sense if the brooch is valuable."

"True."

He took the bag from me and turned the plastic-encased brooch this way and that, as if it might hold some answers. "Why would Nina slip it into your bag in the first place? She didn't want someone to catch her with it?"

"She was scared," I said with certainty. "I saw fear on her face at the airport. Maybe someone was after her, someone who knew or suspected that she had the brooch."

"So maybe it didn't belong to her? And the owner wanted it back?"

"Could be." I leaned into Callum, the entire situation weighing on me.

He handed the bag back to me and ran a hand down my arm. "Why don't we take the brooch to Anton?"

"Anton?" I couldn't place where I'd heard that name recently.

"He owns the jewelry store in town. He can tell us if it's real or not. Then, if it's valuable and we haven't heard back from Brody, we can take it to the police station."

"That sounds like a good plan." Now that I knew the brooch might be related to Nina's murder and the break-in at the farmhouse, I didn't much like the idea of having it in my possession. "How do you know the local jeweler?"

Callum grabbed our coats before replying. "He sold me that necklace I got for my mom for Christmas."

"Right," I said, remembering. "He's got a lot of nice jewelry at his shop."

Before leaving the farm, we stopped at the carriage house to see Auntie O, who'd recently returned home. I showed her the brooch and she was as astonished by my discovery as I had been. Although she had plans to go out again later, she had some time to spare and offered to look after Stardust and the dogs while Callum and I drove into town. With everything that had been going on at the farm lately, I was relieved to not have to leave them alone.

With the animals safe, we hopped in Callum's truck and soon arrived at the jewelry store. The electronic bell sounded as Callum opened the door and held it for me. When we entered the shop, I couldn't see anyone, so I wandered off to the left, browsing, but then Anton emerged from the back room.

"Ah, Callum," he said when he spotted my boyfriend. Then he noticed me. A startled expression flitted across his face before he smiled. "Georgie. Nice to see you again."

After returning his greeting, we showed him the brooch and quickly explained that we were wondering if it had any real value. We added that we were about to turn it over to the police and didn't want to get any more fingerprints on it.

Intrigued, Anton slipped on a pair of white gloves and produced his loupe. He held the brooch up to the light. "Hmm." He checked the back of the setting. "Maker's mark. Yes. Very nice." He then inspected the stones closely, from several angles.

Callum and I waited in silence, but I had to make a concerted effort not to fidget. As eager as I was to hear Anton's opinion, I didn't want to come across as impatient.

Finally, Anton lowered the loupe from his eye.

"Without removing the stones from the setting and weighing them, I can't give you an accurate value," he cautioned. "And, of course, not knowing the provenance of the piece makes a valuation difficult as well."

"We understand," Callum assured him. "Even just knowing if the stones are real is helpful."

"Oh, they are most definitely real, and I feel confident in saying that this piece would have a value at auction of at least $70,000. However, it's entirely possible that the value could far exceed that amount."

My jaw nearly dropped. I looked at Callum. He appeared just as stunned as I felt.

"The quality of the stones is quite impressive, and the piece is absolutely exquisite," Anton continued. "The maker, Daniel Desfontaines, was renowned for his skills back in the teens and 1920s." He carefully slid the brooch back into the plastic bag. "You think this is connected to a crime?"

"It might have been stolen," I said, "but we're not entirely sure."

"We're going to let the police figure it out," Callum added.

"A wise decision." Anton handed the bag to me. "And thank you for bringing it to me. Just holding such an exquisite piece has made my day."

"Thank you for helping us," I returned. "We appreciate it."

"Glad to be of assistance," he said as we turned for the door. "Have a nice evening."

Outside the shop, Callum and I paused on the sidewalk. The sun had disappeared below the horizon, leaving the town steeped in shadows.

"This is crazy," I said, still astounded by what Anton had told us. "I don't think I've ever held something so valuable."

"It could definitely be at the heart of all the recent incidents."

With the brooch safely hidden away in my pocket, I checked my phone. I had a voice message from Brody, so I listened to it as we walked slowly back to Callum's truck.

"Brody says he'll come by the farm in a couple of hours," I told Callum after the message ended.

"So do we go to the station or back to the farm?" he asked.

"The station," I decided.

I wanted to hand over the brooch as soon as possible.

SIXTEEN

We drove straight to the police department, but as soon as we arrived, Callum received a phone call from his niece in Colorado. While he spoke to her out on the front steps, I entered the station on my own and found the place nearly deserted. Tessa's cousin, Valentina, sat at the front desk, tapping away at a computer keyboard, but otherwise the building was eerily quiet.

"Hey, Georgie," Valentina greeted as I approached the desk. Her glossy black hair was tied back in a bun and she wore shimmery green eyeshadow. "What's up?"

"I was hoping to speak to an officer in relation to the recent murder and the break-in at the farmhouse."

"I heard about the break-in," Valentina said. "Freaky. The detectives from the state police are in charge of the murder investigation, but they're not in. And we're stretched thin at the moment. There was an accident on the highway about an hour ago."

"I hope there weren't any casualties," I said.

"Some serious injuries, but no fatalities. So far, anyway." Valentina pointed at the chairs across the lobby. "You're welcome to take a seat and wait, but it could be a long time before anyone's free to see you."

I thought for a moment and decided to head home. Hopefully Brody would still stop by the farm, even if he ended up being later than expected.

I didn't leave the station right away, however. I couldn't pass up an opportunity to seek out some information.

"Any updates on the murder investigation?" I asked Valentina in a low voice, despite the fact that the two of us were alone in the reception area.

She shrugged. "Not many. The victim was from out of town."

"Florida," I said with a nod.

"Right. So the police are a little baffled as to why someone killed her here in Twilight Cove. They probably would have thought it was a robbery gone wrong, because the woman's motel room was ransacked, but she was still alive after that incident. So who knows?"

"Any word on how she was killed?" I asked.

"Sure, but you know I can't share that stuff with the public."

"Right," I said, suppressing a grin.

Valentina was a civilian employee, but she often overheard interesting conversations between police officers. As much as she liked to claim that she was discreet, she loved even more to share intriguing tidbits of information.

I thanked Valentina and let her get back to her work.

Outside, I met up with Callum just as he finished the phone call with his niece, who'd wanted to tell him all about her latest softball game.

When we returned to the farmhouse, we fetched the animals from the carriage house and quickly filled Auntie O in on what we'd learned. Once she was all caught up on recent events, Callum and I faced a dilemma.

"The animals need feeding and all the evening chores need to be done," I said as we entered the farmhouse, "but I don't want to damage the brooch by carrying it around in my pocket."

It wasn't very comfortable to have in my pocket either. It kept poking my leg.

Callum woke up his phone. "I'll tell Brody to come out to the barn to find us if we're not at the house when he arrives."

"And I'll hide this away somewhere safe until he gets here," I said, holding up the bag containing the brooch.

With Flossie and Fancy at my heels, I jogged up to the second floor.

After a moment of consideration, I stashed the brooch in my jewelry box. Then, for good measure, I tucked the jewelry box into a dresser drawer, beneath a pile of socks.

I stepped back and stared at the dresser, knowing that half the drawers were empty. Now that I was no longer keeping secrets from Callum, I could bring up the subject of him moving in with me full-time. Instead of scaring me, the prospect of that conversation excited me. Still, I'd wait to bring it up until after the brooch was out of our hands.

"All right," I said to the spaniels. "Let's hope Brody gets here soon."

"A-woo," Fancy said, before charging out of the bedroom and down the stairs.

Flossie and I followed after her. Stardust didn't want to be left out, so she rode on Callum's shoulder as we headed out to the barn with the dogs. I made sure to lock the farmhouse door before we left. I would have asked Auntie O to keep an eye out for any unusual activity, but she'd already left to meet up with her Gins and Needles group. The informal club consisted of several women who met a couple of times each month to work on knitting, crochet, or needlework projects while enjoying good food, gossip, and cocktails. They took turns hosting the meetings, and tonight's host was Olivia's friend Dolores.

I hurried through my evening chores while Flossie and Fancy ran around one of the back fields, chasing each other in the deepening darkness.

After I finished my farm work, I found the dogs flopped out on the grass behind the barn. "All tuckered out?" I asked.

They barely raised their heads, their tongues lolling out as they rested.

I took that as a yes.

A dark shadow whooshed by my head. I ducked, startled.

Euclid landed on a nearby fencepost.

I pressed a hand to my chest, over my stuttering heart. "Euclid, you scared me."

The great horned owl blinked his eyes and bobbed his head. Then he took off and flew up and over the barn, soaring off in the direction of the house.

A sense of foreboding seeped into my bones.

I jogged into the barn. Flossie and Fancy jumped to their feet and trotted after me. I found Callum in the feed room, measuring out food for the chickens while Stardust supervised from a shelf.

"I just saw Euclid," I said. "I'm going to check on the house. I've got a bad feeling."

"Georgie, hold on," Callum said as I turned to go. He set down the bucket he had in his hand and picked up Stardust. "I'm coming with you."

Together, we walked briskly toward the farmhouse with the

dogs bounding along beside us. Halfway there, the dogs suddenly took off.

"Flossie! Fancy!" I called. "Wait up!"

They slowed their pace, but didn't stop. Flossie let out a sharp bark.

I'd left the porch light on, so I could see why she was upset.

The piece of plywood Callum and Brody had fastened over the broken window was missing.

"No, no, no!" I broke into a run.

"Georgie," Callum cautioned, "we need to stay back. Someone could still be in the house."

I knew he was right, so I stopped and called the dogs over to us. Callum already had his phone out. I took Stardust out of his arms and cuddled her against my chest as he called the police. We watched the house with apprehension. I'd left the kitchen light on and couldn't see anyone moving around inside, but that didn't mean someone wasn't creeping through another part of the house.

"Do you see any sign of anyone in there?" I whispered to Callum.

"Not so far. I'll check the security app after I call the police." He put an arm around me and I knew he must feel as helpless as I did in that moment.

I hated the thought of a stranger invading our private space, our sanctuary. Also worrisome was the thought of the burglar finding the emerald and diamond brooch. I wanted to kick myself for leaving it unattended. At the very least, I should have done a better job of hiding it.

After finishing his phone call, Callum opened the security app on his phone and checked the footage from the surveillance cameras. The one by the back door of the farmhouse showed someone—dressed all in black—using a crowbar to pry the plywood off the window. Then the person climbed in through the opening. Nearly fifteen minutes later, the burglar slipped out the back door, shut it, and then took off. That was mere minutes before Callum and I had discovered the break-in. Euclid must have seen the intruder leaving and flown directly to the barn to warn me.

Although we now knew that the burglar had left the scene, we remained outdoors. It felt like it took forever for the police to arrive, but only five minutes passed before the first cruiser pulled into the driveway, cutting its siren but leaving its lights flashing.

Brody climbed out of the vehicle, along with Officer Jenna Blanchet. We quickly explained about the piece of plywood—which was lying on the floor of the porch—and how we'd found the brooch earlier.

"The burglar left several minutes ago, according to the security video," Callum added.

Brody and Officer Blanchet went inside to look around. I had a key to the carriage house, so I took Stardust over there and locked her in so she'd be safe while we were distracted by the activity at the main house. Flossie and Fancy, however, stuck close to my side.

When Brody and Blanchet came out the kitchen door, they met up with Callum and me at the base of the steps.

"The place has definitely been searched," Blanchet reported.

I wrapped my arms around myself. "Is the brooch gone?"

"I'll have to get you to look and see," Brody said.

He cautioned me not to touch anything, but he allowed me to follow him inside while the dogs stayed in the yard with Callum. My stomach churned at the signs that a stranger with ill intent had rummaged through the house. Kitchen drawers and cupboards stood open, and cookbooks lay strewn about on the floor. In the living room, all the cushions had been tossed off the couch and chairs. No permanent damage appeared to have been done, however.

Upstairs, we proceeded straight to my bedroom. My nausea intensified at the obvious indications that the burglar had invaded the room where I slept. T-shirts had been tossed from the top drawer of the dresser, and socks from the one below it. On top of the mess of clothing on the floor, my jewelry box lay upside down.

Brody took a photo of the jumble and then carefully turned over the wooden box with a gloved hand, revealing a few pieces of jewelry and other trinkets.

Brody nudged a few items aside, but there wasn't anything else to see.

I closed my eyes briefly. My suspicions were confirmed.

I let out a heavy sigh. "The brooch is gone."

SEVENTEEN

Although I felt like a fool for letting the brooch slip out of my hands before I could turn it over to the police, that wasn't the only blow dealt by the burglar. After the police processed the scene, I sorted through the mess in the bedroom and discovered that the thief had also taken two necklaces, three bracelets, and some rings. They weren't worth a lot of money, but they had sentimental value. They'd all belonged to my mom, who'd died when I was three.

Exhausted and upset about the burglary, Callum and I decided to spend the night at his cabin with the dogs and Stardust. I tossed and turned for much of the night, although I tried not to disturb Callum, and morning arrived far too early.

Bleary eyed, we got to work on the farm chores, bringing Auntie O up to speed on the previous night's events as we tended to the sanctuary's animals. Later, when I should have been writing, I decided to drive into town instead. After a sleepless night, I didn't have the energy to think creatively, and I also couldn't relax enough to sit down and focus. Although I needed to clean up the house, I decided to take the dogs for a walk before tackling the mess. Maybe the fresh ocean air would calm the nerves that hadn't stopped jangling inside of me since the burglary.

Flossie, Fancy, and I took a long stroll along Twilight Cove's main beach. By the time we got back to the parking lot, I felt calmer but still tired. I bought myself a latte at Déjà Brew, hoping that would help to perk me up. When I exited the coffee shop, I caught sight of a woman with a sleek brown bob and an expensive wool coat. She looked both ways before crossing the street, giving me a glimpse of her face.

It was Scarlett Nicholson, the woman I'd heard talking on the phone at the hotel. Nina Hartmann's sister.

I made a quick decision. With the dogs' leashes held in one hand and my latte in the other, I jogged across the road during a break in traffic and followed Scarlett. I didn't know what I was hoping to learn by tailing the woman, but her sister had slipped the missing brooch in my bag and I strongly suspected that the piece of jewelry had something to do with Nina's death. I also believed that the brooch was the center of all the incidents at the farm lately. Incidents that had put Callum in danger and had left me feeling uneasy in my own home.

Now that the burglar had the brooch, he or she probably wouldn't bother coming back to the farmhouse, but I couldn't shake the lingering awareness that an intruder had invaded our private space. Besides, my curious nature had me wondering about Nina's murder and the reasons behind her actions before her death.

I remembered how Scarlett had wanted to get her sister's personal effects from the police. Was that simply because of the items' connection to her deceased loved one? Or, was she hoping that the brooch was among Nina's possessions?

Maybe the brooch was a family heirloom. But then why had Nina hidden it in my bag? That action seemed to make more sense if she'd stolen the jewelry and didn't want to get caught with it.

I gave my head a shake. Nothing made sense because I was missing so many pieces of the puzzle.

Up ahead, Scarlett disappeared into a store. I almost turned around and headed back to my car, but then I realized that she'd entered the Treasure Trove. The shop, which sold gifts and metaphysical supplies like crystals, was owned and operated by Fae Hawthorn, a woman I'd met back in the summer. She adored Flossie and Fancy, and always welcomed them in her store.

I took a long sip of my latte so I wouldn't have such a full drink in my hand, and then I tugged open the door. A bell jingled cheerily overhead as the dogs and I stepped inside.

"Georgie!" Fae exclaimed. "How nice to see you again." She hurried out from behind the sales counter to greet the dogs. Her long and curly red hair—so similar to Nina Hartmann's—hung loose, and she wore a peasant blouse, a maxi skirt, and several bangles and beaded necklaces. "And it's always wonderful to see you girls too," she said to the dogs, fussing over them.

They wagged their tails and lapped up the attention.

In the meantime, I glanced around the shop until I spotted the top of Scarlett's head on the other side of a shelf holding journals and greeting cards.

"I heard there was a burglary at your house last night," Fae whispered once she'd finished greeting the dogs. "Are you all right?"

"A little shaken up, but otherwise fine," I said.

"Did the thief take anything?"

I glanced over at Scarlett and noted that she'd moved toward the back of the shop, well away from us. "A few pieces of jewelry."

Fae shook her head. "I hope the police catch the culprit. It's terrible to have your home violated in such a way."

"It's definitely upsetting," I agreed.

"What you need is to cleanse your home."

"How so?" I asked.

"A purification spell—or ceremony, if you prefer that word—will rid your house of the negative energies left behind by the burglar."

A year ago I probably would have dismissed what she'd said as mumbo-jumbo. I'd never really believed in magic or the power of crystals or anything like that until I met Dorothy, the woman Flossie and Fancy had lived with previously. She'd given me a crystal to help with my headaches. To my surprise, it had worked. I might have attributed that to the power of suggestion, but as I'd become aware of Flossie's and Fancy's abilities, I'd had to accept that there were things in the world that I simply couldn't explain. Magical things. So now I wasn't quite so quick to ignore what Fae had to say.

"Is that something you could do?" I asked, hopeful.

Fae offered tarot readings in her shop and seemed to know a lot about crystals and such, so I figured there was a good chance that she had the skills to carry out the ceremony.

"I could," she said slowly, "but since it's your home, it would probably be best if you performed the spell. Not only because you have a greater attachment to the space, but because I think it would have a healing effect on you as well."

"But I have no idea how to do something like that," I said. "And I'm not a witch."

Fae patted my arm as she passed behind me to approach a shelf of books. "We all have the ability to work with the universe's energy, whether we realize it or not."

I'd have to take her word on that.

"Everything is energy, Georgie," she continued as she ran her fingers along the book spines. "This world. The universe. Us. And energy can be manipulated or guided. With the right intention and the right focus, you can send the negative energy out of your home, thereby cleansing it."

She selected a slim volume off the shelf and brought it over to me. "This book has the perfect spell for you. I'm not trying to force a sale upon you, so if you just want to have a peek at the relevant page and put it back on the shelf, that's fine with me." She opened the book, flipped through a few pages, and then handed it to me. "I'm just going to check on my other customer."

As she headed toward the back of the store, where Scarlett was perusing the selection of scented candles, I studied the cover of the book. The title told me that it contained spells for beginner witches. When I skimmed through the cleansing ritual, it didn't seem particularly complicated or difficult. It mostly required concentration and intent. According to the introductory paragraph, the physical items listed for use in the spell would help focus those intentions.

Since spell work was completely new to me, I decided to purchase the book. I didn't think I could memorize all the instructions on the spot, even though they seemed straightforward. The book stated that I would need a white candle and a bowl of water—easy enough to find at home—as well as a besom or a feather. I had no idea what a besom was, but I could definitely find a feather on the farm. There were always some on the ground in the chicken yard.

A clear quartz crystal was listed as an optional item, one that apparently could help me raise my energy. I had one of those at home, purchased from Fae's shop in the past when I was hoping for a boost of creativity—to help me with my writing—and a boost of courage—to help me share my feelings with Callum.

I closed the book and looked down at Flossie and Fancy. They sat at my feet, gazing up at me with their beautiful brown eyes.

"We're going to give it a try," I said quietly.

Fancy stood up and wagged her tail while Flossie pressed her nose against my leg.

I turned at the sound of Fae's and Scarlett's voices drawing closer.

"Thank you for helping me choose this candle," Scarlett said to Fae. "I really need something to help calm me. Losing my sister—and in such a terrible way—has turned my world upside down." She dabbed a finger to the corner of one eye. "She was my sister and my best friend."

"It's such a terrible shame," Fae said with compassion.

"I'm so sorry for your loss," I added as they reached the front of the store.

Scarlett flashed me a sad smile. "Thank you. I appreciate that. The police and everyone I've met in this town so far have been very kind."

"It's too bad you're visiting for such an unpleasant reason." Fae slipped behind the sales counter. "Twilight Cove is a wonderful town."

Scarlett set the candle on the counter next to the cash register. "I just arrived from Tampa on the weekend, and I can already tell this is a lovely place."

She paid for the candle and thanked Fae before offering me another sad smile and leaving the shop.

"So terribly sad," Fae said once we were alone.

"Tragic," I agreed.

I paid for the book and tucked it in my cross-body purse so I'd have my hands free for my drink and the leashes. After thanking Fae for her help, I pushed open the door and followed the dogs out onto the sidewalk.

Scarlett stood just outside the door, focused on her phone. As the spaniels and I passed her, I caught a glimpse of the screen. It looked as though she was checking her email. She opened a message, glanced at it for about three seconds, and then deleted it.

She didn't look up as I passed by, so I didn't have to worry about the puzzled expression that probably crossed my face.

Scarlett had just told Fae that she'd traveled from Florida to Twilight Cove on the weekend. So why did she have an email from a hotel in a neighboring town asking her if she'd enjoyed her recent stay?

EIGHTEEN

My mind whirled on the walk back to my car. Maybe there was a perfectly logical explanation for the fact that Scarlett had recently stayed at a hotel in Britton Bay, a town not far from Twilight Cove. Perhaps rather than flying to Portland and driving down the coast, she'd flown to California and had driven up, stopping overnight in Britton Bay on her way here. She hadn't necessarily lied, and maybe it was overly suspicious of me to even entertain the idea that she had.

It didn't surprise me that I was feeling distrustful these days, after all that had happened at the farm and around town. I wanted to figure out what was going on with the burglaries and the missing brooch so I could feel confident that Callum, Auntie O, and I were once again safe in our own homes, but I knew there was a good chance that I was grasping at straws by suspecting Scarlett of any wrongdoing.

Flossie and Fancy trotted along happily as we headed down the hill toward my car. As we drew close to Déjà Brew, the door opened and four uniformed police officers exited the coffee shop, each with a drink in hand. I said hello as the dogs and I passed them, and then something farther down the road caught my attention. A young man with shaggy, sandy hair was walking in our direction, but as soon as he saw the police officers coming out of the coffee shop, his eyes widened and he spun around. He walked briskly the other way, turning a corner as soon as he had the chance.

My steps slowed and the dogs looked back at me, no doubt wondering why I'd suddenly slackened my pace. I'd seen the young man before, I realized. At Déjà Brew, where he'd reacted in a similar fashion. He'd stepped inside the coffee shop before swiftly turning and retreating. I didn't recall the presence of any police officers at Déjà Brew at the time, but I also couldn't be sure that there weren't any there.

I picked up my pace, and the spaniels happily settled back into a trot. When we reached the next corner, I looked for the skittish guy, but didn't spot him. Other than that time at the coffee shop, I'd never seen him before. I hadn't yet lived in Twilight Cove for a full year and I definitely didn't know everyone who lived in town—not by a long shot—so the fact that I'd never seen him until recently didn't mean he wasn't a local.

Maybe paranoia was getting the best of me. Everywhere I looked, I saw shifty characters.

Once seated in my car, I sent a text message to Genesis, asking if I could watch more of the coffee shop's security footage sometime. Within seconds she responded in the affirmative, inviting me to stop by right then if I wanted. When I told her that I had the dogs with me, she suggested that I enter Déjà Brew through the back door so the dogs and I could go directly into her office.

I grabbed my latte from the cup holder and twisted in my seat to talk to the dogs in the back. "Sorry, girls. One more stop before we head home."

They wagged their tails, apparently unconcerned about my sudden change in plans.

Within a few minutes, we were seated in Genesis' office, her laptop in front of us. I explained what I was looking for, and she found the video for the day and time in question. While Genesis headed out front to help serve customers, I fast-forwarded through the footage until I spotted myself entering the coffee shop. I zipped through the next couple of minutes and then let the video play at regular speed.

"There he is," I said to the dogs when I saw the mystery man opening the door to Déjà Brew.

Just as I remembered, he stopped short on the threshold and then retreated out onto the street.

Fortunately, Genesis had two cameras set up inside the coffee shop. Between them, I had a good view of everyone who was present when the mystery man showed up. I paused the footage now and then, studying faces. I recognized a few locals, but they didn't hold my attention. Two other people did, though. The first was the guy I'd caught staring at Callum and me on Main Street about a week ago. He'd left me feeling distinctly uneasy, but I had no clue who he was. Just like when I'd seen him before, he wore jeans and a gray bomber jacket.

The second person of interest was Hailey, the woman I'd tailed after she approached me at the high school softball game. Did the sandy-haired man's sudden flight from Déjà Brew have anything to do with Hailey or Mr. Bomber Jacket? I had no idea. Neither one had been present on Main Street twenty minutes ago, but there didn't appear to have been any cops in the coffee shop either. I checked the footage again, but unless an officer I'd never met was in civilian clothes, the place had been police-free at the time.

Maybe the sandy-haired guy was simply a skittish criminal who didn't want to run into someone he'd seen at Déjà Brew that day. He probably had nothing to do with any of the incidents at the farm. Nevertheless, I asked Genesis to send me a still of the guy when she came back to the office to check on me. She did so right away. I thanked her, and the dogs and I left her to her work.

Back at the farm, I checked in with Callum to make sure all was well. He assured me that everything was fine and I decided to tell him about all my suspicions another time.

I didn't think I could concentrate on writing in the farmhouse until I shook off the lingering effects of the burglary. While I didn't know if performing the cleansing ritual would help at all, I figured there was only one way to find out.

I sat at the kitchen table with the spell book I'd bought from Fae's shop, going over the instructions. Then I gathered all the items I needed. Since my bedroom was the place that felt the most affected, I decided to start the ritual there. First, however, I opened all the windows in the house—to help the negative energy flow out—and sent the dogs and Stardust out to the barn to hang out with Callum while he worked. I didn't want them getting curious about the candle I was going to burn, especially since I would have my eyes closed part of the time, trying to concentrate.

Once seated cross-legged on my bedroom floor, I set a chamberstick before me and held my smooth quartz crystal in my hand. I closed my eyes and focused on drawing energy from the earth, the cosmos, the breeze fluttering in through the open windows. I imagined the energy giving off a sphere of bright white light, with me at the center of it. To my surprise, I did feel a shift, like a force was gathering inside of me.

Hoping that meant I'd done the first step of the spell correctly,

I opened my eyes and lit the candle. Then I got up and held the chamberstick in my left hand and the chicken feather I'd found in the yard in my right hand. I used the feather to sweep the air toward the open windows, chanting the words I'd memorized from the spell book as I did so. I repeated that in every room of the house, ending in the kitchen, before turning to the next stage of the spell.

Leaving the candle burning on the kitchen counter, I dipped my hand into a bowl of water, focusing on the feel of it against my skin. Then I retraced my path through the entire house, sprinkling water with my fingers as I walked, reciting another chant. I visualized the water droplets spreading positivity and driving out any lingering negativity.

To finish, I thanked the elements of earth, fire, water, and air, and asked them to protect and bless the house. Then, focusing on feelings of gratitude, I poured the water onto a patch of dirt in the yard—it felt right to do that instead of pouring it down the drain—and returned to the house to extinguish the candle.

Tingles danced over my skin and scalp, and I felt . . . glowy. There was no other word for it. I almost found it surprising that I wasn't giving off a bright light like I'd imagined at the beginning of the ritual.

I stood in the middle of the kitchen and turned in a slow circle. Maybe it was all in my head, but the room seemed brighter, the air around me lighter. I felt lighter too.

I let out a sigh of relief and smiled.

Whether it was magic, or my imagination shaping my reality, I'd reclaimed my home.

NINETEEN

"Have you ever seen this guy before?" I asked Callum that afternoon as I handed him my phone.

He studied the latest security footage still that Genesis had sent me. "He doesn't look familiar."

I took my phone back and stared at the picture of the mystery man with sandy hair for a second or two before setting the device aside.

"Did something happen while you were in town?" Callum asked with concern.

He'd just arrived at the house—with the dogs and Stardust—after putting in several hours of work on the farm. While he washed his hands at the kitchen sink, I told him about seeing Scarlett and the mystery man who had practically fled from Main Street at the sight of the police officers.

Callum dried his hands and leaned back against the counter. "I get why you're on edge and suspicious, but I'm hoping the actions of all those people are completely innocent and we have nothing more to worry about."

"But do you really believe that?" I asked, giving Flossie a pat on the head when she leaned against my leg.

"I want to, but you've proven that you have good instincts about these things."

I'd hoped he'd firmly state that he believed we had no reason to be concerned about the actions of Scarlett or the two young men, but even if he had said that, I knew it likely wouldn't have reduced my own suspicions.

Some of my worry must have shown on my face, because Callum took my hand and pulled me in close so he could wrap his arms around me. "Hey," he said into my hair, "I know things haven't been easy since we got back from Florida, but hopefully the police will have some answers soon and we'll be able to relax."

I rested my head on his shoulder. "I hope so too. In the meantime, I cleansed the house, and it already feels better to me."

"Cleansed?" Callum echoed, puzzled.

I told him about the ritual I'd performed. "You'll probably think I'm nuts, but I really think it helped."

"Georgie, that definitely isn't the most out-there thing you've told me in recent times."

I couldn't help but smile at that.

"And I'm sensing a difference in the house too," he added.

I took a step back so I could see his face. "Really?"

He glanced around the room. "I can't put my finger on it exactly, but the place feels . . . better. The way it felt before the burglary." He looked me in the eye. "You never mentioned your own magical abilities."

"That's because I don't have any," I said.

"And yet you performed a spell."

"According to Fae, we all have the ability to work with the universe's energy, whether we realize it or not."

"Huh." He thought that over. "That's not so hard to believe, really."

"Why do you say that?"

"I don't consider myself psychic, by any means, but I've had a couple of eerily accurate premonitions in my life. Maybe that's sort of the same. It could be that we all have some degree of ability in that regard, but some of us are far more in tune with it than others."

I considered that. "I think you could be right." His words had awakened my curiosity. "What sort of premonitions?"

"Nothing earth shattering," he replied. "Once I had a dream about a baseball game playing out a certain way. The next day, things unfolded exactly as they had in my dream. Another time, back in my minor league days, I entered a raffle at a dinner event. When they were drawing the winners, I suddenly had this absolute feeling of certainty that my ticket number would be called next. And it was."

"What did you win?"

"A trip for two to Whistler. I gave the prize to my parents."

"That was sweet."

He gazed into my eyes with deep affection laced with heat. "So are you."

"Sweet" wasn't a word I had ever used to describe myself, but he kissed me before I had a chance to protest, and I quickly forgot about wanting to object. I forgot about everything, except the two of us.

After the kiss, I rested my head on his shoulder again, until Flossie nudged her way between us, her tail wagging. Fancy wiggled into the mix too and Stardust, feeling left out, wound her way around our ankles.

Laughing, we fussed over the dogs and I cradled Stardust to my chest.

"Oh, I forgot to tell you," I said to Callum when I spotted his unopened parcel on the sideboard, "your costume arrived yesterday."

I handed him the large bubble envelope and he tore it open. Fancy grabbed the packaging and ran around the kitchen with it, shaking it wildly. Flossie bounced around and tried to grab it away from her sister. As the spaniels played tug-of-war, Stardust wriggled in my arms. I set her down and she ran over to bat at a scrap of the envelope that had come free of the rest.

"All right," I said, gently taking the packaging out of the dogs' mouths. "That's enough. I don't want you swallowing any of that accidentally."

I used my foot to cover the scrap that Stardust was chasing, not wanting her to inadvertently pounce on my hand with her claws out. She attacked my shoelaces, then rolled over and scampered off to find one of her toys.

As I got rid of the torn envelope, Callum unfolded the pieces of his costume.

I washed the dog slobber off my hands and then picked up the pinstriped waistcoat. "You'd better try it on."

"In case it needs alterations," Callum said with a nod.

"That, and I really want to see you in the costume," I confessed.

He grinned. "I feel the same about you and your flapper dress. If I've got to try mine on . . ."

"All right. We'll both put our costumes on."

As we climbed the stairs to the second floor, the dogs and Stardust clattered up behind us, then pushed us aside to get ahead. In the bedroom, I shimmied into the flapper dress and examined my reflection in the full-length cheval mirror that stood in one corner of the room. The teal lining shimmered in the light where it showed through the black overlay. The black beads and gold sequins sparkled too. I smiled at the sight. I loved the dress just as much as I had the day I bought it.

Flossie let out a happy bark and twirled around on her hind legs.

I laughed and gave her a pat on the head. "You want me to twirl too?"

She barked again and Fancy chimed in with an "a-woo".

I spun around, the fringe at the bottom of the dress flaring out, just as Callum finished buttoning up his waistcoat. He grinned at me from across the room and let out an appreciative whistle.

Fancy piped up again, letting out a long "woo", as if trying to copy Callum.

"Goofball," I said to Fancy with affection.

She wagged her tail. Flossie did too. Stardust, meanwhile, rolled around on the bed, playing with a catnip toy, ignoring the rest of us.

Callum crossed the room to stand before me. "You look incredible, Georgie."

I rested my hands on his chest. "You look really good too. I've never seen you in a waistcoat before. It suits you. No pun intended," I added, when I realized what I'd said.

He grinned again. "Since we're all dressed up with nowhere to go, how about a dance?" He offered me his hand.

I didn't take it. "I can't dance."

"Everybody can dance."

"Not well," I countered. "And I definitely won't be dancing at the fundraising party, or anywhere else out in public."

"All the more reason for me to get my fill right now." He pulled me in close and settled us into a ballroom dance hold.

"Your toes will get squashed," I warned him.

"As long as it's you doing the squashing, Georgie, I don't mind at all."

"You say that now . . ."

He gave me a twirl.

That got the dogs excited again. They ran in circles and jumped on and off the bed, startling Stardust.

Callum tugged me in close once more, rocking me gently on the spot.

"OK, this isn't bad at all," I admitted, relaxing against him.

"Am I going to convert you into a dancer?"

"Nope," I said. "Not publicly, anyway."

"But like this?"

"This we can do again." A happy sigh followed my words.

We stayed like that, swaying ever so slightly together, and my love for Callum welled up in my heart, the emotion so strong I nearly gasped. He was the one and only man for me, I knew.

He was my forever.

Expressing myself verbally had never been my forte. Writing words came so much more easily for me—especially since I knew I could edit them if they didn't turn out right the first time—but I wanted Callum to hear the words that had been swirling around inside of me for a while now.

"Cal?" I tipped my head back slightly so I could see his face

"Mm?" He seemed so content and at peace with me in his arms.

My heart swelled even more, to the verge of almost bursting. "I love you."

He smiled and kissed me gently. "I love you too, Georgie." He said it with his words, his eyes, his touch.

I drew in a breath, determined to finish what I'd started. "You're it for me. My number one."

Fancy protested with an "a-woo" and Flossie let out a sharp bark.

I laughed and amended my statement, "My number one human."

Callum chuckled and pressed a kiss just below my ear. "You're my number one human too," he whispered, his breath tickling my neck, making me shiver.

"I want you to move in with me," I whispered back.

Callum stopped dancing and leaned back just far enough to see my eyes. A slow grin took shape on his face, causing my heart to flutter.

"You want us to live together?" he asked. "Full-time?"

I fiddled with the top button on his waistcoat. "Full-time," I affirmed.

Forever, I added in my head.

Callum's eyes burned brightly with love in the brief moment before he kissed me.

"Does that mean you want to move in with me?" I asked, breathless, when the prolonged kiss finally ended.

"It does." Callum brushed a strand of hair off my face. "But if you need more convincing of my enthusiasm for the idea, I'm happy to oblige."

"Offer accepted," I said with a smile.

He hugged me and swung me around so fast that my feet lifted off the ground.

I laughed and my heart took flight.

TWENTY

Callum and I decided to go out for dinner to celebrate the latest step in our relationship. He offered to take me anywhere I wanted to go. Maybe I should have chosen one of the fancier restaurants in Twilight Cove, but I wanted to go somewhere that felt like us. Somewhere comfortable, friendly, down to earth. Plus, I was craving a chocolate milkshake from the Moonstruck Diner.

"Evening, lovebirds!" Jackie called out when Callum and I stepped into the diner.

Warmth rushed to my cheeks as several pairs of eyes turned our way, but I smiled when Callum gave my hand a squeeze.

The place was nearly full, but Jackie led us to the only free booth and took our drink orders, promising to be back with them soon. Callum reached across the table for my hand and held onto it while we chatted about the day's work on the farm.

Before I'd met Callum, I'd given up hope of ever finding a man who would be the right fit for me, a man I'd feel completely comfortable with. Whether it was fate or luck, I appreciated with my whole heart that Callum had entered my life.

Minutes after seating us, Jackie set two chocolate shakes on the table. As soon as I'd mentioned my milkshake craving to Callum, he'd developed one of his own. I took a sip right away and nearly closed my eyes in bliss.

Heavenly.

"I hear you had a burglar out at the farm," Jackie said, giving her head a sad shake. "I don't know what's going on in this town. A murder and a burglary. I hope that's the end of things, at least for a good while."

"We hope so too," Callum said.

"Are you both all right? Did the burglar take much?"

"They took some jewelry," I said, not wanting to mention the brooch. "But aside from Callum taking a knock to the head, we're fine."

"It's nothing serious," Callum rushed to assure her when she looked at him with concern.

The small cut was healing well, but it had the remnants of a bruise around it. Callum had removed the bandage, and his hair hid the worst of the injury.

"I'm glad to hear that," Jackie said. "Have you heard anything about the poor woman who was killed?"

"Not a lot," I hedged, sharing a glance with Callum. I wasn't sure how much we should share.

"We heard she was from out of town," Callum offered.

Jackie nodded. "I heard that too. From Florida, maybe? I just can't believe she was here in the diner one day and dead the next."

"She ate here before she died?" I asked.

"She didn't stop to eat, but she passed through. Looking back, I wish I'd pressed her for more information. Maybe if I had, she would have gone to the police and she'd still be alive."

"What do you mean?" Callum asked, clearly as confused as I felt.

"Sorry," Jackie apologized. "I skipped over a lot there. She came in one day—the day before she got killed—and asked if there was a back door she could leave through. She said she thought a guy was following her. I asked her if I should call the police, but she said no. She told me she knew the guy and just didn't want to deal with him in that moment. I figured it was an ex-boyfriend or something like that. I should have called the police, even though she asked me not to when I offered."

A chill trickled down my spine. "You couldn't have known that she'd get killed, especially since it sounds like she brushed off the incident."

"I know, but it weighs on me."

I felt bad for Jackie. "Did you tell the police about this?"

"As soon as I found out that the murder victim was a redheaded woman from out of town." She nodded at a camera affixed to the wall in one corner of the diner, near the ceiling. "I showed the police the security footage from that day. They wanted a copy of it and seemed real interested in what I had to say, so I figure the redheaded woman had to be the same one who was killed." She gave her head a quick shake. "Anyway, I didn't mean to bring you down with such heavy conversation. What can I get you folks to eat?"

She took our food orders and sailed off to the kitchen.

Alone again, Callum and I exchanged a long look.

"Someone was following Nina the day before she was killed," I said.

"The murderer?"

"It seems likely, doesn't it?"

Callum stirred his milkshake with his paper straw. "Maybe that information will help the cops find the killer. There could be security footage from other businesses showing someone following her out on the street."

"Let's hope that's the case."

We talked about happier topics while we waited for our food. Like the high school softball team and Callum moving into the farmhouse full-time. He had some exercise equipment in the cabin and we decided that he would leave it in place, so the cabin could be a workout space that doubled as a guest cottage.

When Jackie returned with our food, she set a vegetable pot pie in front of me and a fish burger in front of Callum. As she pulled two napkin-wrapped bundles of cutlery from the pocket of her apron, a small rectangle of paper slid out and fluttered to the ground. I leaned over and picked it up for her.

"A business card for a band?" I asked, glancing at the paper as I handed it back to Jackie.

She sighed before tucking it in her pocket. "A young guy came by earlier today. Wanted to know if his band could play here one evening. I told him we don't do live music. We don't have the space. Besides, people like to enjoy the jukebox while they're here."

"Is it a local band?" Callum asked.

"No, so I wouldn't even be able to ask around to find out if they're any good. Apparently, the guy—Lex was his name—is from back east. He said his band is coming to join him here in Oregon so they can tour around a bit."

Other customers needed Jackie's attention, so she excused herself and left us to our meals.

Later, as Callum drove us back to the farm, our stomachs full, I accessed the internet on my phone.

"What are you looking at?" Callum asked, sending a glance my way before returning his eyes to the dark road.

"I saw the name of the band on that business card that Jackie had. I just want to look it up."

"You thinking of going to a concert?" he asked, a hint of teasing behind his words. He knew I wasn't really one for concerts or other crowded venues.

"Not anytime soon. But Jackie mentioned that the band was from back east. Doesn't it seem like that's where all the recent strangers around town are from?"

"There are a lot of places back east," Callum pointed out. "They're not all necessarily from Florida."

"Sure," I said, my eyes still on my phone. "But this band is."

"Really?" He sent another glance my way and I could tell I'd caught his interest.

As I navigated my way around the band's website, an unpleasant weight settled in my stomach. "You'll never believe this."

"Don't leave me in suspense," he said when I didn't continue right away.

I checked the website again, wanting to be sure that I wasn't seeing things.

Nope. I had it right.

"Lex, the guy who stopped by the diner to talk to Jackie? His last name is Nicholson. Just like Nina's sister, Scarlett."

"That can't be a coincidence," Callum said.

I agreed with him.

I googled the band's name, together with the surname Nicholson. The results included links to the band's website and a Facebook post about one of the group's performances. That, it turned out, was posted on Scarlett's page.

"Scarlett refers to Lex as her son right here in this Facebook post," I told Callum as he turned into our driveway. "So they are related, and they both live in Tampa."

"Maybe Lex tagged along with his mom when she came out here after the murder?" he suggested.

"I suppose that would explain why the rest of his band isn't here yet," I said. "But that's not all. There's a picture of the band here. And I recognize one of the guys."

Callum parked next to the house. "Who is he?"

I turned my phone so he could see the photo. "I'm guessing he must be Lex, since I've seen him here in Twilight Cove. He was the one standing on the street corner, staring at us."

"This was after Nina's death?"

I took a moment to think about that. "It was after we talked to Brody at the police station."

"So, the day after the murder."

I nodded. "But that means . . ."

Callum looked my way and finished the thought. "Lex showed up in Twilight Cove days before his mother, Scarlett, did."

TWENTY-ONE

I texted our discovery to Brody and he promised to look into Lex Nicholson, his whereabouts at the time of the murder, and any connection he might have to the brooch.

The next day, I tried to push aside all thoughts of the murder and burglary. It wasn't easy, but I managed to take control of my mind and focus solely on writing for a few hours. By the time I took the dogs for a long walk in the afternoon, however, all the thoughts I'd kept at bay came rushing back.

Although I felt far more comfortable in the farmhouse since the cleansing ritual, there remained a lingering concern that the burglar could come back. I hoped they had no such intention, now that they had the brooch in their possession, but what if they were worried that I knew too much? After all, the burglar had found the brooch hidden in my sock drawer, so they had to know that I was aware of its existence. Would that matter to them?

I didn't know, and that's what bothered me, especially considering that the intruder and Nina's killer might be one and the same.

If I wanted to untangle the mystery, I needed to come up with a list of suspects and figure out who might have known about the brooch, and who had an opportunity to kill Nina.

As the dogs and I traipsed through the woods, I came up with a list in my head. It didn't take long, considering that I had only three suspects so far. Four, if I really stretched and added the mystery man who hadn't wanted to walk past the police officers outside Déjà Brew. He'd acted shifty a couple of times, but so far, I had no evidence to connect him to the burglary at the farmhouse or Nina's murder. Still, I decided to keep him in mind, just in case none of my other suspects panned out.

The three other individuals on my list were Lex Nicholson, Scarlett Nicholson, and Hailey aka Jane, the woman with the dark blue leather jacket. Since I knew next to nothing about

Scarlett, beyond the fact that she was Nina's sister and Lex's mother, I looked her up online once the spaniels and I had returned to the house. I navigated back to the Facebook profile I'd checked the day before and scoured it for more information about the woman. I managed to find her husband's name—Royce—and learned where she'd gone to high school and college. I also discovered that she and her husband belonged to a country club in Tampa. I didn't, however, come across any references to her sister, the brooch, or jewelry of any kind.

I would have liked to conduct a similar search on Hailey, but I didn't even know her surname—or her real first name, for that matter—so I didn't have anything to go on.

Or did I?

I sent a text message to Genesis, asking if Hailey had paid for her drink with a credit card. If so, Genesis would likely have the woman's name in her sales records. Of course, there was always a chance that Hailey had paid with cash, or that Genesis wouldn't feel comfortable sharing customer information with me, but I had to at least try to find out her identity.

Auntie O knocked at the back door before coming into the farmhouse kitchen. I didn't mind the interruption of my online sleuthing. I wasn't getting very far and I hadn't seen enough of my aunt since my return from Florida.

I got up to give her a hug and then offered to make her a cup of tea.

"That would be lovely, Georgie. Thank you. I feel like I've hardly seen you over the past week."

"I was just thinking the same," I said as I turned the kettle on. "But I've got time for a good visit now."

"A-woo," Fancy said as she and Flossie wagged their tails and rested their chins on Olivia's lap.

She stroked their silky heads. "Of course I'm here to visit you too, sweet girls."

Not to be left out, Stardust hopped up onto my aunt's lap and turned in a circle before lying down with a rumbling purr.

"And you as well, Star," Auntie O said, running her hand over the cat's gray fur.

I smiled as I took two mugs out of a cupboard and dropped a teabag in a stout blue teapot.

"I had a call from Gillian this morning," Auntie O said. "She was wondering if you and Tessa would be willing to drive to Gold Beach on Saturday to pick up the items that Angelica Bergstrom is lending the museum for the party. She'll rent a truck that you can use. I'd go too, but it's Clara's birthday tea that day."

Clara was one of the members of the Gins and Needles group.

"That shouldn't be a problem," I said. "If Tessa isn't free, Cal can probably go with me. I'll talk to him and let you know what he has to say." I poured hot water into the teapot. "And speaking of Callum . . ." A smile touched my lips. "He's going to be moving into the farmhouse full-time."

It took half a second for my aunt to absorb my news. Then she beamed at me. "Oh, Georgie. That's wonderful! Are you happy?"

"So happy." The goofy smile on my face probably conveyed that sentiment even better than my words. "He's everything I could have asked for."

As I sat down at the table, Olivia gave my hand a squeeze. "I'm so pleased for you. You're such a good match."

Still smiling, and silently agreeing with her, I poured our tea.

We spent the next hour chatting about the animals at the sanctuary, the burglary, the high school softball team, and my time in Florida. After Auntie O left to meet some friends for dinner, I checked my phone to find a text message from Tessa.

Apparently, her cousin Valentina had found out a few more tidbits of information. If I wanted to hear them, Valentina was willing to meet me and Tessa once she'd finished work for the day.

I definitely wanted to know what Valentina had learned, so Tessa invited all of us to have dinner at her place. The invitation extended to Callum and the dogs. As much as I wanted to tell Tessa right then about Callum moving in with me, I decided I'd rather share that news with her in person.

I had that chance when Callum and I arrived at Tessa's place that evening. She lived on the top floor of a large Victorian house that had been divided into half a dozen units. We got there before Valentina, so after Tessa had greeted us and the dogs, Callum and I followed her into the kitchen, where she was putting the finishing touches on two homemade pizzas.

"Callum's moving into the farmhouse," I blurted without any preamble.

Maybe that wasn't the most eloquent way to share the news, but it did the job.

Tessa's eyes widened with surprise and a big smile took shape on her face. She threw her arms around me and gave me a squeeze. "That's such great news!" She hugged Callum next. "I'm so happy for both of you!"

Flossie and Fancy added their own approving opinions, making us laugh.

Still smiling, Tessa slid the pizzas into the oven and we wandered to the living area with drinks in hand. Outside the windows, darkness had fallen and rain pattered against the glass. Tessa switched on her gas fireplace, instantly making her apartment extra cozy.

Valentina arrived just as the kitchen timer dinged to signal that the pizzas were ready. I let her into the apartment while Tessa dealt with dinner.

"Good to see you again, Valentina," I greeted as she stepped inside. "This is my boyfriend, Callum."

Valentina's eyes shone as she beamed at him. "Callum McQuade. Can I get your autograph?"

"Tina," Tessa scolded from the kitchen, "he's here as a friend, not to sign autographs."

"I don't mind," Callum assured her.

Valentina pulled a small photo album out of her handbag. When she opened it, I saw that instead of photos, the album held baseball cards in the plastic pouches.

She slid one out and offered it to Callum. "Your rookie card."

"I haven't seen that for a while," he remarked as he took it from her.

I leaned in close to him so I could see the photo. "Aw! Look how young you were!"

He raised an eyebrow. "Are you suggesting that I'm now old?"

"Not at all." I gave him a one-armed hug. "Besides, you're even more handsome today than you were back then."

"Totally," Valentina agreed, gazing at Callum with stars in her eyes.

I couldn't exactly blame her.

"He's taken," Tessa said to her cousin.

"Doesn't mean I don't have eyes," Valentina countered.

Tessa looked heavenward and shook her head while Callum and I laughed. Once Tessa had the pizzas out of the oven, she found a pen for Callum and he used it to sign the baseball card. Valentina thanked him profusely and carefully slid the card back into its plastic pouch.

"No more fangirling," Tessa scolded.

"I'm done, prima." Valentina rolled her eyes. "Yeesh. Can't a girl have any fun?"

Tessa wisely didn't respond. The cousins mostly got along well, but they had a tendency to bicker like siblings now and then.

"All right," Tessa said once we were all seated at the kitchen table with slices of pizza before us. "Time to spill the tea. I'm sure Georgie's ready to burst from the suspense."

"Pretty much," I admitted, getting smiles from the others.

"Woo," Fancy added from beneath the table, where she and Flossie were munching on dog treats that Tessa had given them.

"We all want to hear what you've got to say," Tessa said.

"As long as it won't get you in trouble," Callum amended.

Tessa and I shot him a look, not wanting Valentina to clam up.

"It won't get me in trouble if it doesn't leave this room," Valentina said.

"Which it won't," I assured her.

Valentina's eyes glittered with the delight of having news to share. "That brooch that was stolen from your house, Georgie?" she started. When I nodded, she continued, giving us a juicy piece of intel. "One of the detectives from the state police figured out that it belongs to the dead woman's father."

TWENTY-TWO

"Did she inherit it?" I asked, after I'd absorbed Valentina's news.

She shook her head as she enjoyed a bite of pizza. After she washed it down with a sip of wine, she said, "The old man is still alive and kicking."

"So he gave the brooch to his daughter?" Tessa guessed.

Her cousin smiled smugly as she shook her head again. "Nope. He reported it stolen just days before his daughter got killed."

"Wait. Nina stole the brooch from her own father?" Callum asked.

Valentina shrugged. "Seems that way, doesn't it? Her sister was totally shocked by the idea."

"Scarlett Nicholson?" I checked, making sure there wasn't another sister in the picture.

"That's her," Valentina confirmed. "Before the detective told her that the brooch was in Twilight Cove—thanks to Nina—Scarlett figured a run-of-the-mill jewel thief had stolen the brooch to sell on the black market. Apparently, a window was broken at the father's mansion and someone dressed all in black was caught on the grounds' security cameras."

I fought the urge to shudder. Although it was a generic burglar description, it reminded me of the intruder I'd seen running from the farmhouse. "So Nina either got the brooch back from the thief somehow, or she was the thief."

"It seems a lot more likely that she stole it herself, don't you think?" Tessa said.

"Probably," I agreed. "Maybe she slipped it in my bag because she thought the police were onto her."

"That sounds like a good possibility," Callum agreed. "Do you remember seeing any police at the airport?"

I thought that over before replying. "No, but maybe there were plainclothes officers following her? Or at least she thought there were?"

"That's not all I've got to tell you," Valentina said, after polishing off the last bite of her pizza. She reached for another slice from the pan in the middle of the table. "Whatever the killer used to strangle Nina, it left behind traces of nickel."

She'd clearly forgotten her previous hesitancy to share any details about the cause of death, maybe because we weren't at the police station this time.

"Nickel?" Tessa echoed. "A wire of some kind then?"

"What would nickel wire be used for?" I asked. "Aside from as a murder weapon, I mean."

"It's used in heating elements," Callum said. "And in electrical components for cars and aircraft."

"OK, so maybe that's a clue." I pondered the possible implications.

"The killer might work in a related field, you mean?" Tessa asked.

"Could be," I replied. "Or maybe the killer just found the wire lying around somewhere."

Tessa groaned. "Let's go with the other idea. It's less discouraging."

We all agreed with her assessment.

Although we chatted about the mysteries for a while longer, we didn't make any further progress with solving them. Eventually, the conversation turned to other topics and we spent the rest of the evening simply enjoying each other's company.

I remembered at the end of the meal to ask Tessa about driving to Gold Beach on the weekend. She'd already committed to a family gathering on the day in question, but Callum readily agreed to make the trip with me instead.

After helping Tessa clean up, Callum and I left with the dogs. While Callum drove us home, I checked my phone and found a text message from Genesis. She'd gone through her records at the coffee shop and discovered that Hailey had, unfortunately, paid for her drink with cash. I wrote back to Genesis, thanking her for her help.

"I guess that keeps us at square one," I said with a sigh, after sharing the information with Callum.

"I don't know about that," he said. "I think we still need to look at Lex. He's a solid suspect. It seems awfully strange to me that he was here in Twilight Cove before his mom arrived."

"True," I agreed, feeling a little more hopeful. "Maybe we can figure out where he's staying. At the Gilmore Hotel like his mom?" I thought for a moment. "Jackie mentioned that she knows the owners of the Sea Breeze Motel. Maybe they could tell us something helpful. Like, maybe Nina had visitors at the motel before she died. Her room was ransacked," I added, as I remembered that detail. "I wonder if they could tell us anything about that incident."

Callum agreed that it was worth talking to the motel owners, but he didn't want me approaching anyone about the murder or burglary on my own.

"Even if the killer and the burglar aren't the same person, they're both clearly capable of violence." He gave my knee a gentle squeeze. "I don't want anything happening to you."

"I'll be careful," I promised. "I'll try to avoid being alone with anyone on our suspect list." I smiled when I realized what I'd said. "*Our* suspect list. You're totally into this sleuthing thing now too, aren't you?"

He grinned. "You've pulled me over to the dark side, Georgie."

"Any regrets?"

He glanced my way, his eyes practically burning through the darkness. "None at all."

Warmth bloomed in my chest, along with a sense of elation.

Flossie barked from the back seat.

I twisted around to look at her and Fancy. "Oh, I know you two have got the sleuthing bug. Maybe even worse than I do."

"A-woo," Fancy said, sounding proud.

When we arrived home and climbed out of the truck, a shadow dipped down from the sky, coming to rest on the roof of the house.

I gazed up at the owl from the lawn. "Euclid."

"I wonder if he'd be willing to befriend me," Callum said, standing next to me. "An owl for a buddy? That would be amazing."

"Hoo-hoo," Euclid called from the peak of the roof. Then he took off, swooping down in front of us before beating his wings and flying up into the darkness.

"He hasn't shown any signs of disliking you," I said.

"So there's hope for me?"

"Definitely," I assured him.

I took his hand and, together, we walked into the house. *Our* house.

TWENTY-THREE

I pounded out my screenplay pages the next morning. As much as I enjoyed writing the thriller, I was eager to get on with unraveling the real-life mysteries I'd unwittingly become entangled in. So eager that, once satisfied with my productivity for the day, I immediately hopped in my car and drove to the diner, hoping to catch Jackie between the breakfast and lunch rushes.

I'd timed things well, as it turned out. A few customers sat scattered through the diner, but the place was fairly quiet. A college-age woman was taking care of the customers, and she directed me to the back office when I asked to see Jackie.

When I explained that I was hoping to speak with the owners of the Sea Breeze Motel—and why—Jackie was keen to help.

"I hate that you had your house burgled," she said. "It's just lucky that Callum didn't get hurt any worse. And if you think the burglar might have something to do with the murder . . ." She shuddered. "That's scary."

"I might be chasing shadows, but I feel like I need to do *something*."

Jackie patted my arm. "Honey, I trust your instincts. They've sure helped you unmask criminals in the past."

A lot of my success in that regard was actually thanks to help from Euclid, Flossie, and Fancy, but I wasn't about to mention that.

"I've got about an hour before this place gets busy again," Jackie said. "How about I come with you to the motel and introduce you to Dee? She might be more willing to talk with someone she knows."

"Jackie, that would be amazing. Thank you."

"Anything to help get criminals off our streets," she said as she pulled on her coat. "I love this town and I want to feel safe here."

Although the Sea Breeze Motel was within walking distance, we drove there in my car to save time and to get us out of the damp, blustery wind blowing through town. Even in the few seconds it took to get to my vehicle, a strong gust cut through my clothes with a chill that felt much more like winter than spring.

I parked in one of the several free spots in the motel's lot and Jackie led the way into the office. Inside and to our right was a small seating area. To our left was a coffee station, with a stack of takeout cups bearing the motel's logo. Straight ahead was the reception desk. A woman in her late fifties, with fair skin and dark brown hair, sat there, focused on a computer screen. She glanced up when Jackie opened the door, and smiled as recognition sparked in her gray eyes.

"Jackie! This is a nice surprise!" She hurried out from behind the desk to give her friend a hug.

"Hey, Dee." Jackie returned the embrace. "I missed you at bingo last week."

"I had a touch of a cold," Dee said as she stepped back. "I'm all better now though, so I'll be back with a vengeance next time."

"I've no doubt about it." Jackie put an arm around my shoulders. "Dee, this is Georgie Johansen."

"Olivia van Oosten's niece," Dee said with a nod. "I love the work that you and your aunt do at the animal sanctuary."

"Thank you," I said. "It means a lot to us."

"I hear you had some trouble at the farm though." Her forehead crinkled. "A burglary?"

"That's why we're here," Jackie spoke up. "Georgie's trying to figure out what's going on. She wondered if there was a connection between the break-in at the farm and the woman who got killed. Wasn't her room burgled before she died?"

"Oh, gosh, I hope it's not the same person responsible!" Dee pressed a hand to her chest. "I assumed that the killer was the one who ransacked Ms. Hartmann's room. If the murderer broke into your house . . . that's just terrifying."

"Which is why I can't sit around waiting to see if anything else happens," I said. "I want to be sure that we're no longer in any danger out at the farm."

"I can't blame you for that." Dee frowned. "But I don't know how much I can help you."

"What did Nina Hartmann say to you after she discovered that her room had been ransacked?" I asked. "Any detail could be significant."

Dee thought for a moment before responding. "She came here to the office, quite upset, naturally. She told me that someone had broken into her room through the back window and had gone through all her belongings. She asked if we have video surveillance, which we do, but only at the front of the building."

"But maybe the burglar tried the door to her room first?" I asked, not holding out much hope.

"No," Dee replied, "but I think the person tried to steal a key card. We were short-staffed that day, so I had to leave the office unattended a few times. Our security camera caught someone entering and leaving the office in the early afternoon, but the police didn't seem hopeful that they'd be able to identify the individual. Whoever it was, they were dressed in baggy, dark clothes, with a hood hiding their face."

"But they didn't get a key card?" Jackie asked, beating me to the question.

"Nope," Dee confirmed. "They came behind the desk here and rifled through the drawers, but we keep all the key cards locked up."

"So they gave up and broke the window in Nina's room," I said.

Dee nodded. "I can show you the security footage."

I eagerly took her up on that offer, although it turned out that it didn't do much good. The grainy footage made it impossible to discern any details, and nothing about the mystery person struck me as familiar.

"I did find it a little odd that Ms. Hartmann didn't want me calling the police," Dee said after showing us the footage.

"She was the same when she came into the diner and said she was being followed," Jackie chimed in.

"Did she explain why she didn't want the police involved?" I asked.

"She said nothing was missing and she didn't want to cause a bother," Dee replied. "But I did end up calling the cops. I had to file a police report in order to make an insurance claim."

"Did the police talk to Nina?" Jackie asked.

"She wasn't around by the time they showed up. They wanted her to get in touch with them and I told her that in a voice message but, apparently, she never got around to it, and the next day . . ."

She didn't need to finish her sentence.

"Who found her?" I asked.

"My husband." Dee sighed. "Poor guy. It's been hard on him. He went to check on Nina after noticing that the window in her room had been broken yet again." She gave me a sad smile. "I wish I could help you find some peace of mind, but I really don't know anything helpful."

"That's all right," I said. "I appreciate you talking to me." I was about to wrap up our conversation when I thought of something else. "Is Lex Nicholson staying here? He's Nina's nephew, probably in his early twenties."

Dee shook her head. "There's no one by that name staying here."

Next, I described the other young man with the sandy hair.

"Sorry," she said. "We don't have any young men staying here at the moment."

After thanking Dee for talking to me, I left with Jackie. I drove her back to the diner, but instead of heading home after dropping her off, I sat in my parked car, wishing my trip into town had been more productive. I'd really hoped to find some sort of clue before returning to the farm.

I texted Tessa, asking if she could find out if Valentina knew where in Twilight Cove Lex Nicholson was staying. Then I turned my thoughts to Hailey. I needed to find out more about her too.

With renewed determination, I climbed out of my car and strode up the street.

I'd first seen Hailey at the jewelry store, so that's where I decided to seek out my next clue.

TWENTY-FOUR

When I arrived at the jewelry store, Anton was in the midst of helping another customer. I browsed while I waited, slowly making my way past necklaces, rings, and bracelets. Instead of appreciating the beauty of the pieces on display, however, I felt an ache of loss. Looking at all the jewelry reminded me of the pieces that the burglar had stolen from me. My mom's jewelry was the only physical connection I had to her. She'd passed away when I was so young that any memories of her were fuzzy at best. I had some photos and videos, but there would never be any other heirlooms handed down from her.

Simmering anger bubbled up inside of me when I thought about the burglar likely pawning off the items for a bit of cash. The jewelry meant nothing to him or her, but so much to me. I knew it would be pointless to get caught up in the unfairness of it, but it was hard to stifle those feelings entirely.

As the other customer left the shop, Anton greeted me cheerily. "What can I do for you today, Georgie?"

"I have a question for you, about one of your customers," I said as I approached the sales counter. "The day I bought earrings for my aunt, another woman came into the shop. Her name might be Hailey, or possibly Jane. I ran into her at the school ballpark the other day and was hoping to get in touch with her again. I know she's from out of town, so I'm trying to figure out where she's staying."

"From out of town," Anton said as he pondered the information I'd given him. "You must mean Ms. Lau. I believe her first name was Hailey."

I forced myself to contain my excitement. If that was Hailey's real name, I'd finally made some progress.

"She didn't leave any contact information, but she was carrying a coffee cup with the Sea Breeze Motel's logo on it. I assume that's where she's staying."

"Perfect. Thank you," I said. I thought of another question.

"Do you ever have people come in here trying to sell stolen jewelry to you?"

"It has happened. Of course, no one ever admits that they're trying to sell stolen goods, but if I have any suspicions, I contact the police with my concerns."

"Has anyone tried to sell you any jewelry this week?"

"Not a soul." His voice turned sympathetic. "I heard you had a burglary at the farm. Did the thief take your jewelry?"

"Unfortunately. It belonged to my mom. She passed away when I was young."

"I'm very sorry to hear that," he said with sincerity. "I'll certainly keep my eyes and ears open. If you can provide photos or descriptions of the pieces, that would help too."

"I've got photos." I'd taken them years ago for insurance purposes.

Anton gave me a business card with his email address on it and asked me to send him the pictures. I agreed to do that and thanked him again for his help.

I left the shop with buoyed spirits. I could have tried questioning Anton further, to see if he would reveal the reason for Hailey's visit to his store, but I didn't want to raise any suspicions. As unlikely as it might be, I didn't want him contacting Hailey and telling her that I was asking about her.

I stopped in my tracks on my way to my car. What had Hailey said to Anton when she'd entered his shop? She'd asked him something about buying and selling jewelry.

That couldn't be a coincidence, even though she'd paid that visit to Anton before the burglar stole the brooch and other jewelry from the farmhouse.

Hailey had shown a keen interest in Callum and where he lived, and she'd asked questions about jewelry. Did she know about the brooch? If so, what was her connection to it?

Those questions stayed on my mind as I hurried home. The weather, while a bit chilly, was rain-free, and the sun had even made an appearance. The high school's softball team had a practice that afternoon and I planned to take the dogs to the field to watch. While practices might not be as exciting as actual games, I enjoyed watching Callum coach the teens, and I also liked to see Roxy's progress, both in terms of the sport and her self-confidence.

When I arrived at the farm, I spotted my aunt out beyond the carriage house, surveying her vegetable garden. She hadn't yet started planting, but I knew she'd already been planning for weeks what she wanted to grow.

Flossie and Fancy came running from the direction of the barn and I paused to greet them before carrying on to join my aunt by the raised beds. To my surprise, she wasn't alone. A white duck waddled along the pathways between the beds, occasionally pecking at the ground.

The dogs didn't appear taken aback by the duck's presence. They trotted right up to it and gave it friendly nuzzles with their noses before flopping down on the grass for a rest.

"Who's this?" I asked as I approached the adorable duck.

It quacked and waddled right up to me.

"Meet Quackers," Auntie O said as I stroked the feathers on the duck's neck. "She's our newest resident here at the sanctuary."

To my surprise, Quackers leaned into my touch.

"Aren't you a beauty," I said.

"She loves to be held and cuddled." My aunt gave the duck a gentle and affectionate pat. "I think she believes she's a cat."

Slowly, I gathered the duck into my arms. She didn't resist at all. As soon as I had her against my chest, she snuggled in, the way Stardust did when I held her.

"What a sweetie." I smiled down at Quackers before looking my aunt's way. "What's her story?"

"She lived with an elderly lady about an hour down the coast. Unfortunately, the woman passed away a few days ago and none of her family members are in a position to take in a duck. The two were closely bonded, so Quackers craves human company. She also gets along well with dogs, as you can see."

I set Quackers down on the ground and she immediately waddled over to Flossie and Fancy.

"That's so sad that she lost her human," I said. "She must feel so lost and confused."

"The daughter of the woman who passed away dropped Quackers off today. According to her, Quackers has seemed distressed. She was a little disoriented for the first hour or so after she arrived here, but she's settled down now. She seems happiest when Flossie, Fancy, and I are all with her."

The dogs lifted their heads at the sound of their names. Quackers moved in a slow circle around the lounging spaniels, pecking at the ground as she went, never straying far from Flossie and Fancy.

"We'll take good care of you, Quackers," I said to the duck. "I can promise you that."

"A-woo," Fancy added, sounding like she was voicing her agreement.

That brought a smile to my face, despite my lingering sadness for the poor duck and her recent loss.

When the dogs and I entered the farmhouse a short while later, Stardust gave me a scolding of indignant meows that turned into happy, loving purrs as soon as I picked her up for an apology cuddle.

"I'm sorry you were alone," I said as she snuggled against me. "But don't worry. You're going to hang out with Olivia this afternoon while the rest of us are out."

After a few more cuddles and some tuna treats, Stardust's displeasure was long forgotten. I answered a couple of work-related emails and then started in on baking a batch of chocolate chip cookies. As I worked on the batter, Callum stopped by the house to say he was on his way to the high school. The dogs and I got ready to follow him about an hour later, with me piling freshly baked cookies into a plastic container.

I sampled a couple before leaving the house, of course. My baking skills might not be on par with Auntie O's or Callum's, but I still made a mean cookie. I had to give the animals treats of their own when I sampled the results of my baking. If the sad puppy dog eyes hadn't been enough to convince me to feed them, then the barks, howls, and meows would have done the trick.

When Flossie, Fancy, and I reached the baseball field, all the players waved excitedly. Although I waved back, I didn't kid myself. I knew they were far more excited to see the dogs than me, especially since they couldn't see what was in the plastic container I was carrying.

I settled on the bleachers while Flossie and Fancy stayed down on the grass. They watched the activities on the field for a while, their tails wagging, but eventually they lay down for a snooze. Being the team's mascots was tiring work.

I, too, watched the practice for a while, but I couldn't keep my sleuthing hat off for long. Eventually, I tugged out my phone and accessed the internet, typing Hailey Lau's name in the search bar.

I nearly groaned when I saw how many results popped up for people with the same name. Even when I added "Florida" to the search terms, I ended up with pages of hits. I alternated between watching the softball practice and sifting through all the results. I started with the images, hoping it would be easier to find the right Hailey that way. My eyes had glazed over and I'd sneaked two cookies out of the container by the time a photo caught my eye. I clicked on the picture.

Jackpot! I'd found the right Hailey Lau!

I navigated to the website that was the source of the photo and did a double take.

Even when I read the information a second time, and then a third time, nothing changed.

I'd read it right.

Hailey Lau was a private investigator.

TWENTY-FIVE

It took all my self-control to keep myself from running onto the baseball field to tell Callum about my discovery. At least the practice was wrapping up, so I wouldn't have to wait long to talk to him. As the girls meandered their way off the field, I opened the container I'd brought to the park. Seconds later, the teens swarmed around me, eagerly taking cookies while voicing their enthusiastic thanks.

Flossie and Fancy were on their feet, tails wagging as they gazed up at the girls with adoring eyes. I knew the power of those eyes, so I reminded the teens that the dogs couldn't have any chocolate. That didn't stop a couple of girls from finding bits of cookie that had no chocolate and slipping them to the spaniels.

By the time all the teens had left, two cookies remained.

"For me?" Callum asked, hopeful.

"Better grab them quick," I warned. "I can't promise that they won't disappear if you leave them with me."

Callum snatched up the cookies and snaked an arm around my waist to pull me in close to him. He gave me a kiss before taking a bite of cookie. "Thank you. They're delicious."

"I'll help you pack up the gear," I offered.

The girls had already helped with the task before they left, so it took only a minute for Callum and me to finish the job. We loaded the bags into his truck and could have headed home right then, except I couldn't wait any longer to share my news with him.

"Check this out," I said, handing him my phone, which still displayed the website for Hailey Lau's private investigation firm. "That's the woman who was asking questions about you at the coffee shop. Well, the second woman, after Nina Hartmann. She was also here during the softball game the other day."

"She's a PI?" Callum's face registered surprise and a hint of suspicion. "It says here that she's based out of Orlando. That's a long way from Twilight Cove. And, it's in Florida . . ."

"Right?" I knew his thoughts were heading in the same direction as mine had. "Another person in Twilight Cove from Florida. Definitely not a coincidence."

"OK." Callum handed my phone back. "But why is she here? Who hired her? And why?"

"You took the questions right out of my mouth."

"I wonder if Brody knows her identity."

"I'll text him the link now," I said. "The police definitely need to talk to her, if they haven't already."

Callum walked me to my car, parked across the lot from his truck. "I don't like the fact that she approached you. That's more brazen than asking questions at the coffee shop."

"If she's investigating something—the theft of the brooch, I'm guessing—I doubt she's interested in hurting me."

"But we don't know that for sure," Callum pointed out. "We don't know how desperate she or the person she's working for might be. She could even be the person who broke into the farmhouse."

"True," I conceded. With the text message sent to Brody, I stuffed my phone in my pocket. "This is all so crazy."

Fancy tipped back her head and bayed.

"Even Fancy agrees," I said.

Flossie let out a bark.

I smiled, despite my frustration. "Flossie too."

Callum wrapped his arms around me and rested his cheek on the top of my head. "Hopefully, it will all make sense before long. You know I don't want you putting yourself in danger, but I get why you want to figure this out. This is all driving me a little crazy too. Especially since it feels like not knowing what's going on is contributing to the danger."

I pulled back so I could smile up at him. "Despite the craziness, I love having you on my sleuthing team."

"I love it too," he admitted with a grin. His gaze shifted to something over my shoulder. "Tessa's here."

I turned around to see my best friend hurrying toward us from the direction of the school building.

"I'm glad I caught you!" she called as she drew closer. "I meant to come out sooner, but I got wrapped up in grading papers and lost track of time."

"Is anything wrong?" I asked with concern.

"Not wrong," she replied as she reached us, "but I don't have anything good to report, either. I just wanted to tell you that I asked Valentina about Lex Nicholson, but she has no idea where he's staying in town and she hasn't overheard anyone at the station talking about him."

"It was a long shot, anyway." I tried not to let my spirits slump.

"Georgie just found out something important," Callum said.

"Possibly important," I qualified. "Definitely interesting."

I filled Tessa in and showed her Hailey's website on my phone.

"She's got to know at least something about what's going on," Tessa said when I finished. "I bet she holds a whole lot of pieces to this crazy puzzle."

"But what's the chance she'll share any of them, either with us or the police?" Callum asked.

Tessa looked to me. "If she doesn't want to share, then you know what we need to do, right?"

"Investigate the investigator?" I guessed.

She smiled. "Exactly."

Brody responded to my text message that evening, but he merely thanked me for the tip and didn't give me any hint as to whether the information was news to him or if he thought it could be important to the murder or burglary cases.

That didn't come as a surprise. Brody took his job seriously—as he should—and rarely gave much away, but I would have been lying if I'd claimed not to be at all disappointed.

The following morning, over a breakfast of toast with Auntie O's homemade strawberry jam, I tried to work out a plan of action.

"I know Hailey's staying at the Sea Breeze Motel," I said to Callum as we ate at the kitchen table. "Maybe I can figure out which room she's in and try to have a chat with her."

"Hold up," Callum cautioned. "Remember we decided we didn't know how desperate she might be to do whatever she came to Twilight Cove to do?"

"I remember."

"So please don't go looking for her on your own. It's probably best to let the police talk to her and see what happens after that."

I held back a groan. Fancy, however, didn't. She let out a long one as she sank from a sitting position to lie down next to the table. Then she flopped dramatically onto her side.

I laughed.

"My thoughts exactly, Fancy."

"Hey, my caution comes from a place of love," Callum said as he got up from the table. He kissed my cheek on his way to the sink.

"We know that, right, Fancy?"

She let out a grumble.

"Yes, we do," I said with a smile.

I carried my plate over to the sink and took hold of Callum's hand. With our palms together, I intertwined our fingers.

"I appreciate your love and concern," I said with sincerity. "And I promise not to approach Hailey on my own. So . . ."

A slow smile took shape on Callum's face. "So, you want me to go with you?"

"I always want you with me, but yes. What do you say?"

"When you put it like that . . ."

"You have to agree?" I asked, hopeful.

"Hmm." A dizzying blend of affection and heat flared in his green eyes. "I was thinking more along the lines of I have to do this."

He tilted my chin up, his gaze burning into mine. Then he kissed me, slowly, reverently, making the world around us blur and fade away. I melted into him, into the kiss. The man was a poet with his lips, could write a love letter with his touch.

Maybe he couldn't move objects with his mind or glow with blue light, but he had magic in him nonetheless.

The kiss might have gone on for eternity if Fancy hadn't grumbled and "woo-ed" in complaint.

Callum smiled against my lips. "Somebody's in a mood."

Fancy fussed some more.

"Somebody wants to go sleuthing," I said, still a little breathless.

Fancy jumped to her feet and ran to the back door. She wagged her tail and let out another long "woo".

Callum took a step back, holding my hands, and shook his head. "They really do understand us, don't they?"

Flossie barked and joined her sister at the door.

"Sometimes I think they understand us better than we do." I squeezed his hands before letting go so I could put my breakfast dishes in the dishwasher. "We have to look after all the other animals before we go anywhere," I reminded the dogs.

Fancy let out an impatient "a-woo".

My heart stuttered when Flossie touched a paw to the door and the deadbolt unlocked.

My gaze snapped to Callum's face in the fraction of a second it took me to remember that he now knew about the dogs' abilities. My panic subsided in a sudden rush that left my knees weak. Or maybe that was the lingering effects of the kiss. Callum appeared surprised, but mostly intrigued.

Flossie backed up and stared at the door. The knob turned and the door swung open.

"Incredible," Callum said, as the dogs charged out onto the porch.

"It takes a bit of getting used to." I rubbed his back. "Are you OK?"

"My mind is a little boggled, but I'm fine. It's one thing to hear about what they can do and another to watch them in action."

I smiled. "Just wait until Fancy disappears before your very eyes, or starts to glow."

Callum gave his head a shake. "Life with my favorite girls is certainly interesting."

"Just interesting?" I teased.

"Oh no. That, and so much more."

He kissed me again, in a way that made the air around us hum with the warmth of our love for each other. I fell into the kiss and forgot about everything around us, until Fancy let out a long howl from somewhere outside. Callum and I parted slowly, smiling at each other.

"We should start every day like this," I said.

His grin widened. "That's part of my life plan."

Life plan.

That sounded long-term.

Maybe he saw me as his always and forever, like I did with him.

With my heart full, I took his hand and we set off to tackle the morning farm work.

TWENTY-SIX

After we'd finished the farm chores and had changed our clothes, Callum and I drove into town, with the dogs accompanying us. We made the Sea Breeze Motel our first destination.

After we parked in the motel's lot, we sat for a minute, surveying our surroundings from inside Callum's truck.

"I don't see Hailey's car here," I said after I'd looked at every other vehicle parked in the lot. "Maybe I can ask Dee for her room number."

"She probably won't give it to you," Callum pointed out. "Guest privacy and all that."

"You're most likely right," I conceded. "Maybe we should follow another lead and try to find Hailey later?"

"Probably a good idea," Callum agreed. "I don't think Hailey will tell us who hired her, anyway, even if we get a chance to talk to her."

I rested a hand on his knee. "Ah, the voice of reason."

"Is that code for party pooper?"

"A-woo-woo," Fancy said from the back seat.

Callum laughed. "I thought so."

"I appreciate your sensible input," I assured him. "Tailing Hailey might end up being more worthwhile than talking to her and revealing that we know she's a private detective. If her client is in Twilight Cove, she might lead us right to that person."

"So, you want to wait here until she appears?" He didn't sound thrilled by the idea.

"No." I was feeling far too impatient to sit around in the hope that the private eye might show up and lead us somewhere interesting. "Let's head over to the Gilmore Hotel instead. Maybe we can find out if Lex is staying there."

"If Lex arrived in Twilight Cove before his mother did, does she know he's here?" Callum asked as he drove away from the motel.

"That's a very good question." I sat quietly for a minute, thinking. "I wonder if I can find out more about the Nicholson and Hartmann families. And the brooch. I feel like it's at the center of this tangled web."

"They must be wealthy. Or Nina and Scarlett's father must be, at least, since he owned the brooch."

"And lives in a mansion, according to what Valentina told us."

"But if Nina felt the need to steal the brooch . . ." Callum trailed off.

"Maybe she was having money problems?" I considered that possibility. "Could be. I wonder if there's any way we can find out."

I focused on my phone for the rest of the drive to the hotel. I conducted a few searches, using a combination of words and names, including Nicholson, Hartmann, Tampa, burglary, and brooch. My third attempt brought up a link to an article about the theft of the brooch from Nina and Scarlett's father, published by a news website based in the Tampa Bay area.

I skimmed through the article as Callum turned onto the Gilmore Hotel's property and searched for a free space in the self-parking lot.

"Baxter Hartmann is the name of Nina and Scarlett's father," I said as I scanned the text. "He was a successful real estate developer, apparently, before he retired. That's how he amassed his sizeable fortune." I read another paragraph. "According to this article, the brooch was insured." I continued skimming to the end of the page. "There's no hint here that anyone has accused Nina of the theft, but even if Scarlett now thinks Nina was behind the burglary, she might not want that to be public knowledge."

"Is there any indication that the police in Tampa have any leads?" Callum asked as he shut off the truck's engine.

"The article doesn't say." I tucked my phone away as I realized something. "Oh. Maybe we shouldn't have brought the dogs."

"Woo," Fancy protested from the back of the truck's cab.

I twisted in my seat so I could see the spaniels. "I want you with us," I assured them, "but I don't know what kind of pet policy the Gilmore Hotel has." I remembered something. "But Angelica Bergstrom had Birdie with her, so maybe you'd be welcome." I pulled out my phone again and looked up the hotel's website. "Darn. They only allow dogs under twenty pounds, unless they're service dogs."

Fancy grumbled and Flossie let out an indignant bark.

"Those are some strong opinions," Callum said with a chuckle.

"*We* know you provide important assistance," I said to Flossie and Fancy, "but the hotel still won't consider you to be service dogs. And you both definitely weigh more than twenty pounds." I turned my attention to Callum. "I don't like the thought of leaving them alone in the truck. Do you mind waiting here while I go have a look around?"

"Call me and stay on the line, even if you're pretending that you're not on the phone," Callum requested. "That way, I'll have an idea what's going on. If there's even the slightest hint of trouble, I'm coming in."

I gave him a quick kiss. "Deal."

Fancy grumbled again as I got out of the truck. I smiled when I looked through the window and saw Callum talking to the spaniels.

As I walked toward the hotel's main entrance, I put a call through to Callum. He answered on the first ring.

"I'm going in," I said into my phone as the automatic doors parted for me.

I dropped my hand to my side, but then decided that talking on the phone would give me an excuse to linger in the lobby and get my bearings.

"All right," I said when I put the device back to my ear, "I'm in the lobby. But now what? The desk won't give me Lex's room number, will they?"

"No," Callum replied. "You could try asking them to put a call through to his room. If they agree to do that, you'll at least know he's staying there, but a lot of hotels require you to provide a guest's name *and* room number before they'll connect you."

"It's worth a try," I said quietly as a man in a suit strode past me. "I'll have to hang up for a minute."

"Don't forget to call me right back, Georgie."

I promised I'd remember and disconnected. I looked up the hotel's phone number online and then glanced around. Maybe calling from the lobby wasn't the best idea. I didn't want the desk clerk to catch on to the fact that I was lurking by one of the potted palms. They might wonder why I didn't just approach the desk, and I didn't want them to be able to put a face to the nosy person on the phone if my request somehow raised their suspicions.

Acting like I had every right to be there, I approached the elevators and stepped into the first one that opened its doors. I rode up one floor and then disembarked. The corridor was deserted, just as I'd hoped. I stayed in the elevator alcove and called the front desk.

I hung up, disappointed, less than a minute later.

As Callum had predicted, the employee required me to provide a guest name and room number before they would connect me. They also wouldn't tell me whether or not Lex was a registered guest. So much for my sleuthing attempts. Maybe it was best to call it a day and get back to the farm.

I took the elevator down to the lobby and called Callum back.

"No luck," I reported.

Then I stopped dead in my tracks.

Scarlett Nicholson stood near the front doors, holding her phone to her ear.

"Hold on," I whispered into my own phone. "I've got Scarlett in my sights. I'm going to pretend to text while I eavesdrop."

I gave her a wide berth and then sidled up behind her, leaving a marble pillar between us. I pretended to tap out a message on my phone as I leaned against the pillar and listened in on her phone conversation.

"Our plan is completely falling apart," Scarlett said, her voice hushed and her words clipped. "What are we going to do now?"

She listened for a moment.

"Well, we've got to think of something. And fast. Do you hear me, Royce?" After another short pause she ended the call with a brusque, "I'll call you later."

Still pretending to text, I chanced a casual peek around the pillar. Scarlett's phone rang almost as soon as she ended her previous call. I caught a glimpse of the screen as the name "N. Skidmore" appeared on it.

Scarlett huffed out an impatient sigh. "Not now." She declined the call with a sharp jab of her finger. Then she slid her phone into her designer purse and strode out the front doors, her high heels clicking against the marble floors.

I waited inside the hotel while the valet fetched Scarlett's car. Once she got behind the wheel of a flashy red convertible and zoomed off, I hurried outside and joined Callum and the dogs in the truck.

I shared what I'd overheard.

"Royce is her husband. But what plan could they be talking about?" I wondered.

"It must have had something to do with Nina or the brooch," Callum said. "Don't you think?"

"Probably. I'm sure Scarlett was hoping the brooch would be with Nina's personal effects. Maybe that's what she meant by their plans falling apart? She and her husband were hoping to get the brooch back and return it to Baxter Hartmann?"

"You should tell Brody what you overheard," Callum said as he drove us out of the hotel's parking lot.

"I'll tell him when we see him tonight."

As long as he didn't get delayed at work, Brody would be joining us and several other friends at Genesis' apartment for a games night.

"I'll also ask him some questions," I added.

Flossie whined in the back seat.

"I know," I told her. "He's not likely to answer any of them. But still, it's worth a shot, right?"

"A-woo!" Fancy chimed in.

I had a sneaking suspicion that meant, "Always."

TWENTY-SEVEN

When we arrived at Genesis' apartment above Déjà Brew with a plate of Callum's homemade brownies in hand, Cindy and her brother, Nicholas, were already there. Julia Chen arrived on our heels, and Ava-Kate and Steve McIntosh showed up minutes later. I'd known Julia and Ava-Kate when I lived in Twilight Cove for a year in my teens, but I hadn't met Steve until Tessa had invited me to my first games night with the group back in the summer. Steve's cousin sometimes joined us, but he was currently out of town for work.

Brody showed up last, apologizing for holding up the group, although we all assured him that we didn't mind. He was late getting off work and arrived hungry, so we filled plates with the snacks Genesis had set out on her kitchen island before settling into our gameplaying.

I managed not to bring up the murder or burglary for the first half hour. Actually, I didn't bring up those subjects at all. It was Cindy who asked Callum and me about the latter incident. After we shared what little we knew about the crime and its perpetrator, Nicholas asked if the events at the farmhouse had any connection to the recent murder.

"We're still looking into that," Brody said before rolling the dice.

"Does Lex Nicholson's mom know he's in town? Is he staying at the Gilmore Hotel too?" I asked as Brody moved his piece on the board.

He shot me a suspicious glance. "And why would you be asking me that?" He sounded like he'd already guessed the reason.

"Pure curiosity?" I hadn't meant for my response to sound like a question.

"Uh-huh." He sat back in his chair. "How about you leave the investigating to the police?"

"What fun would that be?" Tessa asked with a mischievous smile.

That made her the target of Brody's quelling stare, but her smile grew brighter and cheekier in the face of it.

Although Brody tried to keep a serious and disapproving expression on his face, his eyes softened, ever so slightly, before he returned his focus to the gameboard.

Tessa's cheeks turned pink and I knew she'd seen what I had. I caught Callum's eye and realized that he'd noticed too. No one else had, as far as I could tell. They were all focused on the game unfolding on the table before us.

I made a mental note to talk to Tessa about Brody the next time the two of us were alone. There was definitely something brewing between them.

I held back a smile. The two of them would make a great couple, of that I had no doubt.

"Who's Lex Nicholson?" Genesis asked as she took her turn with rolling the dice.

Her question brought me back to the conversation I'd momentarily forgotten about.

"The nephew of the woman who was murdered," I replied.

"The son of the murder victim's sister?" Genesis checked. When I nodded, she added, "I heard he's staying at an Airbnb."

"Where did you hear that?" Brody asked, his suspicious gaze now fixed on her.

It had no effect on Genesis. "When I was dropping off the leftover donuts and pastries at the police station yesterday."

Ever since she'd bought the coffee shop, Genesis had made a habit of taking food items that were left over at the end of each day to either the police station, the fire station, or the local food bank.

"The sister was there talking to an officer while her son was sitting—slouching, really—on a chair in the lobby," Genesis continued. "On my way out, I heard the guy ask his mom to drop him off at his Airbnb."

"You don't need to disclose the location of his accommodations," Brody warned, flicking a glance my way.

"I don't know the location, so you don't have to worry about that," Genesis said with a smile.

"Scarlett definitely knows Lex is in town, then." I rolled the dice and moved my game piece along the board, aiming my next words at Brody. "Was Lex questioned by the police? And if so, can you tell us what he had to say?"

"Why would he have been questioned?" Ava-Kate jumped in. "Just because he's related to the woman who got killed?"

"Because he arrived in Twilight Cove even before his mother did," Callum replied.

Ava-Kate's eyes widened. "So he might have killed his aunt?"

"Whoa," Brody cut in. "Can we focus on the game instead of talking about the murder? And, no, Georgie," he added, "I won't tell you what he said when—or if—he was questioned by the professionals whose job it is to conduct the investigation."

I smiled, expecting as much, and unbothered by his emphasis on the last half of that sentence.

Callum clapped him on the back. "Sorry for talking shop while you're off the clock."

"I'm more concerned about certain people trying to investigate on their own and getting into trouble." His eyes skipped from me to Tessa while he spoke.

My best friend met my gaze across the table and smiled.

That didn't go unnoticed by Brody. "Nope," he objected. "No conspiring. No scheming. No sleuthing. Just gameplay."

"Fair enough," I conceded.

We managed to spend the next couple of hours talking about anything but the recent crimes.

Later in the evening, after I was the first player to get booted out of our latest game, I pulled out my phone. As much as I wished I could forget about the unsolved cases, they kept tickling the back of my brain, demanding my attention.

I navigated to the social media pages for Lex's band and scrolled through the numerous posts. They mostly consisted of announcements about upcoming gigs and photos of the band playing at a variety of bars, practicing, or hanging out together.

It wasn't exactly riveting stuff, and my eyes were threatening to glaze over when a comment below one of the posts caught my eye.

The contents of the comment held nothing of interest, but the name of the person who'd written it certainly grabbed my attention.

Nash Skidmore.

Scarlett had declined a phone call from an N. Skidmore.

I clicked on Nash's name and landed on his profile page. When I saw a larger version of his profile photo, my eyes widened.

I looked up from my phone, ready to burst from the excitement of my discovery. The game was nearing its end, so I bit down on my lower lip, not wanting to interrupt.

Finally, the game came to a close, with Cindy as the victor. I was about to say Brody's name when Ava-Kate spoke up.

"Before everyone leaves, Steve and I have some news." She exchanged a smile with her husband and then announced, "We're going to have a baby!"

Cheers and congratulations erupted around the table, and I joined in.

"When is the baby due?" Tessa asked as we all hugged the parents-to-be.

"Early August," Steve said, his beaming smile matching Ava-Kate's.

The excitement about the news bubbled through our group even as we gathered up our coats and filed out the door, calling out our thanks and goodbyes. Tessa and I hugged Ava-Kate again out on the street before she and Steve climbed into their SUV.

We all waved as they drove off, but then I turned my attention back to my recent discovery.

"Brody," I said, once he, Tessa, Callum, and I were alone on the sidewalk. "There's something I need to tell you."

"Let me guess. You've been snooping?" He tried to maintain an unimpressed expression, but I caught sight of a brief twinkle in his eye.

"The preferred term is 'sleuthing'," Tessa corrected him.

"Aren't those one and the same?" Brody asked.

Tessa gave him a playful shove.

"All I did was look at the socials for Lex Nicholson's band," I said. "That's harmless enough."

Brody looked like he wanted to argue, but instead he said, "And what did you find?"

"Ooh, you're officially a source, Georgie!" Tessa exclaimed with delight.

"She's not officially anything, and neither are you." Brody aimed a pointed stare her way.

She simply smiled at him, unfazed.

I found the relevant social media post on my phone and handed the device to Brody. "This guy, Nash Skidmore, commented on one of the band's posts. And, earlier today, I noticed that Scarlett Nicholson declined a phone call from someone by the name of N. Skidmore."

Brody looked from the photo to me. "I probably don't want to know how you noticed that, do I?"

"Never mind that," I said, eager to get to the heart of the matter. I pointed at the screen. "Does Nash look familiar to you?"

Brody studied the photo again. "No, I can't say that he does."

"Oh." His response caught me off guard, but then I realized I'd never told him about this particular individual.

"Hey," Callum said as he leaned in to get a look at the photo, "isn't that the guy you showed me a picture of before?"

I nodded, my excitement returning. "Nash Skidmore, of Tampa, Florida, is here in Twilight Cove."

TWENTY-EIGHT

"But who is he, exactly?" Tessa asked, taking my phone from Brody so she could get a closer look at the photo.

"That, I don't know," I admitted. "But he's yet another person from Florida who's here in Twilight Cove. And I saw his name on Scarlett's phone. So, clearly, he's connected to her somehow and maybe to Nina as well. Plus," I continued, before Brody had a chance to say anything, "he went out of his way to avoid police officers here on Main Street."

I recounted in more detail the two times I'd seen Nash in person.

"OK," Brody said, handing my phone back to me, "but just because he knows Scarlett Nicholson—"

"And Lex, or at least his band," Tessa interjected.

A muscle in Brody's jaw twitched. "That doesn't mean he's involved in the murder or the theft of the brooch."

"What?" Tessa exclaimed with disbelief. "Why else would he be in Twilight Cove?"

"He could be here for an entirely innocent reason," Callum said, although he didn't sound like he truly believed his own statement.

"Exactly," Brody agreed.

"All right, sure, that's possible," I conceded, even though he didn't have me convinced. "But don't you think it's worth looking into?"

"It is," he said. "But *I'll* look into it. Meaning, you don't need to."

"I hear you," I assured him.

"I hope you do."

"You can't blame Georgie for wanting to know what the heck is going on," Tessa said in my defense. "She and Callum got swept into this whole thing by no fault of their own."

"And you can't blame me for wanting Georgie—and Callum—to stay safe," Brody countered.

"You've got me there," Tessa admitted, getting a hint of a grin out of him.

"I want to *feel* safe again," I said. "And not have to worry that someone might target us again for some reason."

Callum slipped an arm around my shoulders. "I feel the same. I'm constantly worrying about Georgie's safety when I'm not with her."

"You are?" That both saddened me and warmed my heart. I leaned against him and put an arm around his waist.

"I get that," Brody assured us. "I really do. My colleagues and I will look into this, I promise you that. In turn, I'd like all of you to promise to do your best to stay out of danger."

"We promise," Callum said.

Tessa and I echoed his words.

"Good," Brody said, satisfied. "I'll see you around."

Tessa waved as they turned toward Brody's truck.

I didn't fail to notice that his hand settled at the small of her back as they walked up the street.

I smiled at the sight.

Yes, Tessa and I definitely needed to have a bestie chat.

Despite the overcast skies the next morning, I started the day in good spirits. After taking care of the sanctuary animals and walking the dogs, Callum and I would drive down the coast to Gold Beach to pick up the donated items from Angelica Bergstrom. I was looking forward to the trip, partly because I loved spending time with my boyfriend, but also because I loved the Oregon coast, and we'd get to see a lot of it on our way to and from the other town.

We'd decided to leave early enough in the day that we'd have time to make a couple of stops along the way to take in the sights. Gillian had provided me with Angelica's phone number, and I texted her to ask if it was all right for us to bring the dogs along for the trip. She'd assured me that was fine, so we bundled into Callum's truck with Flossie and Fancy in the back seat. We stopped off at the museum, where a rented cube truck waited for us. We switched vehicles and set off for Gold Beach.

Callum drove, which meant I got to drink in the views without worrying about watching the road. The gray clouds had parted enough to let the sun shine through, and we stopped briefly at a couple of lookout points to take in the gorgeous scenery and stretch our legs. We also made one quick snack break at a beachside coffee shop.

When we arrived in Gold Beach, we found Angelica Bergstrom's property without any trouble. Although I knew the woman was rich, I wasn't prepared for the spectacular sight of her oceanfront estate.

"Ho-ly," I said, drawing out the word as we turned into the driveway.

Fancy added an "a-woo" from the back of the truck's cab.

We had to pause at a set of iron gates and give our names to someone who spoke to us through an intercom, but then the gates parted and Callum drove farther onto the property. Angelica's mansion was a vast, two-story structure built from logs and stone. I could see a couple of matching outbuildings, one of which looked like a guest cottage, and a gazebo on the acreage.

The voice on the intercom had directed us to park to the right of the mansion. When Callum pulled alongside the large house, an incredible view greeted us. An emerald-green lawn, perfectly manicured, sloped gently downward before dropping off at the low cliffs that lined the shore. I spotted what looked like a staircase that likely led down from the top of the cliff to the beach.

I climbed out of the vehicle and let the dogs out of the cab. Then I stood by the hood of the truck, gazing out at the view of the ocean.

"This is amazing," I said as Callum came to stand next to me.

"Breathtaking," he agreed.

"Hello!" a woman's voice called out.

We walked closer to the enormous back deck, which spanned the entire length of the mansion. Angelica waved to us from just outside a set of French doors, her white Pomeranian, Birdie, tucked under one arm.

"Please, come in this way," she said.

The dogs trotted alongside us as we made our way around the back of the mansion to a set of stairs that led up to the massive covered deck. Angelica set Birdie down and the spaniels touched noses with her, their tails wagging. Birdie gave a little yap and bounced around in a circle.

"She likes them," Angelica said with a smile. "Please, come inside."

Just like when we pulled into the driveway, I wasn't prepared for the sight that greeted us when we stepped indoors. Angelica led us into a space that could have served as a ballroom, considering its size, but which was clearly used as a sitting room. Numerous cozy seating areas had been set up, and an impressive river rock fireplace took up much of one wall. Another wall was almost all windows. Together with the vaulted ceilings, the windows gave the spacious room a bright and airy feel, and the ocean view was nearly as spectacular from the inside of the mansion as it was from the back lawn.

"It's so nice of you to drive all this way to pick up the items for the museum's fundraising party," Angelica said, leading the way through a door on the opposite side of the room from the tall windows.

"We appreciate your generous loan," I said in return.

"It's my pleasure." Angelica headed down a wide hallway. "I love the Art Deco style, and I feel that the theater pieces should be shared so others have the chance to enjoy them too."

"You've got a beautiful home," Callum remarked as Angelica opened a door.

She smiled at him and led the way into the next room. "Thank you. I do love it here."

The space we entered appeared to be a study, though it was so large that it could have housed the entire apartment I'd rented when I lived in Los Angeles. A stately wooden desk sat on a Persian rug, and bookshelves lined one wall. The view of the ocean once again drew my eye, though I soon forced myself to pull my focus back to the room we stood in.

Much of the floor space was currently taken up by an assortment of Art Deco furniture and décor. The jumble included lacquered end tables, leather club chairs, two velvet chaise lounges—one in blood red and the other in black—upholstered benches, lamps, and several statuettes.

"These are the items I'm lending the museum," Angelica said, gesturing at the furniture with a sweep of her arm.

I moved closer for a better look. "They're beautiful. They're not genuine antiques?"

"Just clever reproductions," Angelica confirmed.

"You could have fooled me," Callum said.

Angelica rested a hand on the back of one of the club chairs. "I hope they'll add to the authentic vibe of the party."

"I'm sure they will," I said. "They'll look fabulous in the Elmore house."

I could already picture them there.

"Andreas, one of my employees, will help you load everything onto the truck." Angelica produced a cell phone from the pocket of her flowy linen pants. "I'll let him know we're ready for him."

As she typed out a text message, I turned toward the door, where movement caught my eye. Flossie trotted past the open doorway, glancing at me on her way by. Fancy followed after her, and Birdie took up the rear.

Angelica was engrossed in her phone and hadn't noticed the dogs. Callum, however, looked from the doorway to me, raising his eyebrows in a silent question. I knew he was wondering if one of us should go after the dogs, and I intended to do so, but I had a feeling that I shouldn't call attention to whatever the spaniels might be up to.

"Angelica, is there a washroom I could use?" I asked, taking a step toward the door.

"Of course, dear. Turn to the right and it will be the second door on your left."

I thanked her and slipped out of the room. As I left, I heard Callum asking Angelica about the club chairs. I couldn't help but smile. He might not know exactly what I was up to, but he was keeping Angelica distracted so I'd have a chance to do it.

Even I didn't know exactly what I'd set out to do, beyond following the dogs. I had a sneaking suspicion that they were snooping, but I didn't know why. Pure curiosity, maybe, but I knew from past experiences to pay attention when Flossie and Fancy entered their sleuthing mode. Perhaps they were simply tracking down a cat—if Angelica had any—but even if that was the case, I figured I'd better catch up with them before they found their way into a part of the mansion where they might not be welcome.

As I set off along the hallway, I saw Flossie up ahead, touching a paw to a door on the left, near the end of the corridor. I heard a faint click and the door swung open.

"Flossie!" I whispered, trying to keep my voice low.

She ignored me and nosed the door open wider before disappearing through it.

"Fancy!" I whispered next.

She, too, acted like she hadn't heard, and followed her sister.

Birdie, her little pink tongue sticking out, happily trailed after them.

I glanced over my shoulder to make sure the coast was clear before I passed through the same door. I knew Flossie had unlocked it, and if Angelica kept the room secured, she probably didn't want random dogs and humans wandering in there. I didn't want her getting annoyed and rescinding her offer to loan the items to the museum. I also didn't want her questioning how the door had ended up unlocked, so I hoped to herd the dogs out as quickly as possible, without anyone ever knowing we were there.

"Flossie! Fancy!" I said as I entered a room that offered a view of the front lawn, flower beds, and towering trees.

I stopped short and gazed around. Display cases lined the walls and others sat on pedestals in the middle of the room. It looked like a mini museum. I peeked inside the nearest glass box and saw an Art Deco cigarette case with gold inlay. The next one held a tiara encrusted with sparkling jewels.

No wonder Angelica kept the room locked. It housed her collection of authentic Art Deco antiques. I definitely didn't want to get caught snooping around in here.

"Can we go, please?" I whispered to the spaniels.

They sat in the middle of the room, facing one of the display cases set on a pedestal.

Flossie glanced at me and then stared at the case.

"A-woo," Fancy said, before copying her sister.

Birdie, meanwhile, wandered around the room with her nose to the ground.

I tiptoed across the hardwood floors to reach the spaniels.

"What are you doing in here?" I asked, casting a worried glance toward the door.

Flossie reared up on her hind legs and placed her front paws on the pedestal.

I inched closer to look at the display case.

It was empty, save for a label like the ones I'd seen in the other cases, describing the objects they accompanied.

I read the text on the label, and then read it again.

My heart rate ticked up.

Although the case was empty, the label stated that it was meant to hold the Emerald Mirage, an Art Deco brooch featuring an emerald and diamonds.

TWENTY-NINE

"I don't understand," I whispered to Flossie and Fancy.

Fancy whined and touched her nose to my leg.

"You're right," I said, pulling out my phone. "There's no time to wonder about it right now."

I snapped a photo of the display case and a close up of the label before returning my phone to my pocket. Then I herded all three dogs out of the room.

Thankfully, the corridor was still empty and I was able to return to the study without anyone knowing that I'd been anywhere other than the washroom.

Flossie had locked the door on our way out of the collection room and I hadn't spotted any surveillance cameras, so hopefully no one would ever know that we'd been in there. Nevertheless, nervous energy sparked its way through my body and I had to drum my fingers against my leg to give it a release.

I wanted to tell Callum about the dogs' discovery right away, but I had to hold my tongue. He and Andreas were transporting the items from the study to the truck under Angelica's watchful eye, so I jumped in to give them a hand, hoping it wouldn't be long before I could share my news.

After a half hour that felt much longer to me, we had the truck all packed. We thanked Angelica again and climbed into the cab with the dogs, ready to drive back to Twilight Cove. I waited until we'd reached the highway, but I couldn't keep quiet any longer than that.

"You'll never guess what the dogs found in the mansion," I said to Callum.

He glanced my way before returning his eyes to the road. "I thought the three of you were up to something."

"It was Flossie and Fancy who made the discovery," I said. "I just followed along."

Fancy let out a proud "woo-woo" from the back seat.

I proceeded to tell Callum about Angelica's personal museum

and the case in the middle of the room that held nothing but a label.

"Hold on," he said as I finished. "Are you saying the label described the brooch that Nina put in your bag at the airport? The one that was stolen from the farmhouse?"

"It sounds like it, doesn't it?" I accessed the internet on my phone as I talked. "The label said it was called the Emerald Mirage. I don't know if the brooch Nina stole from her father has a name or not, but I'm going to try to find out."

"But even if it is the same brooch, it belongs to Baxter Hartmann," Callum said. "So why would Angelica have a display case for it?"

"That's exactly what I'm wondering."

"A-woo," Fancy chimed in.

I read through a couple of articles about the theft of the brooch from Baxter Hartmann's residence in Tampa. The first news piece didn't mention that the brooch had a name, but the second one did.

"The brooch Nina stole from her father is called the Emerald Mirage," I told Callum. "It's the same one."

"So, maybe Angelica owned it at one point and then sold it, and never removed the label from the case?" he suggested.

"Or maybe she was hoping to own it in the future?" I shook my head. "Your theory makes more sense."

"Unless . . ." Callum started.

I thought I knew where he was going. "Unless Angelica's behind the theft of the brooch from the farmhouse. Maybe she wanted to add it to her collection and somehow found out it was in Twilight Cove."

"But it wasn't Angelica who broke into the farmhouse the night I was there," Callum said. "She's too short and curvy to be the intruder."

"I can't picture Angelica pulling off a burglary anyway," I said. "I think she'd be far more likely to hire someone to do the job for her."

Callum and I glanced at each other and said in unison, "Hailey Lau!"

I thought for a second. "But would she hire a private detective from Orlando to carry out a burglary in Twilight Cove?"

Callum considered my question. "Maybe she hired Hailey to find the brooch, and Hailey tracked it from Florida to Oregon."

"You could be right about that."

We drove in silence for a few minutes, both of us processing our thoughts.

"I guess I need to talk to Brody about this," I said eventually.

"Definitely," Callum agreed.

"But," I hedged, "that room in the mansion was locked. Flossie got us in there. I can't tell Brody that. And if the police want to question Angelica about the label in the display case, she'd find out that we were snooping around. She might get mad and decide she doesn't want to loan anything to the museum after all."

"She might never have to know that you were in the room," Callum said. "If the police can poke around and find information another way, they might be able to gather their own evidence."

"I hope so."

I didn't like the thought of having Angelica angry with me, but the thought of her taking that displeasure out on Twilight Cove's museum worried me far more. Still, I knew I couldn't keep the information to myself, so I texted Brody right then and there, telling him I needed to speak with him.

He responded shortly before we arrived back at the museum. He was on duty and tied up with work both at the station and out in the field, but he promised to stop by the farm the next day.

Other volunteers met us at the museum and helped unload the truck and transport everything into the Elmore house. With so many helping hands, the job didn't take long at all, but as the last piece—one of the upholstered benches—was moved to the spot Gillian had appointed for it, I sidled up next to her.

"It was so nice of Angelica to lend us all of these beautiful things," I said.

"So generous," she agreed.

"Does she have some sort of connection to the museum?" I asked. "Is that how she knew about the fundraising party?"

"No prior connection," Gillian said, nudging one of the statuettes to the center of a lacquered end table. "She said she saw a notice about the fundraiser in a newspaper. When she realized it was a 1920s-themed party, that's when she decided to reach out to offer us the theater pieces."

Gillian broke off our conversation to thank all of the volunteers, but I didn't mind. I'd already gathered the information I was after. Namely, that Angelica hadn't had a connection to Twilight Cove's museum until very recently.

So I had to wonder: was the fundraising party simply a guise for her recent trip to Twilight Cove? Had she really come to town because of the Emerald Mirage?

Thanks to the volunteers who helped us unload the truck, Callum and I arrived home in plenty of time to take care of the evening farm tasks. In the morning, we tackled the chores again, but then I had the rest of the day free. Sometimes I worked on my screenplays on the weekends, especially if I had a looming deadline or if ideas were rattling around inside my head, clamoring to get out onto the page, but I decided to enjoy a leisurely Sunday.

I texted Tessa, asking if she wanted to get together, and then I wandered away from the barn, heading in the direction of the farmhouse. I was halfway across the lawn when Flossie and Fancy bounded off ahead of me, veering to the left so they could run over to the carriage house. I changed my path too, following after them.

Auntie O was out by her vegetable garden again, pulling out some dead weeds that had shriveled up over the winter. Quackers appeared to be helping her, picking at the ground as she waddled around the garden patch. When the duck saw the spaniels coming her way, she let out an excited series of quacks and gave her wings a flap as she scurried over to greet them.

I smiled when she pecked at Flossie, gently, as if trying to preen her fur. Flossie flopped onto the grass and rolled onto her back. Quackers proceeded to climb all over her while Fancy bounced around and made happy, excited noises.

"That duck is happiest when she's with dogs," Auntie O said as she pulled off her gardening gloves.

"What are the chances of finding her a good home?" I asked as we watched Quackers play with the spaniels.

"Very good, I'd say," she replied. "We've got a potential match already."

"That was fast," I said with surprise.

"They're coming over to visit today, and they don't have far to travel." She smiled. "It's the Dubois family from down the road."

"With the four kids who were our only trick-or-treaters on Halloween?"

"That's them," Auntie O said. "Their grandmother lives on the property too, and they've got two golden retrievers."

I smiled. "Quackers will love that."

"They're bringing the dogs and the kids to see how everyone gets along."

"I hope it works out."

"I think there's a good chance that it will."

"You hear that, Quackers?" I said to the duck, who shook out her tailfeathers before climbing over Fancy. "We might find you a forever home today."

Unsurprisingly, the duck didn't pay me any attention. She was far more interested in the spaniels. Hopefully, she'd have as much fondness—if not more—for the golden retrievers from down the road.

"There's something I wanted to talk to you about," Auntie O said as she sat on one of the patio chairs behind the carriage house.

"Does it have to do with Callum and his offer to fund the sanctuary?" I asked, sitting on a loveseat across from her.

"Good guess." She smiled briefly. "I've been giving it a lot of thought, and I've decided to accept his offer, as long as my lawyer and accountant give it the green light."

"That's great!"

"You really think so?" she checked. "I don't want to complicate matters."

"You won't," I said. "Callum doesn't want to fund this place because of me. He wants to do it because of his love for animals and the work we do here. Even if things didn't work out between the two of us, I think he'd still want to help keep the sanctuary running."

This time her smile reached her eyes. "Then I'll make an appointment with my lawyer and accountant as soon as possible."

I jumped up and hugged my aunt. "I'll let you tell Callum the news."

Tires crunched on the gravel driveway, drawing our attention.

When I peeked around the corner of the carriage house, I saw Brody's truck pulling to a stop over by the main house.

I gave Auntie O another hug and then hurried across the yard to greet Brody. The dogs followed, after covering Quackers with kisses.

I invited Brody into the farmhouse and made him a cup of coffee as I explained about Angelica Bergstrom, her recent visit to Twilight Cove, and what I'd seen at her mansion in Gold Beach. I told him that I found the mini museum by accident when chasing down Flossie and Fancy, who'd gone off to explore the mansion, but I didn't mention that the door had been locked before Flossie got to it.

"Angelica doesn't know I was in there, and I'm hoping it can stay that way," I continued, "but you need to know what I saw when I was in there."

I set a mug of coffee on the table before him and handed him my phone.

"An empty display case?" he said, puzzled, as he studied the photo on the screen.

"Swipe to the next picture and zoom in."

He did so, and his expression transformed from confused to surprised. "Whoa."

"Right?" I said. "Angelica has a connection to the brooch. And if she's linked to the brooch, could she also have something to do with the murder?"

THIRTY

"Well, this complicates an already complicated investigation." Brody rubbed the back of his neck before taking a sip of coffee.

I winced as I sat down at the kitchen table. "I'm sorry. I didn't mean to make things more difficult."

Brody waved off my apology. "It's good to have the information. It's just an unexpected twist, that's all."

"I wasn't expecting it either," I said. "I never even suspected that Angelica had any connection to the crimes in Twilight Cove until I saw that empty display case in her house."

"The detective in charge of the murder investigation has been in touch with the FBI," Brody said before taking another drink.

"The FBI?" I echoed with surprise. "Because of the brooch, or for some other reason?"

"The brooch," he replied. "The FBI thought the Emerald Mirage might turn up on the black market after it was stolen from Baxter Hartmann's mansion."

"But it never did, because Nina had it. Although, maybe she would have sold it if she'd had the chance." I thought for a moment. "Do you think that's how Angelica intended to get hold of the brooch? From the black market?"

"It's a definite possibility."

I let out a frustrated breath. "I wish I'd come across this information some other way. Am I going to get pulled into the middle of things? More than I already have been, I mean."

"I'll try to keep your name out of it where Angelica's concerned, but I can't make any guarantees."

"I understand," I assured him, grateful that he would at least try. I really didn't want Angelica getting angry with me and taking out her ire on the museum.

"I'm going to talk with the FBI agents and see if Angelica's ever been on their radar before," Brody said. "If so, I might be able to nudge the investigation in her direction without bringing you into it."

I crossed my fingers, hoping that scenario would play out.

"Is there any way to find out if Angelica hired Hailey Lau?" I asked. "I have a feeling that Hailey won't be willing to share that information."

"You're most likely right about that. She'll say it's client confidentiality. But maybe they've met here in Twilight Cove and we can find security video to prove that."

"Hailey might have met Angelica at the Gilmore Hotel when Angelica was staying there."

"That's a possibility," Brody agreed. "But I know from past experience that the Gilmore won't give us access to their security footage without a warrant. They're big on protecting the privacy of their guests."

I tried to think of other options to explore. "Hailey's staying at the Sea Breeze Motel. I don't know if Angelica would have met with her there, but it's possible."

"It's definitely worth looking into," Brody agreed. "I know Kevin and DeeDee, the owners of the motel. I don't think they'll require a warrant before showing me their footage."

I was pretty sure he was right about that, since Dee had already shown me some of the motel's security footage, but I didn't want to mention that. Brody wouldn't be impressed that I'd questioned Dee.

Brody stayed long enough to finish his coffee before I walked him out of the farmhouse. As we descended the steps from the back porch, Tessa pulled into the driveway. I waved to her and the dogs ran over to greet her. I said goodbye to Brody, thanking him for coming by, and he paused to talk to Tessa on the way to his truck.

I tried to be discreet as I watched them. Tessa had a smile on her face as they spoke quietly, and Brody rested a hand on her arm briefly before climbing into his truck. Even though I tried not to be obvious about watching them, I didn't fail to notice that Tessa's gaze lingered on Brody until he'd turned his truck around and left the driveway for Larkspur Lane.

"All right," I said when Tessa joined me on the lawn. "I want all the details."

She looked at me with confusion. "Details about what?"

"You and Brody."

"Woo!" Fancy exclaimed as she and her sister sat by our feet.

I thought Tessa might deny that there was anything between her and Brody, but instead her cheeks turned pink and she said, "Is it that obvious?"

"To me it is," I said with a smile. "Something's changed between the two of you recently."

The pink in her cheeks grew brighter, but a smile bloomed on her face. She tucked an arm through mine as we climbed the porch steps.

"We kissed, Georgie!" she confided in a low voice.

I stopped dead at the top of the stairs. "What? When? That's amazing! Tessa!"

She laughed. "I was as surprised as you are. And it just happened last night. He asked if he could see me after my family gathering yesterday. We ended up going for a walk on the beach. And, Georgie . . ." She seemed ready to burst from excitement.

As for me, I was nearly in agony from the suspense. "Tessa, tell me!"

She beamed with joy. "He told me that he's in love with me."

It took me half a second to absorb that news. Then I threw my arms around Tessa and gave her a squeeze. She laughed as she hugged me back, the sound full of pure joy.

"Tessa, I'm so happy for you!" I exclaimed before releasing her.

"Thank you. I'm elated."

"What did you tell him in return?" I asked.

"That I'm in love with him too, and have been for a while."

I realized then that I had tears of happiness on my cheeks. Tessa did too. I wiped mine away as we sat down on the porch swing, and she did the same.

"This is the best news ever," I declared.

"Thank you for being so pleased for me," Tessa said, giving my hand a squeeze. "I'm so glad you moved back to Twilight Cove. I didn't realize until you came back last summer that you were the bestie I'd been missing from my life."

"Same," I said, blinking away a fresh batch of happy tears. "So, what happens now?"

Tessa shrugged, but with a smile. "We're going to spend more time together. Go on dates. Hang out. See what happens."

"And is this a secret?"

"Not anymore. I wanted you to be the first to know, but now that I've told you, we're not going to hide it."

"A-woo-oo!" Fancy cried as she put her front paws on Tessa's knee and gave her a kiss on the cheek.

Tessa laughed and hugged Fancy. "Thank you. It's amazing to have such good friends to share happy news with."

Flossie let out a bark and rested her chin on Tessa's leg, gazing up at her with adoring eyes.

Tessa stroked her glossy fur. "What updates do you have to share about all the crazy crimes that have been happening?" she asked me. "I'm guessing that's why Brody was here."

"You guessed right." I filled her in on the trip to Gold Beach and what I'd seen in Angelica's personal museum.

Tessa's jaw dropped when I showed her the photo of the label in the otherwise empty display case.

We tossed theories around about the murder and the theft of the brooch, but we didn't cover any new ground. Too many pieces of the puzzle were missing to get a real picture of what was going on. Frustration simmered at the back of my mind, but I tried to keep it there, instead focusing on my happiness for Tessa and Brody.

My best friend left the farm in the early afternoon, after visiting the sanctuary animals and having lunch with me. Shortly after her departure, I joined Auntie O out in the driveway to welcome the Dubois family from down the road. The four children, three adults, and two dogs arrived in a van and spilled out of the vehicle with big smiles on their faces.

Flossie and Fancy were overjoyed to have so many visitors, both of the human and canine variety. The Dubois children were equally as thrilled to see the spaniels. Eventually, when greetings had been exchanged and the dogs and children had calmed down, we strolled over to one of the enclosures near the barn, where Quackers was waiting to meet her prospective new family.

The children were delighted by the mere sight of the adorable white duck. Despite their excitement, they were on their best behavior when Auntie O let them into the enclosure to meet

Quackers properly. They stayed calm and let the duck approach them, which she did quite happily and readily. The golden retrievers, named Honey and Bailey, watched with interest for a minute or two before turning their attention to all the interesting smells around the outside of the enclosure.

Jason Dubois, the children's father, assured us that both golden retrievers had been around ducks in the past and had always treated them gently. Once the children were well acquainted with Quackers and the duck seemed entirely at ease, Olivia let one dog into the enclosure at a time. I held my breath, hoping all would be well and we wouldn't have to intervene to keep Quackers safe.

I soon saw that I needn't have worried. Honey and Bailey were as good with the duck as Flossie and Fancy were, and Quackers took to them immediately. She pecked at their fur and climbed all over them when they lay on the ground. Whenever the dogs got up and walked away from Quackers, she let out a series of quacks and scampered after them.

After a good long visit, Auntie O let Quackers out of the enclosure, and the dogs followed. Tired out from all the excitement, Flossie, Fancy, Honey, and Bailey stretched out on the grass for a snooze. Quackers climbed over Honey—with no reaction from the dog—and snuggled up with Bailey.

We were all tickled pink by the sight and each one of us adults snapped several photos with our phones. Callum emerged from the barn in time to witness the sweet scene, and he took a couple of pictures too. We all chatted together for a while longer, and then the Dubois family piled back into their van, with Auntie O promising to get back to them with a decision within twenty-four hours.

Really, it didn't even take twenty-four seconds of my aunt, Callum, and I discussing the matter to decide that we had indeed found the perfect home for Quackers. Auntie O picked up the duck for a cuddle and spoke to her quietly.

"You're going to love your new family," she said, stroking the duck's feathers.

"I think she already does," I said with a smile.

I gave Quackers a gentle pat on the head before Auntie O set her down on the ground to mosey around the yard with Flossie and Fancy.

I let Stardust out of the farmhouse to join them, and the four animals capered about, playing, exploring, and enjoying life. Auntie O disappeared into the carriage house to make a happy phone call to the Dubois family and I leaned against Callum as we watched our cat and dogs interact with Quackers.

"It's nice when things work out well," I said.

Callum slid an arm around my waist and rested his chin on my head. "I couldn't agree more."

"The match between Quackers and the Dubois family isn't the only thing that's worked out well." I told him about Tessa and Brody, unable to keep from smiling as I did so.

"It's about time," Callum said with a grin.

"Right?" I wrapped my arms around him. "But at least they got there. That's what matters."

He gave me a quick kiss. "Just like we got there."

"There and beyond," I said, smiling again.

"Yes," he agreed, holding me close and sounding utterly content. "There and beyond."

THIRTY-ONE

I spent the following day wrapped up in my screenwriting work. I added numerous pages to my latest thriller script, signed a shopping agreement with a producer for another project, and wrote a basic outline for a Christmas romcom I hoped to write in the upcoming weeks. While the unsolved mysteries never left my thoughts entirely, I immersed myself in my work, putting all my energy into writing instead of trying to untangle the complicated criminal cases.

It wasn't until the middle of Tuesday morning that my focus shifted back to the investigations. I'd just wrapped up a solid couple of hours of writing when I checked my phone and found a text message from Brody, asking if I could come by the station that day to view some security footage from the Sea Breeze Motel. I responded right away, and after a few more texts back and forth, we decided that I'd stop by the station in an hour.

"You know what this means?" I said to Stardust and the dogs after I'd filled them in on the text exchange. "Brody might have found evidence of a link between Angelica and Hailey."

"A-woo!" Fancy exclaimed, while Flossie danced around in a circle.

Stardust attacked Fancy's wagging tail and a wild game of chase ensued, first with the dogs pursuing Stardust, and then with the roles reversed. By the time I left the farm, my animals had calmed down and were hanging out peacefully with Auntie O.

I, however, had anticipation building inside of me. Maybe the police were about to find the person or people responsible for the recent crimes. Then I could feel at peace again and not have to worry about prowlers, burglars, or potential stalkers anymore. That would be worth celebrating.

I tried not to get ahead of myself, but when I arrived at the police station and sat waiting in an interview room, my right leg kept jiggling, a result of the restless, anticipatory energy zinging through me. When Brody joined me in the room, bringing a tablet with him, I sat forward, eager to see what he had to show me.

"This footage is from the Sea Breeze Motel two Fridays ago," he said as he tapped the screen of the tablet. He angled the device toward me and let the footage play. "Let me know if you recognize anyone."

The video provided a view of the outdoor entrances to the motel rooms on the ground floor. After a few seconds of nothing, a woman in a blue sweater and black pants approached one of the doors. Even if she hadn't had a white Pomeranian in her arms, I still would have recognized her.

"That's Angelica Bergstrom," I said, a note of excitement creeping into my voice. The woman knocked on the door, and seconds later someone opened it. "And that's Hailey Lau."

Hailey stepped back and Angelica entered the motel room. Once Hailey shut the door again, Brody stopped the footage.

"So they do know each other," I said, my excitement growing. "Why would they meet up unless Angelica was the one who hired Hailey?"

Brody shut off the tablet. "I suppose there could be another reason, but it seems unlikely."

"So, what happens next?"

"This video gives us a basis for questioning Angelica Bergstrom, but that doesn't mean she'll admit to anything."

Some of my excitement faded. "Especially if she hired Hailey to do something shady, like steal the brooch." I paused to sort through my thoughts. "Do you think Angelica could want the brooch badly enough to have someone commit murder on her behalf?"

"Some people will stop at nothing to get what they want," Brody said. "Even when most of us can't understand why they'd want whatever it is they're after."

A hint of worry invaded my thoughts. "If Angelica won't admit to anything, where does that leave the investigation?"

"We'll still have things to look into," he assured me. "Tracking Hailey's movements, for instance. Angelica's too."

I wanted to ask if he thought Hailey could be the individual caught on camera sneaking into the motel's office, but I decided against raising the question. Revealing that I'd seen that footage would likely only get me a lecture about conducting my own investigation.

"By the way, I'm really happy for you and Tessa," I said as Brody walked me out of the station.

His face broke into a grin. "Thank you. She's amazing."

"She really is," I agreed with a smile and a surge of happiness.

After saying goodbye to Brody, I jogged down the front steps and climbed into my car. When I reached Ocean Drive, the road that ran parallel to Twilight Cove's main beach, I lowered the car windows so I could breathe in the fresh coastal air. It had a frosty bite to it, but it was wonderfully crisp and revitalizing.

As I drove past an oceanfront restaurant, a bright red convertible—with its top up—caught my attention. It looked just like the car I'd seen Scarlett driving away from the Gilmore Hotel.

Before I had a chance to question my actions, I flicked on my turn signal and left the road for the restaurant's parking lot. I decided I'd take a quick look inside. If I couldn't spot Scarlett, I would turn around and leave. If I did see her there, what then?

As that question swirled around in my head, I entered the restaurant. The spacious dining room had floor-to-ceiling windows that looked out over the ocean. During warmer months, diners could eat out on the large deck, but the weather still wasn't quite right for that. The place was about half full, with a low murmur of conversation and the occasional clink of silverware reaching my ears.

Maybe my sleuthing instincts were better than I realized. Scarlett was seated at a table within easy view of the restaurant's entrance, and she wasn't alone. Her son, Lex, sat across from her.

"Are you looking for a table?" a hostess with glossy black hair asked as she approached, carrying a stack of menus.

"Um," I stalled, glancing at Scarlett and Lex. They appeared to be more than halfway through their meals. "Actually, I was thinking of ordering some takeout."

"Would you like to take a look at the menu?" The hostess offered me one.

I thanked her and sat down on a padded bench that provided me with a view of Scarlett and Lex. Unfortunately, I couldn't overhear their conversation. I placed an order for fish and chips as well as a crispy cod burger before sitting down again for what I was told would likely be a fifteen-minute wait. Five minutes into that time, mother and son got up from their table.

I woke up my phone and bent my head, pretending to be engrossed in my social media feeds.

"They'll probably make me pay for the broken window," Lex grumbled as he walked by with his mother.

"That wouldn't be right," Scarlett said. "You're not the one who broke in. I'm sure the host has damage protection."

"They'd better," her son grouched as they disappeared out the door.

I didn't have time to process that snippet of their conversation right then. I was too intent on getting a chance to hear more. A few seconds after they exited the restaurant, I followed them outside, hanging back near the door until I spotted them crossing the parking lot toward the red convertible. I tried to look casual as I skirted around the corner of the building and entered the space between a silver pickup truck and a dark blue minivan with tinted windows. I paused when I'd nearly reached the rear of the minivan, pretending to rummage through my purse, looking for something, just in case someone was watching.

The red convertible—likely a rental car—was parked nearby, and the minivan conveniently shielded me from Scarlett's and Lex's view. I'd noticed just before I darted between the two vehicles that she had her phone to her ear. As I kept up my pretense of searching through my purse, I listened carefully.

"Yes, it's been such a terrible blow, losing Nina," Scarlett said, sounding as though she was on the verge of tears. "She was my friend as well as my sister." After a brief pause, she spoke again. "Thank you. I deeply appreciate your condolences. We'll talk again when I'm back home."

She ended the phone call and the convertible beeped, likely because she'd unlocked it.

I heard two car doors open, one after the other.

"Why do you do that?" Lex asked.

"Do what?" Scarlett said in response.

"Pretend that you liked Aunt Nina, when the two of you couldn't stand each other."

I chanced a peek around the back of the minivan.

Scarlett fished a pair of sunglasses out of her designer purse and slipped them on. "Because, Lex," she said, "we don't air our dirty laundry in public."

She climbed into the car. Lex turned his head my way and I quickly ducked out of sight. I heard the car's engine roar to life as I huddled in my hiding spot. Before Scarlett could drive by and spot me lurking, I hurried back between the truck and minivan and walked briskly toward the restaurant's front door.

Inside, I sat down to wait again, my mind replaying the conversation I'd just overheard between Scarlett and her son. It wasn't the first time I'd heard Scarlett suggest that she and Nina had been close. However, thanks to Lex, I now knew that was nothing more than a charade.

Was that somehow relevant?

It certainly strengthened my suspicion that Scarlett had been eager to get hold of Nina's personal belongings because she was hoping to find the Emerald Mirage among them, but that didn't necessarily mean that she had anything to do with her sister's death. Maybe she'd known—or at least suspected—all along that Nina had stolen the brooch from their father, and was simply trying to retrieve it.

But why wouldn't she just say that to the police? Why put on such an act?

Then there was the fact that someone had broken into the Airbnb where Lex was staying. There seemed to be a lot of that going around. Nina's hotel room had been ransacked before her death, we had the intruder at the farmhouse, and now a burglar had struck at the Airbnb. Was the same person responsible for all of those incidents?

I wondered if anything had been taken from the place where Lex was staying. I considered texting Brody, to ask if Lex had reported the incident to the police, but he'd probably wonder how I'd heard about it. As much as I wanted the information, I wasn't keen to admit that I'd been following people and eavesdropping.

One of the restaurant's servers brought me my takeout order in a paper bag with delicious smells wafting from it. I quickly paid and headed for home.

"If the same person is behind all of the break-and-enter

incidents, does that mean that Lex couldn't be the burglar?" I mused out loud as Callum and I lunched on the food I'd brought back to the farm. I'd already filled him in on everything I'd overheard and learned that day.

"Unless he's trying to throw suspicion away from himself," Callum said.

"True, and we don't know if it's one burglar at work or multiple people." I tasted a delicious bite of battered fish. "I wish I could believe that the break-ins had nothing to do with the murder, but I've got a feeling everything is related."

"I'm inclined to agree," Callum said, picking up the crispy cod burger I'd purchased for him. "But tonight, let's try to forget about all that and enjoy ourselves."

The museum's fundraising party would take place that evening, and I'd been looking forward to the event for weeks.

I smiled at Callum as I reached for my drink. "Sounds like a good idea to me."

THIRTY-TWO

The party was already in full swing when Callum and I arrived at the Elmore house that evening. While the thought of attending a large, busy party caused my nerves to flutter—because of my introverted nature—having my arm tucked through Callum's helped to calm me. Once we stepped inside the Elmore house and left our outerwear at the coat check, any lingering nerves got overshadowed by my admiration of the historical house's transformation.

The last time I'd been there, I'd seen some of Angelica Bergstrom's Art Deco reproductions in place, but volunteers and museum staff had clearly been busy since then. The house had been decorated with an eye-catching and extravagant gold and black 1920s theme. Shimmery gold fabric covered the buffet and end tables, and Art Deco adornments had been added to the frames of mirrors and around doorways.

The color scheme extended to arrangements of artificial flowers and pampas grass, and to helium balloons tied up in bunches, floating near the ceiling. At least three dozen gold and black balloons created a border around an Art Deco photo backdrop that was clearly popular. Couples and groups posed in front of it, and when our turn came, Callum and I did the same.

Once the volunteer in charge of taking photos handed our phones back, we wandered deeper into the house. A small band in the largest parlor played ragtime music, and couples danced in time to the lively beat.

Callum and I bypassed the dance floor—I'd meant it when I said I wouldn't dance in public—and threaded our way through the crowd of partiers to reach the food and drink table. We skipped the bar and opted for the alcohol-free sparkling punch before tasting a couple of the scrumptious finger foods on offer.

As we sipped our drinks and worked our way deeper into the large house, I spotted Tessa and Valentina seated side by side on the black velvet chaise lounge that Angelica had loaned the museum. They each had a colorful cocktail in hand.

When Tessa saw Callum and me crossing the room, she jumped up, careful not to spill her drink. She wrapped me in a one-armed hug and I did the same to her.

"You look amazing, Georgie," Tessa said. "You too, Callum."

"And you," I added. "You finally got to wear that dress you bought last year."

"And I love it." She twirled and the light glinted off the silver threads in the flapper dress that she'd purchased at a local antiques shop.

Valentina joined us then and I complimented her dress too. She was decked out all in gold, from her high-heeled shoes to her glittery headband.

"No Brody?" I asked, searching the crowd for him.

"He's coming, but he's going to be a bit late." Tessa nudged her cousin. "Before he gets here, tell Georgie what you were just telling me."

Valentina gestured for us to follow her into a less crowded corner of the room. "We don't want this reaching the wrong ears." She glanced around and lowered her voice. "Apparently, Nina Hartmann didn't steal the brooch from her father."

"Then how did she get it?" Callum asked.

Valentina shrugged. "Good question. No one seems to know. But Nina had a solid alibi. When the burglar was breaking into her father's mansion, she was presenting at a conference in Miami. Something to do with her job in the medtech field."

"Maybe she was working with an accomplice?" I suggested.

Valentina shrugged again. "Could be."

Something across the room caught her eye and her face lit up. "There's Joey Maxwell. I'm gonna go say hi."

With a flutter of her fingers, she set off across the room like a panther on the prowl.

Tessa shook her head as she watched her cousin go. "Joey's her latest crush. I bet he doesn't know what he's in for."

We decided to get another bite to eat, so the three of us made our way through the crowd and into the spacious dining room, where the large table had been pushed up against one wall. On the way there, we passed Angelica Bergstrom, who was in conversation with Anton from the local jewelry store.

I wished I could come up with a way of subtly questioning Angelica about the empty display case at her mansion and her connection to the private investigator. My mind came up blank in that regard, so I simply smiled at her and Anton as I passed by.

I couldn't help but wonder if her previously empty display case now held the Emerald Mirage. I wanted to ask Brody if the police had spoken to Angelica about Hailey Lau and the brooch, but he'd yet to appear, and I didn't know if he'd answer my question even when he did show up.

We spent the next hour enjoying the food and drink while mingling with friends, neighbors, and other townsfolk. Aunt Olivia arrived with a couple of members of her Gins and Needles group, and Genesis and Cindy also appeared. With such good company around me, the time seemed to fly by.

While I was in the midst of chatting with Cindy and Genesis, I spotted Brody entering the Elmore house. He searched the crowd until his eyes lit upon Tessa. The change in his expression when he saw her made me smile. That was the look of a man in love.

After he'd spent a few minutes with Tessa, the two of them came over to join Callum and me with Cindy and Genesis. Brody was dressed similarly to Callum in a pinstriped waistcoat and trousers. Genesis had gone for that look too, while Cindy wore a blue flapper dress with silver beading.

"Has there been any progress with the murder investigation?" Genesis asked Brody.

I was glad someone else had raised the question. It saved me from having to do so.

"We're still chasing down leads," Brody said.

"What about the burglary at the farmhouse?" Cindy asked. "Has that person been caught?"

"Not yet." Brody cut a look my way. "But that doesn't mean that any of you should decide to play Nancy Drew."

"Would we do that?" Tessa asked with feigned innocence.

Brody tried to fix her with an unimpressed gaze, but he couldn't hold the expression. He did, however, shake his head when the rest of us laughed.

By the time we'd been at the party for a couple of hours, my feet were getting sore. I wasn't used to wearing high heels and I was looking forward to getting home and kicking them off. After downing another glass of punch, I set off in search of the restroom. When I returned, I couldn't spot Callum, Tessa, or Brody amid the crowd, which had only grown in size since we'd arrived at the party.

I noticed Anton over by the food table in the dining room, chatting with a woman I didn't recognize, but I didn't see Angelica Bergstrom anywhere. Not that it mattered. I still couldn't think of a way to subtly interrogate her. Besides, what if, after talking to the police, she knew or suspected that I'd snooped around her personal museum? She might not want to speak to me at all in that case.

I wandered through the various rooms and noticed two women coming through the back door from the spacious wrap-around porch. I decided to check outdoors for Callum and my friends. Maybe they'd decided to get some fresh air. The inside of the house was getting quite warm and stuffy with so many people packed into the rooms.

As soon as I stepped outside, I shivered. Rain poured down from the dark sky, highlighted by the glow of the porch lights, and the chilly, damp breeze cut easily through the thin fabric of my dress. A young couple in 1920s costumes smiled at me on their way back inside the house. Otherwise, the back section of the wrap-around porch was deserted. I peeked around one side of the building, and then the other, but nobody else was hanging out on the porch.

A gust of wind sent a spattering of rain flying at an angle, allowing it to sail under the overhang to spray me with icy drops. I shivered again and turned for the door, eager to get back inside where it was warm.

As I took a step, I heard a scuffling sound from somewhere nearby. I was about to look over my shoulder, but before I got the chance, something slammed into my left side, sending me flying.

THIRTY-THREE

I barely had a chance to register a jolt of fear before I hit the porch floor and toppled down the steps to the wet grass. Footsteps pounded closer and another shot of fear cut through me. The noise of the party grew louder and somebody gasped.

"Hey!" a man yelled.

As I raised myself up on my elbows, movement flickered in my peripheral vision. A shadowy figure raced across the lawn and disappeared into the shadows.

"Oh my gosh! Are you OK?" a twenty-something woman asked as she picked her way down the steps in her high heels.

She and her male companion each took hold of one of my elbows and helped me to my feet.

"What happened? Did that person hurt you?" the man asked.

I realized then that I recognized him from around town, but I didn't know his name.

"They knocked me down the stairs," I said, getting my bearings. "Thank you for helping me."

My legs were trembling, and my left elbow and both knees felt banged up, but otherwise I was fine.

"Do you want me to call the cops?" the man asked.

"That's OK, thanks," I said. "One of my friends is a police officer. I'll talk to him in a minute."

The couple had left the door open and I caught sight of Callum making his way through the crowd. When he spotted me, his face clouded with worry and he picked up his pace. Brody and Tessa trailed behind him.

"Georgie, are you OK?" he asked as he stepped out onto the porch. "I got worried when you didn't come back." He took in my somewhat bedraggled appearance. "What happened?"

"I'm all right," I said to begin with. Then, once Tessa and Brody had joined us outside, I outlined what had happened. It didn't take long. I didn't exactly have many details to share.

"When we came outside, she was on the ground at the bottom

of the stairs," the woman who'd helped me said. Then she introduced herself as Janine, and her companion as Garrett.

Garrett took up the tale next. "Someone dressed in black took off across the yard. They were gone before I realized what had happened." He shook his head. "I should have gone after whoever it was."

"No," Brody disagreed, "you did the right thing by staying here. You don't know if the person was armed or not."

I had to suppress a shudder at the thought of my assailant having a weapon. What would have happened if Janine and Garrett hadn't opened the door when they did? I didn't want to think about the possibilities.

Callum put an arm around me and I leaned against him, glad for his warmth and solidity.

"You're shivering," he said before kissing the top of my head. He addressed Brody next. "I should get her home so she can get out of these wet clothes."

"I'll get an officer to come by the farm to take your statement," Brody said as he walked with us along the porch to the front of the house.

He and Tessa waited with me while Callum fetched our coats from inside. When he returned, Callum helped me into mine, and I pulled it close around me in an attempt to ward off the chill that had settled into my bones.

"Are you sure you're OK?" Tessa asked, giving me a hug.

"Just a few bruises and a bit of a scare," I said.

She studied me with worried eyes. "This is all too much. I hate that you're being targeted."

"I was hoping we were done with all that, now that we don't have the brooch," I said.

"Maybe one or more of the players involved doesn't realize that someone stole the brooch from you?" Tessa glanced at Brody as she raised the possibility.

"Have you been questioning people?" he asked me. "Maybe someone's worried about you getting too close to the truth."

I shook my head. "I don't know who would think that. I talked to Dee at the Sea Breeze Motel the other day, but other than that I've mostly just looked at security footage and overheard a few things."

Callum put an arm around me again. "Let's get you home."

The rain was pouring down even harder now, so Brody and Tessa waited with me while Callum fetched his truck and drove it up the driveway to pick me up. This wasn't how I wanted the night to end, but I decided to try my best not to let the frightening incident overshadow all the fun memories from earlier in the evening.

During the ride home, I texted Auntie O about what had happened and assured her that I was fine and safely on my way back to the farm with Callum. She was still at the party and word of what had occurred out on the back porch would soon reach her, if it hadn't already. I wanted her to get my version of the story, not one that could possibly get exaggerated as it was passed from person to person.

While sending that text, I noticed that I had a new message waiting for me from earlier in the evening.

"Conrad Rigsby messaged me while we were at the party," I said.

"Is something wrong at the farm?" Callum asked.

Conrad lived across the road from us and rarely ever sent us text messages.

Worry fused into a solid rock in my chest as I read what our neighbor had written. "He saw someone hanging around the farmhouse just after Auntie O drove away. He'd heard about the break-in so he called the cops, but when he crossed the road to keep an eye on the prowler, whoever it was got spooked and took off."

"And then came to the party and attacked you?" Callum theorized.

I considered that possibility. "Could be. But *why* attack me? I don't have the Emerald Mirage anymore and I really don't think I've asked enough questions around town for the culprit—or culprits—to get worried."

"If someone was lurking around the farm again and coming after you, that makes me think they don't know that you don't have the brooch."

"So multiple people are trying to get their hands on it?" That was not a comforting thought.

"Seems like there's a good chance of that."

I stared out the windshield, my thoughts and emotions churning. "How can we ever feel truly safe with all this going on?"

Callum reached over and gave my knee a squeeze before returning his hand to the steering wheel. "It's got me feeling uneasy too. I don't want you to be alone on the farm until this is all figured out."

"I hate not feeling safe in our own home."

"We'll get that sense of security back," Callum said, sounding so certain that some of my hope returned. "Maybe the prowler got caught on camera."

"I should have thought of that as soon as I read Conrad's text." I opened the app on my phone, but there was nothing to see. "The cameras haven't been triggered at all this evening."

"The prowler didn't get close enough to the house, then," Callum concluded.

That was a relief, since the dogs and Stardust were at home alone.

"It might not have helped even if they had," I said. "All anybody ever sees is a figure dressed in black."

Callum turned the truck into the farm's driveway. "We'll figure this out, Georgie."

I managed a slight smile. "We? Are you going all Frank Hardy on me?"

He laughed. "I don't know about that, but I'm also not keen on sitting back and doing nothing. Not anymore. Not when you keep getting targeted. We just need to be careful about what we do next. I want you to be safe, not ending up in even more danger."

"I feel the same about you."

My spirits lifted and the last of the trembling in my limbs ebbed away when Flossie, Fancy, and Stardust greeted us with exuberant enthusiasm. They'd barely had a chance to calm down when a police cruiser pulled into the driveway. Officer Escobar, whom I'd met before, joined us in the farmhouse's kitchen to talk about what had happened at the fundraising party.

As I recounted the incident to Escobar, Callum made hot drinks for all of us. He set a mug of coffee in front of Escobar and a cup of peppermint tea in front of me. When I breathed in the fragrant steam rising from my cup, the aroma triggered a sudden memory.

"Perfume!" I exclaimed.

Officer Escobar looked up from his notebook, and Callum paused on his way past my chair with his own cup of tea in hand.

"Perfume?" Callum echoed.

"I smelled perfume on the person who attacked me at the Elmore house," I explained, excited by the recollection. "It was faint, but kind of flowery."

Escobar made a note of that.

Callum took the seat next to me. "So it was a woman?"

"It definitely smelled like a woman's perfume, not a man's cologne," I said.

I didn't have any other details to add, and Officer Escobar soon left the farm. He promised to make a report about the incident, but my excitement about my memory faded quickly after his departure.

"Short of going around town and sniffing all of our suspects, I'm not sure the perfume clue is going to help us much," I said with a growing sense of frustration.

"Let's think about who our female suspects are," Callum suggested.

I tried to pull myself together. He was right. The clue did potentially narrow down our list of suspects. I was tired, and my fatigue was fogging my brain, but I tried to think carefully.

"Angelica Bergstrom is one," I said, "but she was inside the Elmore house earlier, wearing an apricot dress. She would have had to change into an all-black outfit and then just hope that I wandered outside at some point."

"So it probably wasn't her." Callum took a drink of tea as we continued to think.

"There's Hailey Lau and Scarlett Nicholson," I said.

He nodded. "My money's on Hailey. She must not know that someone already took the brooch from the house. She probably came here in the hope of breaking in to look for it. When she got scared off by Conrad, she decided to go after you directly."

"Hoping that I would tell her where to find the brooch?"

"Probably."

I posed another question. "How did she know I was at the Elmore house?"

"Maybe she's been following you. Or maybe she just knew that half the town would be there tonight."

I rubbed my forehead, my thoughts getting jumbled as exhaustion crept deeper into my mind and body.

Flossie whined and rested her chin on my knee.

I stroked the glossy fur on her head. "Don't worry, girl. Everything will be OK."

"Yes," Callum said, taking my hand and pulling me to my feet. "It will. And for now, let's try to get some sleep."

"Sleep sounds good," I agreed as I slid one arm around his waist and rested my other hand on his chest. "But first, I could use a distraction."

I gave him a lingering kiss that brought a smile to his face.

He trailed a line of kisses up my neck to my ear, and then whispered, "I'm always happy to oblige."

THIRTY-FOUR

Usually, when I was at home working on my writing, I left the back door of the house unlocked. However, the incident at the fundraising party had left both Callum and me on edge. When he asked me the next morning to keep the house locked whenever I was there alone, I agreed. I hated not feeling completely safe in the place that had become my sanctuary, but I didn't want to take any foolish chances until whoever was responsible for all the recent crimes was safely locked away, whether that was one individual or multiple people.

I also didn't want to take any foolish chances while conducting my own, unofficial investigation into the crimes, but that didn't mean I couldn't do anything at all. Like Callum, I couldn't bear the thought of simply waiting for the police to figure things out. They were more than competent, but they also had their hands full with multiple cases and they didn't have savvy, magical animal detectives to help them along.

Before I could turn my mind to solving crimes, I had to put in a few solid hours of work while Callum tended to the sanctuary animals out in the barn and pastures. Then, after school let out for the day, the Dubois family came over to collect the newest member of their clan. I nearly shed a tear as I gave Quackers a final cuddle, and Auntie O definitely did, but we were both happy for the sweet duck.

Honey and Bailey, the two golden retrievers, came along with their humans to take Quackers home. I was happy to see that the dogs and duck got along just as swimmingly as they had during their first meeting. One of the kids told me that Honey and Bailey had a kiddie pool that they would gladly share with Quackers. They also had a pond on their property, where the duck would have lots of room to swim. The children's parents promised to send Auntie O videos and updates. They also told us we were more than welcome to come by their farm to visit and see how Quackers was getting on.

I stroked the duck's white feathers one last time and then Flossie and Fancy each gave her a sniff and a kiss before Mr. Dubois coaxed Quackers into the dog crate the family had brought to transport her down the road. When the family drove off a short while later, I stood in the driveway with an arm around Auntie O's shoulders.

"It's a happy ending to one chapter of Quackers' life and the start of a wonderful new one," I said, giving her a squeeze.

She rested her head on my shoulder for a moment. "You're absolutely right, Georgie. This is why I do this job; to help animals get the lives they deserve."

"It's still hard to say goodbye, though."

She wiped away one last tear. "Difficult and rewarding all at the same time."

As we wandered toward the carriage house, my aunt shifted the subject of our conversation to our recent troubles. Although I'd texted her about what had happened to me on the museum's back porch the night before, and about the news Conrad Rigsby had sent me, we hadn't yet had a chance to discuss the events face-to-face.

Auntie O was dismayed and even a little angry that these incidents kept happening. I assured her that Callum and I were taking extra care to stay safe and I urged her to do the same. She promised me that she would.

Auntie O had plans to meet friends for dinner, and Callum was at the high school to coach the softball team, so I planned to join him there. Darkness would fall before he got home, and I wasn't eager to stay alone at the farm after daylight had faded. He didn't want me doing that either.

I double-checked that every window and door was locked up tight and that the cameras were working. I even took Stardust over to the carriage house, since the main house seemed to be the target of every prowler and burglar so far, and I didn't want her there alone if someone broke in again.

With all those precautions taken, the dogs and I drove into town. I sat on the bleachers to watch the softball practice while the dogs lay in the grass, none of us much caring when it started spitting rain. I preferred to get rained on than to stay at home without Callum, jumping at every creak of the old house.

Part-way through the practice, Tessa emerged from the school building and joined me on the bleachers after greeting Flossie and Fancy.

"I just got an interesting text message from Valentina," she said as she sat next to me.

"To do with the murder? The burglary?"

"The murder. She overheard a couple of detectives talking about Lex Nicholson. Apparently, he's got an alibi."

I absorbed that news. "Did Valentina share any details about his alibi?"

"He was video chatting with his bandmates during the entire window of opportunity."

"The police confirmed that?"

Tessa nodded. "All three of his bandmates corroborated the story."

I turned that information over in my mind. "OK, so Lex didn't have a chance to kill Nina. And he probably doesn't wear women's perfume, like the person who attacked me last night."

"So that's one name we can cross off our suspect list," Tessa said. "That's some progress."

"I suppose he could still be the burglar, but since his Airbnb was broken into, maybe not." Mentally, I struck a line through Lex's name, relieved that our pool of suspects was at least a little smaller.

Tessa left for home soon after that, without us making any further progress with our theories. When the practice ended, I helped Callum load the equipment into his truck. We decided to swing by the pizza parlor to pick up some dinner on the way home, since we both had growling stomachs. I left the parking lot first, with the dogs in the back seat of my car, and Callum followed behind us.

The drive to the pizza parlor took us past the Sea Breeze Motel. Despite the fact that dusk had fallen, the security lights in the motel's parking lot provided enough illumination for me to recognize someone emerging from one of the ground-floor rooms.

I made a split-second decision, flicking on my turn signal and pulling in to the lot. Fortunately, Callum reacted quickly enough to follow me onto the motel's property. I parked in the nearest free space and jumped out of the car, the dogs clambering out after me.

"What's going on?" Callum asked as he climbed out of his truck, which he'd parked next to my car.

"It looks like Hailey's leaving town," I replied in a low voice. "Can you call Brody and ask if the police have had a chance to talk with her?"

"Be careful, Georgie," he cautioned as he pulled out his phone.

I forced myself not to run, since I didn't want Hailey to feel like I was ambushing her, but a sense of urgency crackled through me like electricity because she was moving luggage from her motel room to her car.

With effort, I managed to walk casually across the lot. Hailey had a large tote bag over her shoulder and was lifting a rolling suitcase into the back of her vehicle. She glanced my way and I raised a hand in greeting, acting as if I was just casually strolling along. Flossie and Fancy, however, didn't take their cue from me. They bounded off ahead, racing up to Hailey and dancing around her as if she were their long-lost best friend.

I picked up my pace. "Sorry about that," I apologized as I reached Hailey. "Flossie, Fancy, settle down."

"That's all right," Hailey assured me, giving each spaniel a pat on the head. "I like dogs."

"Sit," I said to Flossie and Fancy.

They obeyed, but kept their gazes fixed on Hailey.

"You were just in town for a visit?" I asked, pretending that I didn't know why she'd come to Twilight Cove.

"And on my way home now." She offered me a half smile. "Georgie, right?"

"That's right." I glanced over my shoulder in time to see Callum end his phone call. I gestured for him to join us, hoping to buy some time in case the police wanted to intercept Hailey before she skipped town. "I'll introduce you to Callum McQuade."

She smiled, but I could tell the expression was forced. I didn't know if she was worried about something or just annoyed that we were delaying her departure.

Callum rested a hand on the small of my back when he reached us.

"Hailey, this is Callum McQuade. Cal, this is Hailey . . ." I smiled at her. "Sorry, I never caught your last name."

"Chang," she lied after a split second's hesitation, her smile growing even more brittle.

"Good to meet you," Callum said, not giving any hint that he knew she'd given us a false name.

"And who are these beauties?" Hailey asked, turning her attention to the dogs. Her expression became much more relaxed and natural.

I glanced down at the spaniels. I recognized the focused look in Flossie's eyes a mere second before the straps of Hailey's tote bag suddenly slipped off her shoulder. The bag crashed to the ground, spilling its contents onto the pavement.

Hailey dropped to a crouch, scrambling to gather up her belongings.

"Let me help you with that," I said, crouching down too.

"That's all right!" she said with a frantic edge to her voice.

I froze for the briefest of moments before standing up and taking a step back.

There, among the jumble of makeup and other small personal items, sat the gleaming brooch known as the Emerald Mirage.

THIRTY-FIVE

Hailey grabbed for the emerald-and-diamond brooch, but Fancy snatched it up first and danced out of her reach.

"Hey!" the private eye exclaimed, anger burning in her eyes. She made a swipe at the piece of jewelry, but Fancy bounded off behind the nearest vehicle.

I heard the approach of a car, but I didn't pay any attention to whoever might have arrived until Brody said, "What's going on here?"

When Hailey saw Brody in his police uniform, her face blanched. Then her expression turned to stone.

"Nothing," she said in a flat voice. "That dog just stole something of mine." She turned her eyes on me. "If you get it back for me, I'll be on my way."

"Fancy, come here," I called, my voice calm despite the racing of my heart.

She trotted into view and moseyed right up to me.

Hailey made another move to grab the brooch from Fancy's mouth, but I stopped her with a hand to her wrist.

"Let go of me!" she seethed, shaking off my grip.

"Fancy, show Brody what you've got," I said to my dog.

Obligingly, Fancy dropped the brooch right by the toes of Brody's boots.

The emerald and diamonds glinted in the light from the nearest security lamp.

Hailey took a step back. "It's not what you think."

Brody held up a hand. "Stay right where you are, Ms. Lau."

He produced a plastic evidence bag and turned it inside out so he could pick up the brooch without getting any fingerprints on it.

"Detectives from the state police have been trying to reach you," Brody said to Hailey.

Her lips formed a firm line. "I've got nothing to say to them, or you. I'll only speak to a lawyer."

"That will be arranged," Brody assured her. He unhooked a set of handcuffs from his belt. "Hailey Lau, you're under arrest for possession of stolen property."

She didn't resist, and Brody soon had her seated in the back of his cruiser.

"I'll need you both to come by the station," he said to Callum and me once he shut the door on Hailey.

Callum rested an arm across my shoulders. "We'll be right behind you."

We watched Brody drive off, and then climbed into our own vehicles for the short trip to the station.

Brody wasn't thrilled that I'd stopped to talk to Hailey instead of simply alerting him to her departure and staying well away from the motel. I had to admit that would have been the wiser choice. Nevertheless, I didn't regret what I'd done because of the resulting revelation, not that I mentioned that bit to Brody.

When we left the station a while later, I crouched down in front of my dogs and hugged them. "Good girls. You're both so clever."

They wagged their tails, looking pleased with themselves.

"Fancy grabbed the brooch away from Hailey, but what did Flossie do?" Callum asked.

Flossie barked, sounding a little indignant.

"I'm pretty sure she caused Hailey's bag to fall," I replied.

She barked again, sounding like she was confirming my statement.

Callum met her gaze straight on. "How did you know Hailey had something important in her bag?"

Flossie wagged her tail and sat down at his feet, looking up at him with an enigmatic expression.

One corner of Callum's mouth turned up in a grin. "Not sharing that secret, huh?"

Her tongue lolled out of her mouth and I could have sworn she was grinning.

Callum shook his head. "You certainly are special dogs."

"A-woo," Fancy said as she and her sister wagged their tails.

"Probably hungry dogs too," I added.

That was met with excited barks and yips.

Callum laughed. "Then let's go get that pizza."

* * *

The sun shone so brightly the next day that I shed my jacket while taking care of the sanctuary's animals after breakfast. Signs of spring were popping up all over the farm. Trees sprouted new leaves, bright yellow daffodils dotted the flowerbeds, and the first tulips showed just a hint of color.

The weather was too lovely to work inside when not absolutely necessary, so I carried the tools I needed out of the barn so I could groom the donkeys in their pasture. I took care of Tootsie and Twiggy, and had just started in on brushing Hamish's coat when a truck drove onto the farm.

I raised a hand in greeting when I recognized Brody climbing out of the driver's seat. I brushed my hands on my jeans, ready to go meet him, but he started across the yard and called out, "I'll come to you!"

I returned to brushing out Hamish's coat. With his long strides, it didn't take long for Brody to reach the pasture.

"Day off?" I asked when he approached the fence.

He'd arrived in his personal vehicle and he wore jeans and a T-shirt rather than his police uniform.

"And planning to make the most of it." He leaned his forearms against the top rail of the fence. "I already went for a run on the beach, and I'm going to spend some time in my studio before having lunch at the diner."

Brody was a talented woodcarver and painter. He sometimes sold his Native American art at the local farmer's market, and I had one of his carvings—a beautiful orca—on the mantel in the living room.

"I'm hoping I can convince Callum to come shoot some pool with me on the weekend," he added.

I smiled as I saw my boyfriend coming out of the barn and walking over our way. "Looks like you'll get a chance to ask him."

After Callum greeted Brody, he climbed the fence and hopped down into the pasture to clean out Hamish's hooves.

"How are you feeling today, Georgie?" Brody asked as he watched us work.

"I'm fine, thanks," I replied. "I've got a few bruises, but nothing worse than that."

"I'm glad to hear it, but I'm sorry that happened to you."

I gave him a smile of thanks as I continued brushing Hamish's coat. "I'm hoping you don't have any bad news to share."

"Well, it's not the best news," Brody admitted. "I thought you'd want to know that we didn't find your missing jewelry among Hailey's possessions. The only stolen property was the Emerald Mirage."

I paused in my grooming and ran a hand down Hamish's neck. "Do you think she already pawned my jewelry?"

"I'm not sure. She swears she never broke into the farmhouse. Says she's never set foot on this property."

"Then how did she get the brooch?" Callum asked.

"She wouldn't say, and I feel like we're still missing a lot of pieces of the puzzle."

I got back to brushing Hamish. "Has Hailey been arrested for Nina's murder?"

"Not yet. She swears she had nothing to do with that either."

Callum finished cleaning out one hoof and moved on to another. "Did she admit to anything at all?"

"Not at first," Brody replied. "She was pretty tight-lipped last night, but I dropped by the station on my way here and got the latest news. Angelica Bergstrom came in to speak with the lead detective. She admitted that she hired Hailey to find the Emerald Mirage."

"And steal it for her?" I guessed.

"Pretty much, although she phrased it differently. I think the word she used was 'reclaim.' She insists that the brooch is rightfully hers and Hailey was simply getting it back for her."

I brushed at a particularly stubborn clump of dirt that had dried on Hamish's coat. "How could it be hers when it was stolen from Baxter Hartmann?"

"Angelica Bergstrom's father apparently owned the brooch up until about ten years ago," Brody explained. "It was passed down from his mother, who received it as a gift from some European princess she nursed through a near-fatal illness. According to Angelica, her father lost the Emerald Mirage in a bet with Baxter Hartmann, a bet that she claims was underhanded."

"So she thinks her father was basically scammed out of the brooch?"

"That seems to be her opinion."

"Sounds like a flimsy story, legally speaking," Callum said. "Will it let Hailey off the hook?"

Brody shook his head. "The charges haven't been dropped. Where things go from here will be up to the lawyers and the judge. Angelica has already hired a lawyer to represent Hailey."

I paused in my work so I could look directly at Brody. "Do you think Hailey's lying about not breaking into the farmhouse?"

"It's hard to say when there are still so many unanswered questions," he replied, "but the brooch was taken from your house and found in her possession. There's a good chance she's the burglar."

"And the murderer?" Callum asked.

Brody shrugged. "We're still chasing a lot of leads in that case."

I was used to his non-answers, but they still managed to disappoint me almost every time. Although, I couldn't be too upset on this occasion because he'd already willingly shared more than I'd expected.

"We've got officers checking with all the pawnshops in nearby towns," he continued. "There's still a chance that we could find your jewelry, Georgie."

"A slim chance?" I guessed.

He acknowledged that with a tip of his head to the side.

"A slim chance is better than none," I said with a sigh.

I tried not to think about never getting my mom's heirlooms back. I didn't want my spirits taking a dive. From the concerned way that Callum was watching me, I figured he was worried that might be happening. I sent him a quick smile to let him know that I was OK.

Brody's expression, meanwhile, grew more serious. "That's not all I wanted to talk to you about."

Apprehension tensed my shoulders. "Now you've got me worried."

"No need to worry if you don't try investigating on your own."

"Hey, I'm just grooming a donkey here," I said with a smile.

That got a skeptical twitch of one eyebrow, but he let it slide. "I ran a background check on Nash Skidmore."

"What did you find out?" Callum asked.

"He's a criminal," Brody replied, his response blunt. "So I'd advise you to steer clear of him." His gaze was on me when he said that.

Unease threaded its way through my body. "What kind of criminal are we talking about?"

"DUI, assault, uttering threats," he said. "He's done some jail time. Most of the charges on his rap sheet arose from a couple of barroom brawls."

Curiosity overrode my unease. "Why would Scarlett be associated with a guy like that? He's closer in age to her son than her, and it sounds like they come from completely different walks of life. Yet he phoned her the other day."

"I asked Mrs. Nicholson if she knew anyone by the name of Skidmore," Brody said. "The question definitely took her by surprise, but she answered readily enough. It turns out that the N. Skidmore she knows is Nathaniel Skidmore."

"Any relation to Nash?" Callum asked the question before I got it off my tongue.

"He's Nash's father. He, meaning Nathaniel, works for the company that insured the Emerald Mirage for Baxter Hartmann."

I took a moment to absorb that information. "So what's Nash doing here in Twilight Cove?"

"I don't have an answer to that question, and I don't want you going looking for one," Brody said. "He's a dangerous guy, known to carry a knife and prone to fits of temper."

"But aren't you curious about what he's doing here?" I pressed.

"Sure, and my colleagues and I are going to look into that. Because it's our job."

I voiced what he'd left unsaid. "And not mine."

"Exactly." He smiled to soften his words. "I just want you to stay safe, Georgie."

"I want the same," Callum said.

"So do I." When I saw a hint of skepticism on Brody's face, I added, "I'll do my best to stay away from Nash Skidmore."

"Glad to hear it," he said.

After he and Callum made plans to play pool on the weekend, Brody returned to his truck and drove off.

"Why do I feel like the sleuthing gears are turning in your head?" Callum asked, watching me once we were alone with the donkeys.

"Because you know me so well?" I smiled. "Don't worry. I'll keep my word to Brody."

"But?" Callum prodded.

He really did know me well.

"But," I continued, "that doesn't mean I can't have a look around online."

THIRTY-SIX

As soon as I'd finished looking after the sanctuary's animals, I returned to the farmhouse and grabbed my laptop. Stardust frolicked on the lawn, pouncing on bugs—real or imaginary—and generally being silly, while Flossie and Fancy watched over her. I settled in one of the comfy wicker chairs on the back porch and accessed the internet.

It didn't take long for disappointment to sink in. Nash Skidmore had multiple social media accounts, but they didn't reveal a whole lot about him. He seemed to spend a lot of time hanging out at bars and clubs, he occasionally attended baseball and football games, and four-letter words dominated his vocabulary. None of that gave me any insight as to why he'd come to Twilight Cove. He'd posted online only once since his arrival, and that post consisted of a photo of the meal he'd bought from one of the food trucks parked by the town's main beach.

I sought out information on his father, Nathaniel, next. Unlike his son, Nathaniel didn't have a social media presence that I could find. His name appeared on the website for his employer, a large insurance company, but I couldn't find any other details about him.

Setting my laptop aside, I sipped at a glass of ice water and watched as Stardust climbed over Flossie and Fancy while they rolled about in the grass. When I had been spying on Scarlett in the lobby of the Gilmore Hotel, Nathaniel Skidmore's unanswered phone call had likely had to do with the theft of the Emerald Mirage from Scarlett's father. Why she'd declined the phone call, I didn't know, but maybe she simply hadn't wanted to be delayed. After all, she'd sped off in her rental car soon after.

What interested me far more than that phone call was the reason for Nathaniel's son's presence in Twilight Cove. I didn't believe for a second that it was coincidental. Nash easily could have known about the theft of the brooch from the Hartmann mansion in Tampa. The news of the burglary was online, and there was a chance he could have heard about it straight from his father. Or from Lex. Nash had commented on a social media post from Lex's band, so there was clearly a connection there, to some degree. Could Nash somehow have found out that the Emerald Mirage was in Twilight Cove?

But how? Through his father? But how would Nathaniel have known that?

Maybe he was more likely to have come by that information from Lex.

Fighting back a wave of frustration, I drained the last of my water and picked up my laptop again. This time, I tried to find out everything I could about Nina Hartmann and Scarlett Nicholson. The deep dive into Nina's online presence resulted in zero clues. It was evident from her social media posts that she'd loved animals, and she'd volunteered at a dog and cat shelter in Tampa Bay. That resonated with me and made me feel even more saddened about her senseless death. The world needed more animal lovers. She also had a penchant for crocheting and country music, but none of that helped me with my unofficial investigation.

I focused on Scarlett next. From her social media posts, I gleaned that she enjoyed an expensive lifestyle, with frequent spa visits, and lots of time spent at a country club. She was also well educated, with an MBA from the University of Florida. I had to dig beyond social media to discover that her husband, Royce, was an engineer and that they'd started their own company together several years ago. The company was involved in the manufacture of certain components for the aerospace industry.

When I read that tidbit, dots connected in my head. Valentina had shared that the wire used to strangle Nina had left behind traces of nickel. What was it Callum had said about nickel wire? It was used in electrical components for aircraft.

My pulse ticked up as I considered the possible implications of that information. Scarlett might have access to nickel wire through her company, and she'd seemed eager to get her sister's personal effects. Perhaps Scarlett had arrived in Twilight Cove earlier than she'd admitted—spending a night or two in Britton Bay—so she could get her hands on the Emerald Mirage. She could have searched Nina's motel room and failed to find the brooch. Then, she either confronted her sister or took her by surprise, killing her with a piece of nickel wire.

But why would Scarlett carry nickel wire around with her? That seemed an unlikely thing for her to do, unless the murder of her sister was premeditated.

The thought of her killing her own family member sent a chill down my spine, but soon another question popped into my head.

Why would Scarlett kill Nina before she had the Emerald Mirage in her possession?

A possible answer to that question bubbled to the surface of my mind.

Maybe she'd somehow forced Nina to tell her what she'd done with the brooch. Then, once Scarlett had that information, she killed Nina, and later broke into the farmhouse to find the Emerald Mirage, taking some of my jewelry to make it look like a random burglary.

Scarlett had posted several pictures of herself playing tennis at her local country club. She was certainly athletic enough to run from the farmhouse at the speed the prowler had fled at, but did she have the right build to be the intruder?

I really wasn't sure. Everything had happened so fast, and I'd only ever caught a fleeting glimpse of the burglar. The footage from our new security cameras hadn't revealed any helpful details either. Besides, there was always the chance that Scarlett wasn't working alone.

Of course, I didn't have any evidence that she had an accomplice, and I didn't exactly have any solid links between Scarlett and the crimes. Still, the information I'd uncovered felt too important to dismiss.

I grabbed my phone, about to text Brody with what I'd learned, but I stopped myself. I'd heard about the traces of nickel left behind on Nina's neck from Valentina, and she could get in serious trouble if the police found out she'd leaked that information. She might even lose her job.

I didn't know how I could tell Brody about the potential connection between Scarlett and nickel wire without revealing that I knew about the evidence found on Nina's body. I didn't like holding information back from the police, but I reassured myself slightly when I realized that the cops likely already had the information I'd found. They'd probably looked into Nina's family members and would have drawn the connection between the nickel wire and Scarlett and Royce's involvement in the aerospace industry. Or so I hoped, anyway.

My mind was spinning and my eyes hurt from staring at the screen of my laptop for so long. A dull headache was threatening to grow in intensity, so I jogged up to my bedroom to grab the smooth purple stone I'd left on my bedside table. It was the crystal that Dorothy had given me to help with my headaches.

As I ran my thumb over the smooth surface of the amethyst, I made my way back downstairs. I found Flossie, Fancy, and Stardust lounging on the porch, tired but content after their play session. I refilled their outdoor water dish and then sent a text message to Tessa, asking if she could arrange another meeting with Valentina. Maybe I could find out if the police had taken a serious look at Scarlett as a suspect and, if so, what conclusions they'd drawn about her potential guilt. If Valentina reported that the police had already investigated Scarlett and dismissed her as a suspect, then I could turn my attention to other potential culprits.

Even though my headache was quickly fading, I couldn't bear to stare at a screen any longer, so instead of writing, I helped Callum repair a section of fencing in the goats' pasture. Then the two of us took the dogs for a long walk through the woods and down to the beach. By the time we returned to the farmhouse for a late lunch, I had a text message from Tessa. Valentina wanted to attend jam night at the Sea Glass Tavern that evening, but she was happy to have us join her there.

Callum and I would have liked that idea even if I hadn't hoped to get investigation-related information from Valentina, so I texted Tessa back to say we'd meet her and her cousin at the local pub. Callum and I arrived before our arranged meeting time so we'd have a better chance of snagging a table at the popular eatery. On our way toward one of the few remaining empty booths, I smiled at some familiar people, including Anton, from the jewelry shop, and Fae, the owner of the Treasure Trove. They sat at separate tables, each with several companions around them.

When Tessa and Valentina arrived a short while later, we ordered food and drinks, opting to start with a platter of nachos to share between us. Once our server had left us with our drinks, Valentina leaned over the table and whispered, “Tessa tells me you’ve got the victim’s sister pegged as a suspect.”

“As one of several possibilities,” I said. “Do you have any information on her that you can share?”

She lowered her voice even further. “This is for your ears only.” She glanced around to ensure that no one was listening in. Then, satisfied, she smiled like the cat who got the cream. “I’ve got a juicy tidbit for you.”

THIRTY-SEVEN

"Don't leave them in suspense," Tessa scolded, giving Valentina a sharp nudge with her elbow when she didn't immediately share what she knew.

Her cousin shot her a sidelong glare. "I'm getting to it!" She waited another two beats, getting an eye-roll out of Tessa. "Scarlett Nicholson and her husband own a company."

"Georgie and Callum already know that," Tessa said.

I'd filled Tessa in on my research via text messages, but I wasn't sure it was wise of her to mention that Valentina's revelation wasn't actually news to us.

Sure enough, Tessa earned another glare from her cousin.

"But do they know that the company is in serious financial trouble?" Valentina asked with an edge to her voice.

"Definitely not," I said quickly, hoping to defuse the tension between the cousins.

Valentina smiled and her aggravation vanished. "Apparently, they made some terrible business and investment decisions. They lost millions of dollars. Their company's probably going bust."

A buzz of excitement hummed through my bloodstream as I considered that news. "That's very interesting."

"Are you thinking that Scarlett and Royce are behind the theft of the brooch from Baxter Hartmann?" Callum asked.

"I think it's a solid possibility," I replied. "They must have known it was insured. Maybe they figured they could steal it, sell it on the black market, and at least lessen their financial difficulties. Meanwhile, Scarlett and Nina's father would receive the insurance payout and wouldn't be any worse off, financially speaking."

"I don't know the exact value of the Emerald Mirage," Valentina said, "but I heard one of the detectives say that the fact that it was once owned by a princess makes it way more valuable than it would be without that history."

"So it really could help the Nicholsons with their financial troubles," I concluded.

We paused our conversation when our server brought the platter of nachos to our table. We all dug in right away, resuming our hushed chat once we were alone again.

"But then how did Nina end up with the brooch?" Tessa asked as she scooped up guacamole with a cheese-covered nacho. "Could she have been in on the plan with Scarlett and Royce?"

"Possibly." I mulled over the idea as I enjoyed a delicious nacho topped with cheese, black olives, salsa, and guacamole. "Maybe all three were in on the plan together, but then someone else found out that Nina had the brooch and came after her. Or, Nina wasn't in on the plan, but got wind of it, and tried to steal the brooch back from her sister."

"Only to get followed and murdered by Scarlett," Tessa added.

"You should have been cops," Valentina said before munching on a nacho.

"Dealing with crooks and felons all day?" Tessa grimaced. "No, thank you."

"Is that any different than dealing with teenagers all day?" her cousin asked.

Tessa shrugged. "Some days, not so much."

We all smiled at that before getting back on topic.

"There's another possibility too," I said. "Maybe Nina was in on the plan with her sister, but then double-crossed her and tried to take off with the brooch so she could sell it and keep all the money for herself."

"That's a lot of possibilities." Tessa took a long drink of her soda.

I sighed, and added guacamole to another nacho. "Too many."

"Is there any way we can rule one or more of them out?" Callum asked.

I considered his question. "I'm not sure, but maybe we could find out if Scarlett has an alibi for the time of the murder."

"Her alibi is that she wasn't in town," Valentina said.

"But do the police know that she stayed in Britton Bay for at least one night before she came to Twilight Cove?" I spoke again before she had a chance to respond. "I wish I knew how many nights she spent there. If it was just one, it could have been a stopover on her way here."

Callum picked up my line of thinking. "But if she was there for multiple nights, she probably lied about when she arrived in the area."

"Exactly," I said.

"The police would have checked her flight itinerary," Valentina said.

My shoulders sagged. Of course they would have done that.

Another thought occurred to me. "But I don't know when she stayed in Britton Bay. Could she have come to Oregon, killed Nina, flown back to Florida, and then flown out this way again once the police informed her of her sister's death? If she did that, the police might only know about her most recent flight."

"That would be devious of her," Tessa remarked.

"*Someone* has been devious," I pointed out.

"I'm not sure if this is helpful," Valentina said, "but I overheard one of the detectives calling the Gilmore Hotel and asking to be put through to Scarlett Nicholson's room."

I perked up at that. "Did the detective mention her room number?"

Valentina smiled. "Yep. Room 302."

I filed that information away in case it came in handy at some point.

We left the conversation there for the time being, as our server had returned with our main courses. Shortly after that, the live music portion of the evening got underway. Mick, the owner of the Sea Glass Tavern, and his nephew, Hayden, got up on stage with their guitars. They played a couple of songs together, and then invited other musicians to join them on stage.

I took a sip of ginger ale and nearly spat it out when I recognized the young man climbing the two steps to the stage, an acoustic guitar in hand.

"That's Nash Skidmore," I whispered to my companions.

"The guy Brody warned you about?" Callum asked, narrowing his eyes at the shaggy-haired young man.

"What's the deal with him?" Valentina asked. "I haven't heard his name around the station."

I quickly explained how I'd seen Scarlett decline a phone call from someone with the last name "Skidmore" and "N" as their first initial. Then I told them that Brody had informed me that the call had come from Nathaniel Skidmore, Nash's father, who worked for the insurance company that had insured the Emerald Mirage.

"The plot thickens," Tessa said, watching the musicians on stage.

Nash seemed to stumble over a few notes and faltered entirely at times, but the others carried the song along and he joined in again here and there. He clearly didn't have the same level of skill as the other musicians up there, not that it really mattered.

He stayed on stage for another song before bowing out and placing his guitar in its case. He snagged the only free stool at the bar and ordered a beer. I watched him for a minute, noting that he appeared to be on his own.

Anton from the jewelry shop and a man I didn't recognize joined Mick and Hayden on stage next. It wasn't easy to hold a conversation with music playing, so we focused on enjoying our food and the entertainment.

After polishing off our meals, Valentina raised the suggestion of dessert. I was full, but still craving a little something sweet, and Tessa and her cousin raved about the pub's heavenly tiramisu. We ended up ordering two servings of the dessert. Tessa and Valentina shared one, while Callum and I ate the other. I didn't think I'd be able to manage more than a bite or two, but the tiramisu was so delicious that I downed a third of it before leaving the rest for Callum.

"This was a fun evening," Tessa said, once we'd all finished eating.

By then, the music had ended, but the murmur of multiple conversations still surrounded us.

"It really was," I agreed. "Thanks for suggesting we meet here, Valentina. And thanks for sharing your intel with us."

"Intel? What intel?" she asked, feigning innocence.

"Right," I said with a smile. "My mistake."

Valentina tapped the side of her nose and winked as she shimmied her way off the booth's bench seat.

I gave Tessa a hug, and she and her cousin left through the pub's front door.

Callum and I had parked in the small lot out back, so we headed down the hallway to the rear exit.

"That food was amazing," Callum said as he held the door open for me. "But I wouldn't mind taking the dogs for a walk before bed."

"Me too." I pressed a hand to my stomach. "I don't think I can fall asleep until I'm not quite so full."

As the door drifted shut behind us, Callum hit the key fob to unlock the truck.

A dark shape swooped through the air, startling me.

I realized a split second later that Euclid had landed on the nearest utility pole. I could make out only the shadowy outline of a great horned owl, but I knew without seeing any details that it was my friend.

He let out a "hoo-hoo" that caught Callum's attention.

"Is that Euclid?" he asked, looking up at the owl.

"Yes," I replied, already moving toward the utility pole. "And I think he's trying to tell us something."

Euclid remained on his perch when I reached the base of the pole.

"What do you want me to see?" I asked him, glad that Callum and I were the only two people in the parking lot.

Of course I received no response, but I knew I should look around. I switched on the flashlight app on my phone and shone the light at the ground. As I moved the beam of light around, it illuminated a small object lying on the pavement. I picked it up and saw that it was made of yellow plastic, in the shape of a triangle with a rounded top.

I ran my thumb over the smooth surface as Callum came over to take a look.

"That's a guitar pick," he said as soon as he laid eyes on the object.

I flipped it over on the palm of my hand.

My breath caught in my throat.

"What's wrong?" Callum asked, noticing my reaction.

I stared at the name FENDER, written on the guitar pick in black lettering.

I'd seen that same style of F before, on a different color of plastic.

I pointed at the letter. "This same F was on that piece of plastic I found across the road from the farmhouse."

"The one the dogs led you to?"

I nodded. "I think the prowler dropped a broken piece of a guitar pick."

THIRTY-EIGHT

"The broken guitar pick could have been lying by the road for a long time," Callum said as he steered his truck out of the parking lot.

"True," I agreed. "But at least two of my suspects play guitar. So there's a chance it could have been dropped by the burglar."

"Also true," he conceded. "And those guitar-playing suspects are Nash and Lex?"

I nodded. "But Lex has an alibi for the time of the murder."

"Could he still be the burglar?"

"It's possible. Especially if he's working with an accomplice."

"Like his mother?"

"Maybe." I tried shoving all the mental puzzle pieces together in my head, but I couldn't get everything to fit. "I'm so confused."

"And yet, less confused than I am, I'm sure," Callum said.

"I don't know about that."

"Maybe things will make more sense in the morning," he suggested. "Are you going to tell Brody that the purple plastic is from a guitar pick?"

"I'll tell him. The police might have already figured it out, but I should make sure he has the information." I let out a heavy sigh laced with frustration. "I really felt like Scarlett was my strongest suspect, but now I'm wondering if that dubious distinction should go to Nash."

"He's got a criminal record, so it doesn't seem like a stretch that he could be involved."

"But how do we prove it?" I asked, feeling lost.

"That," Callum said, "is a problem best tackled after a good night's sleep."

Unfortunately, morning didn't bring any helpful epiphanies. I'd surprised myself by sleeping soundly after only a minimal amount of tossing and turning. Nevertheless, my sound slumber hadn't shaken loose any revelations from my subconscious.

After breakfast, I texted Brody, letting him know that the piece of purple plastic he'd taken into evidence had come from a Fender guitar pick.

Nice catch, he wrote back a while later. I thought the F looked familiar, but I couldn't place it.

I considered asking if he believed that was a good clue, but I knew he wouldn't tell me his thoughts on the matter. More likely, he'd just warn me off from investigating again, so I refrained from texting him any questions. It took effort, but I managed.

After I'd finished my morning farm jobs, I settled on the back porch with a glass of water and my laptop. The sun beamed down from the sky, providing enough warmth to sit outside as long as I wore a sweater. I wanted to make the most of the sunshine, since I could see a bank of dark, roiling clouds moving toward us. According to the weather app on my phone, we had several days of heavy rain coming, with the possibility of thunderstorms. Judging by the incoming clouds, that weather system was nearly upon us.

I felt safe out on the porch with the dogs nearby, Olivia at the carriage house, and Callum in the barn. I lost myself in my work and added several pages to my latest script before standing up to stretch my legs. Stardust was snoozing on the kitchen windowsill, but the dogs had been napping at my feet. They jumped up when I did, and then took off across the yard toward the carriage house. I realized why when I noticed Callum near the back of the small dwelling with Auntie O. They shook hands, then hugged.

My aunt greeted the dogs before heading back inside, but Callum started across the yard toward me. I descended the porch steps and met him on the lawn.

"Were you sealing the deal with Auntie O?" I asked, after he gave me a quick kiss.

He grinned, his green eyes alight with happiness. "She's agreed to let me set up a trust fund for the sanctuary, and she's cleared the plan with her lawyer and accountant."

I gave him a joyful hug. "I'm glad it worked out. I'm happy for Auntie O, the sanctuary, and for you, because I know this is something you really wanted to do."

"I love the sanctuary, and what's the point of having a lot of money if you can't do some good with it?"

I rested a hand on his chest, feeling like I was brimming over with love and affection. "That heart of yours is made of pure gold."

He wrapped his arms around me. "Yours too."

I rested my head on his shoulder, smiling. "Does that make us a perfect match?"

"It's one of many, many things that make us a perfect match," Callum said into my hair.

"A-woo," Fancy howled.

Flossie chimed in with a bark.

Off in the distance, an owl hooted.

Coincidence? Maybe.

"What are your plans for the rest of the day?" Callum asked as I reluctantly stepped out of his embrace.

We walked together toward the house, hand-in-hand.

"I'd like to find out more about Scarlett," I said. "I'd really like to eliminate a name or two from my suspect list, but I'm not sure how to do that. What about you?"

"I was thinking lunch."

Flossie woofed her approval.

I smiled. "I should probably work that into my plans too. Sleuthing on an empty stomach might not be the best idea."

Once in the house, we put together a meal of grilled cheese sandwiches and tomato soup. As we ate, an idea popped into my head.

"I've thought of a way to get a chance to talk to Scarlett," I said to Callum.

"While staying out of danger, I hope."

"Of course," I assured him. "You can even come with me, if you'd like."

"I definitely don't want you talking to murder suspects by yourself."

"Maybe you could help me come up with some good questions to ask her," I said. "I'm not quite sure how to get the information I want out of her."

Callum reached across the table to give my hand a squeeze. "We'll figure something out."

I gave him a grateful smile and then outlined my plan as we finished our soup and sandwiches. I couldn't exactly ask Scarlett outright if she'd been in Twilight Cove when her sister was murdered, not without incurring her (potentially murderous) wrath, anyway.

I could, however, ask her some more subtle questions and watch her reaction when she answered them. If I could find a way to get a look at her phone—maybe while Callum distracted her—that would be even better, but I knew there wasn't much chance of that happening. Any bit of information we could gather would help, though, so we decided to simply do our best and see how things played out.

After lunch, we drove into town and stopped at the Treasure Trove. Fae sold gifts like scented candles and pottery handmade by local artists, as well as crystals, tarot cards, and local interest books. I knew she always had a couple of gift baskets on hand as well, filled with local products like jam, crackers, cheese, and handmade soap. I purchased one such gift basket and, after Fae had a quick visit with the spaniels, we continued on our way to the Gilmore Hotel.

"I'd like the dogs to come with us," I said as Callum found a free spot in the self-parking lot at the hotel. "But it'll be obvious to the staff that Flossie and Fancy are over the size limit."

Fancy "a-wooed" her disapproval from the back seat.

"We agree, Fancy," Callum said over his shoulder. "All dogs should be allowed."

"I'll go in the front door on my own," I decided.

"I don't want you visiting Scarlett by yourself," Callum objected.

"I won't," I assured him. "I'll find a side or back door that you can sneak through with the dogs."

"And if you get caught creeping around the hotel?"

I'd already considered that possibility. "I'll just claim I got lost."

Although I managed to sound unconcerned, nerves fluttered uncomfortably inside of me. I wasn't a rule breaker by nature and didn't relish the thought of getting caught where I didn't belong, but I wanted answers. I needed to find out who was behind all the recent crimes. Until the people responsible were behind bars, I'd always be looking over my shoulder. Plus, Scarlett could leave town at any time. The same was true for all of my suspects, so I figured it was now or never.

With the gift basket in my arms and my heart cantering in my chest, I walked into the lobby, trying my best to look as though I had every right to be there. I made a beeline for the hallway near the elevators, since it would likely lead me deeper into the building. The corridor turned to the right, then to the left before I found myself near a couple of empty conference rooms. Surely, I'd come across an exit soon, but so far, I'd had no such luck.

Approaching voices sent my heart stumbling. I ducked into one of the conference rooms and pressed my back to the wall behind the door. Through the narrow space between the door and the frame, I saw two women, dressed in the dark blue uniforms of the hotel's employees, walk briskly down the hall, chatting about what sounded like an upcoming business conference that would be hosted on the premises.

I remained frozen in my hiding spot until their voices had faded away entirely.

Then I mustered my courage and peeked out into the hall.

To find three sets of eyes staring at me.

THIRTY-NINE

My heart leapt in surprise.

I pressed a hand to my chest, nearly dropping the gift basket, as relief rushed in to replace my momentary surge of fear.

"You scared me half to death," I whispered to Callum as he met up with me in the hall.

Flossie and Fancy trotted up to me and sat at my feet.

"Sneaking around doesn't give you an adrenaline rush?" Callum asked with a grin.

"It's more like it ages me prematurely."

"Nah." Callum gave me a quick kiss. "You're still as youthful as ever."

"A-woo," Fancy piped up, as if she were agreeing.

I pressed a finger to my lips as I looked down at the dogs. "You need to stay quiet or we'll all get kicked out of the hotel."

Fancy grumbled, but then fell silent.

"How did you get in here, anyway?" I asked Callum.

"We found a side entrance. Next thing I knew, Flossie had unlocked it and opened the door."

Flossie swished her tail and lifted her chin, looking proud of herself.

"I was afraid she'd set off an alarm," Callum said, "but luckily that didn't happen."

I glanced over my shoulder, worried we'd get caught if we lingered there in the hall too long. "Let's get this over with. My nerves are already shot."

Callum relieved me of the basket and we got moving. We managed not to run into anyone on our way to the stairwell, which—luckily for us—was located just off the lobby, so the hotel employees working at the front desk couldn't see us as we slipped through the door. After jogging up to the third floor, I had to pause to catch my breath and calm my nerves.

"Are you sure you want to go through with this?" Callum asked, sensing my anxiety.

"I want to," I said. "I just wish I were braver. My pulse is racing."

"I'll be right here with you," Callum promised. "I won't let anyone hurt you."

I smiled and kissed him. "To be honest, I'm more worried about getting in hot water with the hotel staff."

Callum grinned. "The sooner we get moving, the less likely we are to get in trouble."

He had a good point. Loitering in the stairwell would only increase the chances of someone coming across us and reporting to management that we'd brought oversized dogs into the building.

I drew in a steadying breath, let it out slowly, and then eased open the door to the hallway. The coast was clear, so I walked quickly to room 302 and knocked before I had a chance to chicken out.

I took the gift basket from Callum and he rested a hand at the small of my back. Flossie and Fancy sat on either side of us, waiting patiently.

Just as I was beginning to wonder if the room was empty, the door swung open.

"Yes?" Scarlett said, her expression distracted and impatient. As she took in the sight of me, recognition flashed in her eyes and the muscles around her mouth relaxed. "We met a few days ago at one of the local shops."

"That's right," I said. "Sort of, anyway. I'm Georgie Johansen, and this is my boyfriend, Callum McQuade."

She nodded slowly, as if trying to figure out what we were doing at her door. "What can I do for you?"

I held out the gift basket. "This is for you. A gift from the town. We're so sorry that it was tragic circumstances that brought you here."

Some of the tension eased out of Scarlett's shoulders as she accepted the basket from me. "How kind." She stepped back. "Will you come in for a moment?"

"Thank you. We won't keep you long," I said, already following her into the suite. "Do you mind if our dogs come in as well?"

"Are they allowed in the hotel?" she asked over her shoulder, leading us from the short entry hall to an open room.

"Um . . ." I glanced to Callum for help.

"Nobody stopped us on the way up here," he said.

I held back a smile, appreciating how he'd managed to answer without lying.

Scarlett set the gift basket on a desk in the suite's sitting room, which also featured a gas fireplace, a comfy-looking couch, and two armchairs. A small kitchen sat to the left, and to the right, a hallway led to what I assumed were the bedrooms and bathrooms, however many of them the suite contained. Straight ahead, French doors led to a balcony with a distant view of the ocean.

"This looks lovely," Scarlett remarked as she peeked through the clear plastic wrapped around the gift basket.

"All the products are locally made," I said.

"This was so kind of you. I'll have to return to this town one day, under happier circumstances."

"Is this your first time in Twilight Cove?" Callum asked.

"It is," she replied. "I haven't spent much time in Oregon, but I appreciate the beauty of this area, even in this dark time."

"Will you be staying much longer?" I asked as I tried to take in the details of the room without being obvious about it.

A backpack sat on one of the armchairs and a hardshell guitar case was propped up next to the desk. Signs that Lex was now staying with his mother? Or was Scarlett a musician too?

"I'm planning to head home tomorrow," she replied. "There's nothing more I can do here. If the police need further information from me, they can contact me in Tampa. That's where we'll have the funeral, once . . ." She fought to compose herself before continuing. "Once the police release my sister's body."

My heart ached for her. If she wasn't involved with her sister's death, then her grief might be genuine, even if she and Nina hadn't been the best of friends.

"We're so sorry for your loss," Callum said, his voice full of kindness.

Scarlett offered us a wavering smile. "Thank you."

Flossie and Fancy sniffed around the sitting room. I almost told them to sit, but decided against it. I didn't want to hinder their snooping.

I gestured to the guitar case. "Are you a musician?"

"I haven't got a shred of musical talent, I'm afraid," she replied. "That's a gift for my husband. I picked it up at a cute little shop just down the coast from here."

"Is your husband here too?" I asked. "I heard that your son is."

"My husband's at home in Florida. My son, Lex, is hoping to line up some gigs for his band here on the west coast." Scarlett's gaze shifted to the small kitchen. "Can I offer you some coffee or tea?"

Callum looked my way, letting me take the lead.

"No, thank you," I declined. "We don't want to impose."

A cell phone sitting on the coffee table rang.

Scarlett grabbed it and checked the screen. "I'm so sorry, but I need to take this. I won't be long."

She disappeared into one of the bedrooms as she answered the call.

"Anything?" I whispered to Flossie and Fancy.

As if she'd been waiting for me to ask, Fancy trotted behind one of the armchairs. She reared up on her hind legs, placing her front paws on the back of the chair, and snagged a silk scarf with her teeth.

"Careful with that," I cautioned quietly.

I was no fashion expert, but the scarf looked expensive.

Fancy sat down in front of me with the silk in her mouth, looking up at me expectantly.

"Why is this important?" I asked as I carefully took the scarf from her.

Fortunately, she hadn't left more than a drop or two of slobber on it.

I glanced at Callum, but he shrugged. I ran the black-and-gray silk through my fingers, not recognizing the dark, two-tone floral pattern. I caught a hint of a scent, and lifted the scarf to my face, breathing in through my nose.

My chest tightened and suddenly I couldn't get air into my lungs.

"Georgie?" Callum's voice sounded like it was coming from far away.

He snaked an arm around my waist and put a hand to my face.

"Georgie? What's wrong?"

Looking into his green eyes helped to reel me back to the present, to ground me.

"The perfume on the scarf," I said, my voice faint.

Only then did I realize that the silk accessory lay pooled at my feet. I didn't even remember dropping it.

"What about it?" Callum asked.

When I saw the worry in his eyes, I gave myself a mental shake. "It's the perfume I smelled when I got knocked over at the museum's party."

Understanding flashed in Callum's eyes. He snatched the scarf off the ground and flung it over the back of the armchair, before darting back to my side and slipping an arm around my waist again. A mere second later, Scarlett exited the bedroom.

"I'm sorry about that," she said as she returned to the sitting room.

Grateful for his support, I leaned against Callum, although I tried not to be too obvious about it. The scent of the perfume, and the memory it triggered, had left my legs weak.

"No worries," Callum said, sounding completely normal. "We should be on our way."

I glanced down at the dogs and saw that Flossie was staring hard at the backpack sitting on the same armchair as the scarf. The zipper moved and panic flashed through me. I cut my eyes to Scarlett, but she was looking at us, not the backpack.

"Thank you so much for bringing the gift basket," she said. "It was so—"

The backpack tipped off the chair and fell to the floor, spilling its contents on the rug.

Something glinted in the light streaming through the French doors.

I drew in a sharp breath and pointed at the jumbled mess on the floor.

"That's my stolen jewelry."

FORTY

"There must be some mistake," Scarlett insisted, though her voice sounded weak and panic flashed in her eyes.

"No," I countered. "That jewelry belonged to my mom. It was stolen from my house last week."

Scarlett clutched the silver necklace at her throat and shook her head. She opened her mouth, about to speak again, but then she pressed her lips tightly together.

Beside me, Callum was already on the phone with the police.

Scarlett tapped at her own device. "I'm calling my lawyer. You should leave."

"I don't want to let that jewelry out of my sight," I said.

I didn't want to give her a chance to get rid of the evidence before the police arrived.

Flossie and Fancy sat down on either side of the fallen backpack, as if intending to guard the small pile of spilled items.

"I'm contacting hotel security next," Callum said after ending his first call.

Scarlett held a clipped conversation on her phone as she paced the small kitchen. By the time she finished the call, two men from the hotel's security team, dressed all in black, had arrived at the suite.

We quickly filled them in on the situation. Scarlett maintained that there had to be some sort of mistake or misunderstanding, but the security officers weren't interested in her claims. They intended to stay on the scene until the police arrived and just wanted to keep the situation calm in the meantime.

Satisfied that the security officers would guard the evidence, Callum and I retreated to the hallway with the dogs to await the arrival of the police. Two officers showed up within minutes and we once again had to explain what had transpired. While Callum and I spoke with one of the officers out in the hallway, the dogs' heads turned in unison to look at something behind me. When I glanced that way, I saw nothing other than the stairwell door drifting shut. Flossie and Fancy relaxed and sat down to wait patiently, so I got back to the conversation with the officer.

After Callum and I had shared all the relevant information we could think of, the police told me they'd have to take my jewelry into evidence. I'd expected that, so the news caused me only a flicker of disappointment.

"At least you'll get it back eventually," Callum said once the police had allowed us to leave.

"That's a relief," I agreed as we took the stairs down to the ground floor.

We left through the side entrance, thankfully never running into any other hotel staff. Aside from telling me that dogs over twenty pounds weren't supposed to be in the building, the security officers hadn't taken any action against us, for which I was grateful. I didn't want to press our luck in that regard by walking across the lobby on our way out of the building.

When we got back to the farm, I felt too restless to focus on writing, so I helped Callum with some tasks in the barn instead. In the early evening, we met up with a bunch of our friends at the baseball field so we could practice for the local fun league. I was a little nervous about playing in actual games, which would start in another couple of weeks, but I also didn't want to sit on the sidelines while all my friends took part.

Since Callum had played baseball professionally, he wasn't permitted to be on a team, but he was allowed to coach us. With him there to offer guidance and support from the sidelines, I thought I might be brave enough to get over my nervous jitters and play on the team with my friends.

After the practice, Tessa and Brody helped Callum and me load all the equipment into Callum's truck. While we worked, we filled our friends in on what had transpired at the hotel. Brody had another day off and hadn't heard the latest news from the police station. He promised to let me know if he found out any information about when I might get to have my jewelry back.

By the time we drove away from the park, with Flossie and Fancy in the back seat, the last remnants of daylight had faded away. The storm clouds that had been amassing above us for hours finally opened up as we left the parking lot, sending rain down in sheets.

"It's the perfect night to cozy up in front of a fire," I said as Callum switched the windshield wipers on.

Flossie gave a woof from the back seat as thunder rumbled overhead.

"Maybe with some brownie pudding?" Callum suggested. "It won't take me long to whip some up."

"Yum." My stomach growled at the mere thought.

"A-woo," Fancy spoke up.

"No chocolate for you two," I said over my shoulder. "But I'm sure we can scrounge up a dog-appropriate treat."

Flossie woofed again, this time with great excitement.

"Sounds like we're all on board with that plan," I said, smiling.

That smile faded when I saw Callum's worried expression.

"What is it?" I asked.

When his eyes flicked to the rearview mirror, I twisted in my seat to look behind us.

Bright headlights nearly blinded me.

"They've got their high beams on," I said, shading my eyes.

"And they're going way over the speed limit," Callum added. "They came out of nowhere."

The lights zoomed closer, growing ever brighter. I tensed, gripping the edge of my seat, expecting the car to slam into us from behind. At the last second, the vehicle swerved into the other lane, never bothering to signal.

I maintained my grip on the seat. "Do they have a death wish?"

The vehicle—an SUV—was now in the lane meant for oncoming traffic.

Callum slowed the truck to make it easier for the other vehicle to pass us, but instead of zipping out in front of us, the SUV slowed to keep pace with us.

"What the heck?" My pulse racing, I peered through the passenger window, trying to see into the other vehicle.

Lightning flashed, illuminating a frightening sight.

My heart nearly stopped. "Callum! They've got a gun!"

Brakes squealed and thunder rumbled.

Lightning flashed again.

A gunshot cracked through the storm.

FORTY-ONE

The truck swerved and bounced before jolting to a stop.

"Georgie?" Callum's voice cut through my state of shock.

"I'm OK," I gasped. Releasing my seatbelt, I whipped around in my seat. "Flossie? Fancy?"

The dogs had tumbled down into the footwell, but they bounced back up onto the bench seat. I didn't have a chance to process my relief that they seemed unharmed. Callum had already opened the driver's door.

"We need to run," he said, his voice urgent. "Now."

I realized in that split second that the SUV had stopped. It had shot ahead of us when Callum slammed on the brakes, but it wasn't far away. The bullet had missed us and the truck, but the driver could fire another one at any moment.

I scrambled across the seat and tumbled out the driver's door. Callum had already let the spaniels out of the cab and stood by the truck's bed, stuffing something into his pocket. As soon as I was steady on my feet, he grabbed my hand and we ran for the woods at the side of the road.

As we plunged into the tree line, I glanced toward the SUV. Someone was clambering out of the driver's seat, into the bright beams of light coming from Callum's truck.

I recognized our assailant in the fraction of a second before another shot rang out, nearly as loud as the clap of thunder that followed it.

I inhaled sharply and tripped over a tree root. I would have fallen if not for Callum holding me up. We kept running, but between the darkness and the rain we couldn't see much and soon had to slow our pace.

"It's Lex Nicholson," I whispered to Callum.

His grip on my hand tightened.

I could hear the dogs crashing through the underbrush ahead of us. Then I heard a similar sound behind us.

"He's coming!" My words almost caught in my throat.

Up ahead and to our right, a blue light flared before disappearing.

"This way." I pulled Callum in the direction of the now-extinguished light.

I knew it was Fancy, trying to guide us. I wished she could stay lit up, but I knew that would only lead Lex straight to us and the dogs. No doubt Fancy realized that too.

We stumbled clear of the underbrush, finding ourselves on a narrow trail. We picked up our pace, running as fast as we dared in the darkness.

The trees parted and a black expanse stretched out before us.

The ocean.

"We need to hide," Callum said, still gripping my hand.

Fancy's blue glow lit up briefly again. This time Callum saw it too.

"Fancy?" he asked in a low voice.

I nodded and we ran that way as the light blinked out.

The dogs waited for us at the top of a steep, rocky slope that led down to the water, where waves crashed against the boulders. Flossie and Fancy hopped from rock to rock, leading the way down the bluff. Callum nudged me ahead of him, and I scrambled to follow the dogs, with Callum right on my heels.

"I know you're out here!" Lex's voice rang out, muffled by the lashing rain and crashing waves.

I tensed and hunkered down as lightning flashed, worried that Lex would see us in the momentary brightness.

When no gunshot sounded, I resumed following the dogs.

Thunder clapped right overhead, startling me. I slipped on the slick rocks and fell to my knees, listing to one side. I nearly toppled off the big boulder I was kneeling on, but then Callum was there, steadying me with his strong arms.

"You OK?" he whispered, his words barely audible over the pouring rain.

I nodded and climbed carefully back to my feet before stepping down to the flat rock where Flossie and Fancy waited. They led us down a little farther, and then in behind a giant boulder.

I crouched down and hugged Flossie and Fancy, only then realizing that my entire body was trembling. Spray from the pounding waves showered over us, barely distinguishable from the rain.

Callum pulled out his phone and pressed the emergency button. We stayed hunkered down as he had a hushed conversation, requesting help from the police. My heart thudded the entire time, worried that Lex would hear Callum's voice.

Luckily, the rain and thunder provided good cover for any other noises. Unfortunately, that also made it hard to hear if Lex was nearby.

Callum tried his best to explain where to find us, but we'd stopped along a stretch of road with woods on either side. At least the police would know where to start searching when they found the abandoned vehicles.

A shower of rocks tumbled down the slope just forty feet away from us.

Panic shot through me.

Callum abruptly ended his phone call and shut off the device so the glow from the screen wouldn't give away our position. I peeked around the boulder. A flash of lightning lit up the area, giving me the chance to see Lex clambering down onto the rocks, the gun still clasped in one hand.

"We need to move," I whispered to Callum.

It wouldn't take long for Lex to find us here in our hiding spot.

By the time the words made it out of my mouth, Flossie and Fancy had already leapt to another rock. Staying low, Callum and I followed them across the slope, slowly climbing higher again. The spaniels led us to another large boulder, where we once again hunkered down.

The pouring rain plastered my hair to my head, and droplets ran down my forehead into my eyes. I wiped the water off my face, but new rivulets formed right away.

A rock tumbled somewhere nearby and Lex let out a loud curse.

He was getting close. Too close.

Below us, the waves lashed angrily against the rocks.

Above us, the slope was too steep to climb directly up.

Callum pressed a kiss to my temple before whispering, "You need to get back to the truck. I'll distract him."

"No!" I whispered, reaching for his wrist.

But I was too late. He was already picking his way across the rocks. Fancy scrambled along with him while Flossie stayed pressed to my side. As he disappeared around a bend in the bluff, my heart ached. I didn't want us separated.

I was about to follow after Callum and Fancy when Lex's voice rang out, dangerously close.

"Come out, come out, wherever you are!"

The taunt sent slivers of ice into my veins.

I peeked ever so carefully around the boulder.

Lex stood on a rock, about thirty feet away now, just a little higher than my position.

"Why are you doing this, Lex?" Callum's voice boomed out from somewhere above us.

Lex's head whipped in that direction.

I ducked back behind the boulder, my heart hammering. I knew Callum was trying to give me a chance to escape, but I hated the thought of him putting himself in more danger.

"Why do you think?" Lex yelled back.

Flossie pressed her nose to my hand. I put an arm around her, shivering from cold and fear. If we tried to move out of our hiding spot now, Lex would spot us for sure, and he wouldn't have any trouble picking us off with his gun.

"That nosy girlfriend of yours should have minded her own business," Lex shouted. "Spying at the restaurant, at the hotel. She should have let sleeping dogs lie."

"Why kill your aunt in the first place?" Callum called back.

This time, his voice came from a little farther away.

Thunder rumbled around us, muffling all other noises.

I chanced another peek around the edge of the boulder and had to bite back a gasp.

Lex had climbed farther down the bluff. Another few steps and he'd see me and Flossie.

"You haven't figured that out?" Lex hollered through the rain.

"You wanted the brooch." Callum's voice was a little closer now, coming from beyond the clifftop.

"Still do, since your girlfriend stole it back."

He thought I had the brooch again? No wonder he'd tried to return to the farmhouse on the night of the museum's party.

As I watched from my hiding spot, Lex started climbing upward, away from me and Flossie.

"As soon as I've dealt with both of you, I'll search your house until I find it," he yelled through the noise of the storm.

"Are you planning to sell it on the black market?" Callum's question nearly got drowned out by another roll of thunder.

"Of course I'm going to sell it!" Lex slipped on a rock and let out a string of curses. He regained his footing and resumed climbing. "I don't need some freaking piece of jewelry! I need money!"

He climbed up over one more rock and reached the top of the bluff.

"What for?" Callum called.

In the next flash of lightning, I saw a cruel, triumphant smile creep onto Lex's face.

Then he raised his gun and fired.

FORTY-TWO

My heart hammered and a wave of nausea crashed through me.

I wanted to yell Callum's name, to run and find him, but if I moved, Lex would fire at me next.

I listened for Callum's voice, desperately hoping he was unharmed. I heard nothing but the crashing waves and the raging storm.

When I peeked around the boulder again, Lex had disappeared from sight.

"Be careful," I whispered to Flossie.

Then I crept out from behind the large rock and started to climb.

My fingers were so cold and wet that it was hard to grip anything, but I made my way slowly upward and to my left. Flossie climbed along behind me, hopping from perch to perch like a mountain goat.

Every second that passed without hearing Callum's voice, without any sign of Lex's current position, made my stomach churn harder.

I still hadn't heard either man by the time I reached the top of the bluff. I was about to peek over the clifftop when an angry roar from Lex tore through the night. Thunder rumbled, almost as if the sky were imitating him.

His obvious rage lit a spark of hope inside me.

He wouldn't be so angry if he'd managed to fell Callum.

I chanced a careful look over the top of the bluff.

Lex stormed out of the tree line, his hair and clothes plastered against his skin.

Somehow, Flossie and I needed to get past him, to get to the truck.

My hand closed around a loose rock.

Channeling everything I'd learned about throwing from Callum, I hurled the rock as far as I could, sending it horizontally along the bluff. It clattered against the rocks, just loud enough to draw Lex's attention. He whirled around in that direction, putting his back to me.

Raising his gun, he crept closer to the bluff.

A dark shape swooped down out of the sky. Sharp talons skimmed over Lex's head.

He shrieked and ducked.

Euclid flew back up into the sky, disappearing into the darkness.

Lex teetered on the edge of the bluff. I got ready to scramble up to level ground, but then Lex regained his footing.

I ducked back down out of sight, frustration surging through me.

Then a most welcome sound met my ears.

The wail of a siren.

No, multiple sirens.

Lex swore and ran for the tree line.

I clambered up off the rocks and Flossie bounded up with me.

The sirens were too far off, I realized with dismay. Lex would get away before the police arrived.

Callum popped up from behind an old tree stump. Then something white streaked through the air, hitting Lex square in the back.

He cried out as he fell face first into the mud.

Flossie and Fancy tore over his way and pounced on him.

I ran through the rain, desperate to keep my dogs safe from Lex's gun.

Callum beat me there.

Lex lay on the ground, groaning. Flossie and Fancy had their front paws planted on his back. They let out fierce growls whenever he so much as twitched.

The gun lay about a foot from his left hand. Callum kicked it farther away as the sirens drew closer.

I launched myself at Callum, throwing my arms around him.

"Are you hurt?" I asked.

"I'm fine," he said into my hair as he hugged me close. "You?"

"I'm OK." I looked down at Lex as he groaned, the dogs still growling. Then I glanced up at my boyfriend. "What did you do?"

"Got him with a fastball." Callum grinned as rivulets of rain ran down his face. "I might be retired, but I've still got it."

I smiled and hugged him harder, tears of relief joining the rain streaming down my cheeks.

The sirens cut off and voices shouted through the trees.

The cavalry had arrived.

FORTY-THREE

"Did you miss your calling as a pitcher?" Tessa asked Callum the next afternoon.

We'd gathered at the field again for another practice with our friends. We hadn't played any baseball yet, though. Everyone wanted to hear what had happened the night before from Callum and me.

Callum grinned as he tossed a ball into the air and caught it in his glove. "I pitched in high school, but I always preferred batting and playing the outfield."

I smiled, remembering how effectively he'd taken Lex down.

After the police had taken custody of Lex, Callum had told me that he'd grabbed a baseball from one of the equipment bags in the bed of the truck before we'd taken off into the trees. He'd hoped to get his hand on a bat to use as a weapon, but his hand had closed around a ball and he didn't have time to take anything else.

"Is it true that you threw the ball at a hundred miles per hour?" Cindy asked, sounding awed. "That's what I heard at the coffee shop this morning."

"I think it was more like eighty-five," Callum said.

Which still sounded impressive to me. To Cindy too, judging by her expression.

Genesis shook her head in amazement. "That guy is lucky he's in jail and not the hospital."

"I'm not sure Lex sees it that way," I said.

Tessa frowned. "I can't believe he killed his aunt. And just because he wanted some money?"

"To fund his music career."

We all turned at the sound of the new voice. Brody, wearing his police uniform, joined us where we'd gathered by home plate.

Tessa greeted him with a quick kiss, which garnered some whistles and whoops from our group. Her cheeks turned pink, but she had a smile on her face, and I did too. Seeing her happy made me happy.

"Lex thought he and his band would have their big break if they could just record an album and tour the country," Brody explained. "He wanted his parents to fund all that, but they were broke."

"Thanks to their failing business," Callum said.

Brody nodded. "Scarlett and Royce were desperate for money too. They decided to steal the Emerald Mirage from Scarlett's father so they could sell it on the black market while Baxter Hartmann collected the insurance money. Except, Nina somehow figured out what they'd done. We think she might have recognized Royce on the security video from her father's mansion. The burglar had a somewhat distinctive gait when he was running."

"So Nina stole the brooch from her sister?" Cindy asked.

"She was trying to set up a cat shelter," Brody said by way of confirmation. "We think that's why she wanted the money she'd get from selling the brooch."

"A noble motive," Cindy said, "but not the best way of going about things."

"And, unfortunately, it got her killed," Brody added.

"Lex knew she'd taken the brooch?" Callum guessed.

Brody gave a short nod. "And followed her to the airport. She must have realized he was tailing her."

"So she slipped the brooch into my bag, hoping to retrieve it later," I said.

"But then Lex just tracked her here," Brody continued. "So did Hailey Lau, the private investigator Angela Bergstrom hired once she heard about the theft of the brooch. Ms. Lau figured out that Nina had the brooch when she hacked the phones and computers belonging to Nina, Scarlett, and Royce. She found that Nina had been searching for potential buyers online."

"What about Scarlett?" I asked. "Did she arrive in Twilight Cove earlier than she admitted?"

"No, but she spent a couple of nights in Britton Bay on the way here after flying into Los Angeles. Even with money troubles and her sister's death, she couldn't resist spending a day there shopping."

"That's nuts, even though they do have cute shops in Britton Bay," Tessa said. "So it was Lex who broke into the farmhouse?"

"He's admitted to that," Brody confirmed. "He followed Nina

there when he first got to town. Initially, he didn't know what she was doing at the farm, but when he tried to steal the Emerald Mirage from her motel room, he didn't find it."

"So it was him who was caught on the motel's surveillance footage, trying to steal a key card," I concluded.

Brody nodded. "He used layers of baggy clothing to make himself look heavier than he is. When ransacking Nina's room didn't get him what he wanted, Lex confronted her and she told him she didn't have the brooch on her. Lex killed her and discovered that she'd told the truth. He took her phone and checked the internet history, which showed that she'd researched Callum to find out where he lived. From that, Lex put two and two together and realized why she was watching the farmhouse. He started watching it himself—ditching Nina's phone at one point—waiting for a chance to break in and find the brooch."

I shook my head. "Talk about a dysfunctional family." I brought up something that had been bothering me. "Lex had an alibi for the murder."

"A false one, it turns out," Brody said. "His bandmates lied for him, told us they'd all been video chatting at the time. Lex told them he was innocent but needed an alibi, otherwise the police would keep him here and he'd miss the gig they have scheduled in Nashville next week."

"He's definitely going to miss it now," Callum remarked.

"What about the perfume I smelled when I was attacked at the Elmore house?" I asked. "I thought that pointed to Scarlett as the culprit."

"Lex borrowed his mom's scarf to cover his face that night," Brody explained.

"And the murder weapon?" Tessa glanced my way after raising the question.

I'd wanted to ask about that too, but I didn't want to get Valentina in hot water for sharing the detail about the traces of nickel left on Nina's body. Tessa had cleverly left her cousin's name out of the conversation.

"Lex used one of his spare guitar strings to strangle his aunt," Brody replied.

I cringed. "Gruesome."

"I'll say," Tessa agreed.

Everyone else concurred as well.

I thought of another question. "Was it Hailey who broke into Lex's Airbnb? Is that how she ended up with the brooch?"

"That was her," Brody replied. "Angelica wanted Hailey to get her the brooch, even if it meant breaking a few laws."

"But if Hailey figured out that Lex had the Emerald Mirage, didn't she realize he'd probably killed Nina?" I asked.

"She won't admit it, but I'm sure she must have had her suspicions, at the very least," Brody said. "After all, she claims she guessed that Lex might have the brooch because she'd observed him acting suspiciously. Ultimately, I guess she was just more worried about doing the job she'd been hired to do and getting paid by Angelica."

"That's crazy," Tessa said, and I had to agree.

I raised more of the questions that had been troubling me. "What about Nash Skidmore? Why was he in Twilight Cove? Was he looking for the brooch too?"

"Nash overheard his dad on the phone, talking about the theft from Baxter Hartmann's residence," Brody explained. "Nash knew Lex and was hoping to join his band. He caught a glimpse of Lex's phone one day and realized he was hoping to sell the brooch. So, Nash figured Lex had it. He followed Lex to Twilight Cove, taking care not to let Lex see him here, hoping to steal the brooch and sell it himself. He likes living a partier's lifestyle, but isn't so fond of working to pay for it."

Cindy shook her head. "All that trouble caused by greed."

We fell silent, a cloud of heavy emotions hanging over us.

"Ugh," Tessa said after a long moment. "Let's forget about the bad guys for now. Callum and Georgie are alive and well."

"A-woo!" Fancy chimed in from my side.

"And Fancy and Flossie too," Tessa added. "We should celebrate that."

That got a woof of approval from Flossie.

"And I know the perfect way," Callum said with a grin. "Let's play ball!"

FORTY-FOUR

After everyone else had left the field, Callum and I stayed behind so I could get in some extra batting practice. I really didn't want to embarrass myself by striking out every time I stepped up to the plate once the fun league games got underway. Callum believed wholeheartedly that I wouldn't, but I wasn't so confident, and I knew I'd feel better with more practice under my belt.

Flossie and Fancy watched from the sidelines as Callum threw me some easy pitches. I hit most of them, even sending a few into the outfield.

"Make it a little harder now," I requested. "The opposing team's pitcher isn't going to go easy on me."

"So you want a ninety-mile-per-hour fastball?" Callum teased. "Or maybe a killer curveball?"

I made a face. "How about just one step harder than what you've been throwing me?"

He laughed. "All right, slugger. Get ready."

I took up my stance and waited for him to throw the pitch.

When my bat connected with the ball, it felt different than all the other times. More powerful, yet smoother.

I stood and watched as the ball sailed through the air.

And kept going.

My jaw nearly dropped when the ball flew right over the back fence before hitting the ground.

"A home run?" The bat fell from my hands. "Did I really do that?"

"What are you waiting for?" Callum called from the pitching mound. "Run the bases!"

I tipped off my batter's helmet and took off toward first base. We might not have been playing in an actual game, but that didn't stop a thrill of elation from rushing through my bloodstream. Flossie and Fancy cantered along with me and I laughed when they each made sure to touch a paw to first base before continuing on.

Callum cheered as we rounded the next base. I slowed down enough to bunny hop onto third base, and then I jogged down the line to home plate.

Callum waited there for me and I launched myself into his arms. He swung me around and gave me a kiss before setting me on my feet.

"Did you ever think you'd see the day when I, Georgie Johansen, hit a home run?" I asked, still in a state of shock.

"I knew I would," Callum said, his green eyes full of pride. "Just like I've known for a long time that this would happen."

He released his hold on me and got down on one knee.

"What are you doing?" I asked, the gears in my head screeching to a halt.

Flossie and Fancy sat on either side of him as he produced a small velvet box from his back pocket.

I stared at him, my mind frozen and unable to comprehend what was happening.

"Georgie," Callum said, taking my hand in one of his, "I first told you that I love you on a night when the aurora borealis lit up the sky. But *you* are the light of my life. You challenge me, center me, complete me."

I gaped at him, finally understanding as his words wrapped around my heart.

"Is this really happening?" I whispered.

"Woo-woo!" Fancy offered her assurance.

Callum grinned. "It's happening, Georgie. I've stood on baseball fields thousands of times, all across the country, but this is different. Because this time it's not about the game, it's about you and me. About us. I've hit grand slams, I've heard thousands of fans chant my name, but none of that compares to this moment. Will you be my teammate, my partner for all our future innings, Georgie?"

He opened the box to reveal a ring. Tiny diamonds glinted in the daylight, but the real showstopper was the blue-green stone in the center.

It was stunning, all the more so because of what it meant.

"You want to marry me?" My words came out faint, but tinged with awe.

Callum laughed. "Georgie, there's nothing I want more."

"Oh, my gosh." My hand shook as I pressed it to my mouth.

He squeezed my other hand. "Do you have an answer for me?"

"Yes!"

His eyes twinkled. "Yes, you have an answer for me, or yes is your answer?"

"Yes!" I practically shouted, then realized I still hadn't clarified. "That's my answer! Of course I'll marry you, Callum McQuade!"

My heart nearly burst at the sight of the pure joy in his eyes.

"I had this ring custom-made just for you," Callum said as he slid it onto my trembling finger. "The stone is alexandrite. It changes color depending on the light. It reminds me of the aurora borealis, which reminds me of you."

I stared at the ring on my finger as the gems sparkled in the sunshine.

Then my gaze returned to Callum as he stood up.

I threw myself into his arms. He laughed and spun me around again.

When he set me on my feet, he kissed me.

It was a sweet yet passionate kiss, full of promise, full of always and forever.

Fancy howled.

Flossie barked.

In the distance, an owl hooted.

Life had thrown me a lot of curveballs through the years, but from the aurora borealis to the lines on the field, everything had guided me here.

To this moment.

To this man.

Home.

Acknowledgments

It's taken a village to bring the Magical Menagerie Mysteries to life, and I'm truly grateful to each and every person involved. Special thanks to Jessica Faust, Laurie Johnson, Piers Tilbury, Lianne Slavin, Sianna King, and the entire team at Severn House. Thank you to my review crew, my readers, and everyone in the book community who helps to spread the word about cozy mysteries.

The home of great genre fiction

Discover more must-read stories:
visit severnhouse.com or scan the QR code below

Sign up for monthly updates on our latest books:
severnhouse.com/newsletter

Find us on social media:
@severnhouse
@severnhouseimprint